Accra Noir

Edited by
Nana-Ama Danquah

Brooklyn, New York

This collection consists of works of fiction. All names, characters, places, and incidents are the product of the authors' imaginations. Any resemblance to real events or persons, living or dead, is entirely coincidental.

Published by Akashic Books

Series concept by Tim McLoughlin and Johnny Temple
Accra map by Sohrab Habibion

ISBN: 978-1-61775-889-8
Library of Congress Control Number: 2020935791

First printing

Akashic Books
Brooklyn, New York
Twitter: @AkashicBooks
Facebook: AkashicBooks
E-mail: info@akashicbooks.com
Website: www.akashicbooks.com

For my cousin Kwasi Twum—
thank you for always staying in stride with me.
For hiking mountains, going to raw-food retreats,
eating lots of sushi, and braving a colonic,
all so I would know that I am not alone.
I love you.

They broke the sheds and built a town
Which grew stronger as city or state.
The city advanced as Accra has shown,
And the infant town conquered its fate.

—Dr. J.B. Danquah,
from the poem "Buck Up, O Youth!" (1938)

ALSO IN THE AKASHIC NOIR SERIES

ADDIS ABABA NOIR (ETHIOPIA), edited by MAAZA MENGISTE

ALABAMA NOIR, edited by DON NOBLE

AMSTERDAM NOIR (NETHERLANDS), edited by RENÉ APPEL AND JOSH PACHTER

ATLANTA NOIR, edited by TAYARI JONES

BAGHDAD NOIR (IRAQ), edited by SAMUEL SHIMON

BALTIMORE NOIR, edited by LAURA LIPPMAN

BARCELONA NOIR (SPAIN), edited by ADRIANA V. LÓPEZ & CARMEN OSPINA

BEIRUT NOIR (LEBANON), edited by IMAN HUMAYDAN

BELFAST NOIR (NORTHERN IRELAND), edited by ADRIAN McKINTY & STUART NEVILLE

BELGRADE NOIR (SERBIA), edited by MILORAD IVANOVIC

BERKELEY NOIR, edited by JERRY THOMPSON & OWEN HILL

BERLIN NOIR (GERMANY), edited by THOMAS WÖERTCHE

BOSTON NOIR, edited by DENNIS LEHANE

BOSTON NOIR 2: THE CLASSICS, edited by DENNIS LEHANE, MARY COTTON & JAIME CLARKE

BRONX NOIR, edited by S.J. ROZAN

BROOKLYN NOIR, edited by TIM McLOUGHLIN

BROOKLYN NOIR 2: THE CLASSICS, edited by TIM McLOUGHLIN

BROOKLYN NOIR 3: NOTHING BUT THE TRUTH, edited by TIM McLOUGHLIN & THOMAS ADCOCK

BRUSSELS NOIR (BELGIUM), edited by MICHEL DUFRANNE

BUENOS AIRES NOIR (ARGENTINA), edited by ERNESTO MALLO

BUFFALO NOIR, edited by ED PARK & BRIGID HUGHES

CAPE COD NOIR, edited by DAVID L. ULIN

CHICAGO NOIR, edited by NEAL POLLACK

CHICAGO NOIR: THE CLASSICS, edited by JOE MENO

COLUMBUS NOIR, edited by ANDREW WELSH-HUGGINS

COPENHAGEN NOIR (DENMARK), edited by BO TAO MICHAËLIS

DALLAS NOIR, edited by DAVID HALE SMITH

D.C. NOIR, edited by GEORGE PELECANOS

D.C. NOIR 2: THE CLASSICS, edited by GEORGE PELECANOS

DELHI NOIR (INDIA), edited by HIRSH SAWHNEY

DETROIT NOIR, edited by E.J. OLSEN & JOHN C. HOCKING

DUBLIN NOIR (IRELAND), edited by KEN BRUEN

HAITI NOIR, edited by EDWIDGE DANTICAT

HAITI NOIR 2: THE CLASSICS, edited by EDWIDGE DANTICAT

HAVANA NOIR (CUBA), edited by ACHY OBEJAS

HELSINKI NOIR (FINLAND), edited by JAMES THOMPSON

HONG KONG NOIR, edited by JASON Y. NG & SUSAN BLUMBERG-KASON

HOUSTON NOIR, edited by GWENDOLYN ZEPEDA

INDIAN COUNTRY NOIR, edited by SARAH CORTEZ & LIZ MARTÍNEZ

ISTANBUL NOIR (TURKEY), edited by MUSTAFA ZIYALAN & AMY SPANGLER

KANSAS CITY NOIR, edited by STEVE PAUL

KINGSTON NOIR (JAMAICA), edited by COLIN CHANNER

LAGOS NOIR (NIGERIA), edited by CHRIS ABANI

LAS VEGAS NOIR, edited by JARRET KEENE & TODD JAMES PIERCE

LONDON NOIR (ENGLAND), edited by CATHI UNSWORTH

LONE STAR NOIR, edited by BOBBY BYRD & JOHNNY BYRD

LONG ISLAND NOIR, edited by KAYLIE JONES

LOS ANGELES NOIR, edited by DENISE HAMILTON

LOS ANGELES NOIR 2: THE CLASSICS, edited by DENISE HAMILTON

MANHATTAN NOIR, edited by LAWRENCE BLOCK

MANHATTAN NOIR 2: THE CLASSICS, edited by LAWRENCE BLOCK

MANILA NOIR (PHILIPPINES), edited by JESSICA HAGEDORN

MARRAKECH NOIR (MOROCCO), edited by YASSIN ADNAN

MARSEILLE NOIR (FRANCE), edited by CÉDRIC FABRE

MEMPHIS NOIR, edited by LAUREEN P. CANTWELL & LEONARD GILL

MEXICO CITY NOIR (MEXICO), edited by **PACO I. TAIBO II**

MIAMI NOIR, edited by **LES STANDIFORD**

MIAMI NOIR: THE CLASSICS, edited by **LES STANDIFORD**

MILWAUKEE NOIR, edited by **TIM HENNESSY**

MISSISSIPPI NOIR, edited by **TOM FRANKLIN**

MONTANA NOIR, edited by **JAMES GRADY & KEIR GRAFF**

MONTREAL NOIR (CANADA), edited by **JOHN McFETRIDGE & JACQUES FILIPPI**

MOSCOW NOIR (RUSSIA), edited by **NATALIA SMIRNOVA & JULIA GOUMEN**

MUMBAI NOIR (INDIA), edited by **ALTAF TYREWALA**

NAIROBI NOIR (KENYA), edited by **PETER KIMANI**

NEW HAVEN NOIR, edited by **AMY BLOOM**

NEW JERSEY NOIR, edited by **JOYCE CAROL OATES**

NEW ORLEANS NOIR, edited by **JULIE SMITH**

NEW ORLEANS NOIR: THE CLASSICS, edited by **JULIE SMITH**

OAKLAND NOIR, edited by **JERRY THOMPSON & EDDIE MULLER**

ORANGE COUNTY NOIR, edited by **GARY PHILLIPS**

PARIS NOIR (FRANCE), edited by **AURÉLIEN MASSON**

PHILADELPHIA NOIR, edited by **CARLIN ROMANO**

PHOENIX NOIR, edited by **PATRICK MILLIKIN**

PITTSBURGH NOIR, edited by **KATHLEEN GEORGE**

PORTLAND NOIR, edited by **KEVIN SAMPSELL**

PRAGUE NOIR (CZECH REPUBLIC), edited by **PAVEL MANDYS**

PRISON NOIR, edited by **JOYCE CAROL OATES**

PROVIDENCE NOIR, edited by **ANN HOOD**

QUEENS NOIR, edited by **ROBERT KNIGHTLY**

RICHMOND NOIR, edited by **ANDREW BLOSSOM, BRIAN CASTLEBERRY & TOM DE HAVEN**

RIO NOIR (BRAZIL), edited by **TONY BELLOTTO**

ROME NOIR (ITALY), edited by **CHIARA STANGALINO & MAXIM JAKUBOWSKI**

SAN DIEGO NOIR, edited by **MARYELIZABETH HART**

SAN FRANCISCO NOIR, edited by **PETER MARAVELIS**

SAN FRANCISCO NOIR 2: THE CLASSICS, edited by **PETER MARAVELIS**

SAN JUAN NOIR (PUERTO RICO), edited by **MAYRA SANTOS-FEBRES**

SANTA CRUZ NOIR, edited by **SUSIE BRIGHT**

SANTA FE NOIR, edited by **ARIEL GORE**

SÃO PAULO NOIR (BRAZIL), edited by **TONY BELLOTTO**

SEATTLE NOIR, edited by **CURT COLBERT**

SINGAPORE NOIR, edited by **CHERYL LU-LIEN TAN**

STATEN ISLAND NOIR, edited by **PATRICIA SMITH**

ST. LOUIS NOIR, edited by **SCOTT PHILLIPS**

STOCKHOLM NOIR (SWEDEN), edited by **NATHAN LARSON & CARL-MICHAEL EDENBORG**

ST. PETERSBURG NOIR (RUSSIA), edited by **NATALIA SMIRNOVA & JULIA GOUMEN**

SYDNEY NOIR (AUSTRALIA), edited by **JOHN DALE**

TAMPA BAY NOIR, edited by **COLETTE BANCROFT**

TEHRAN NOIR (IRAN), edited by **SALAR ABDOH**

TEL AVIV NOIR (ISRAEL), edited by **ETGAR KERET & ASSAF GAVRON**

TORONTO NOIR (CANADA), edited by **JANINE ARMIN & NATHANIEL G. MOORE**

TRINIDAD NOIR (TRINIDAD & TOBAGO), edited by **LISA ALLEN-AGOSTINI & JEANNE MASON**

TRINIDAD NOIR: THE CLASSICS (TRINIDAD & TOBAGO), edited by **EARL LOVELACE & ROBERT ANTONI**

TWIN CITIES NOIR, edited by **JULIE SCHAPER & STEVEN HORWITZ**

USA NOIR, edited by **JOHNNY TEMPLE**

VANCOUVER NOIR (CANADA), edited by **SAM WIEBE**

VENICE NOIR (ITALY), edited by **MAXIM JAKUBOWSKI**

WALL STREET NOIR, edited by **PETER SPIEGELMAN**

ZAGREB NOIR (CROATIA), edited by **IVAN SRŠEN**

FORTHCOMING

JERUSALEM NOIR, edited by **DROR MISHANI**

PARIS NOIR: THE SUBURBS (FRANCE), edited by **HERVÉ DELOUCHE**

PALM SPRINGS NOIR, edited by **BARBARA DeMARCO-BARRETT**

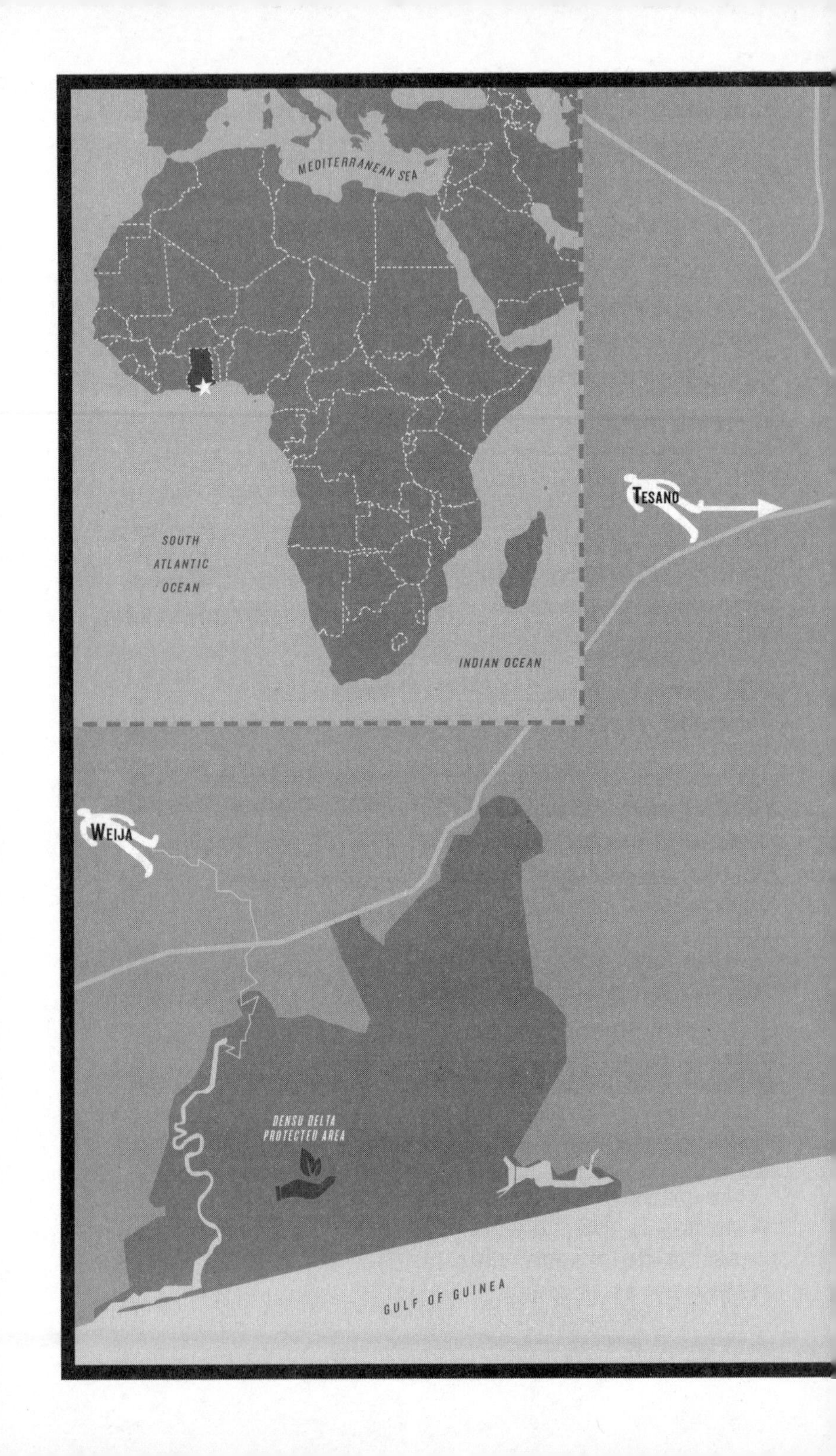
MEDITERRANEAN SEA
SOUTH
ATLANTIC
OCEAN
INDIAN OCEAN
TESANO
WEIJA
DENSU DELTA
PROTECTED AREA
GULF OF GUINEA

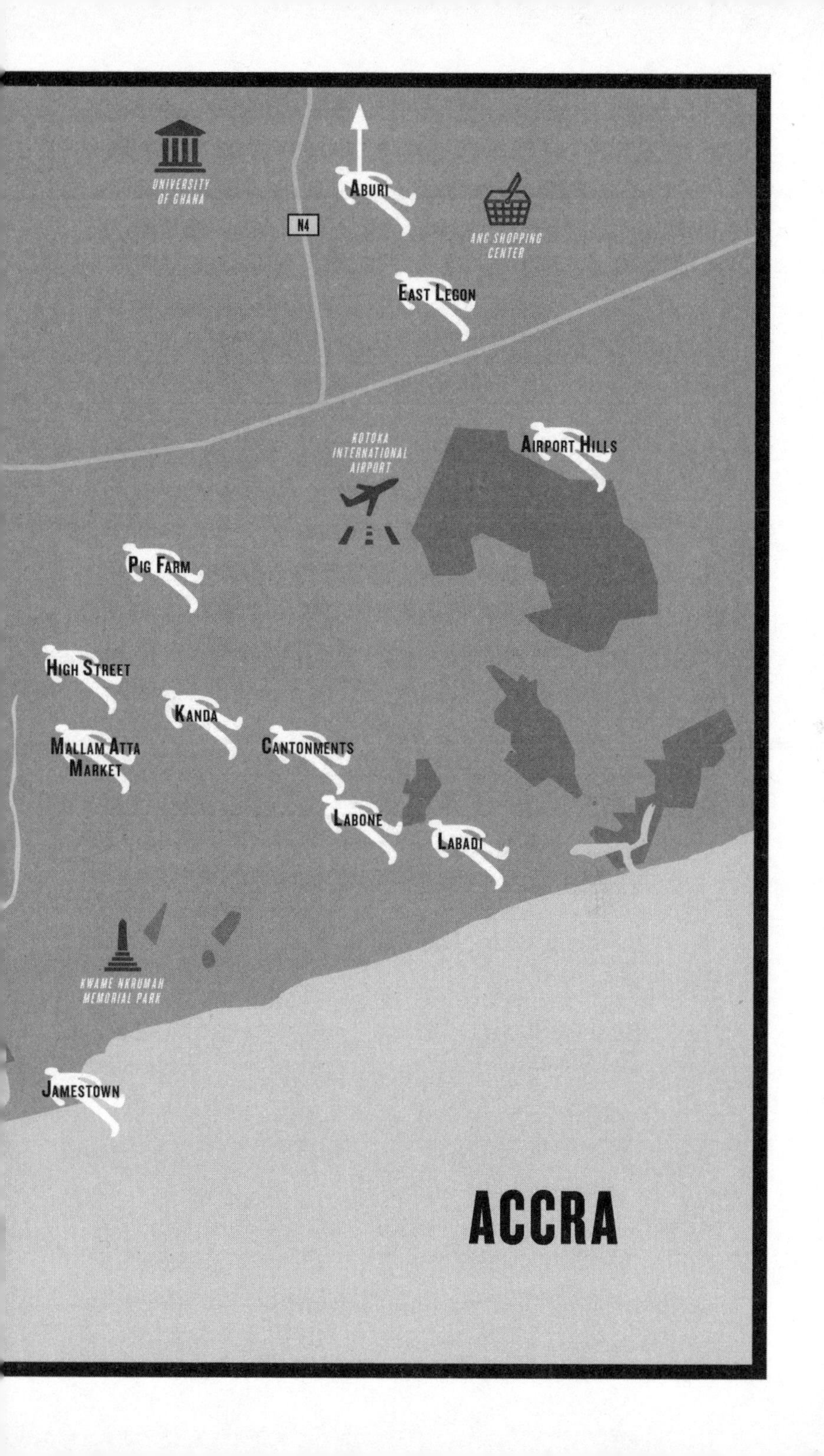
University of Ghana
Aburi
N4
ANC Shopping Center
East Legon
Kotoka International Airport
Airport Hills
Pig Farm
High Street
Kanda
Mallam Atta Market
Cantonments
Labone
Labadi
Kwame Nkrumah Memorial Park
Jamestown
ACCRA

Table of Contents

INTRODUCTION

Cry Your Own Cry

Accra is the perfect setting for noir fiction. The telling of such tales—ones involving or suggesting death, with a protagonist who is flawed or devious, driven by either a self-serving motive or one of the seven deadly sins—is woven into the fabric of the city's everyday life. Allow me to explain.

Accra is a city that stands at the center of the world. Of course, this is technically untrue. The center of the world is at the meeting point of those two imaginary lines that divide the globe into hemispheres, separating north from south and east from west—the equator and the prime meridian. It's the intersection of 0° latitude with 0° longitude. Accra's geographic coordinates are latitude 5° 33' 21.6" north and longitude 0° 11' 48.8" west; not quite the center of the world, but remarkably close. Those few degrees of distance notwithstanding, Accra has long served as the meeting point of east and west, north and south, as a cultural crossroads.

Accra is one of the most well-known cities in Africa. It's the capital of Ghana, which in 1957 became the first sub-Saharan (read: black) nation to gain independence from colonialism. But the city, in all its globalism, predates the nation. Prior to becoming a sovereign land, the area now known as Ghana was the Gold Coast, a British colony formed in 1867. Ten years later, Accra was installed as its capital. For nearly a century, in addition to being a political and financial center, the city was a major hub of trade. People came from Europe and other African nations to trade everything from gold and salt to guns and slaves.

Accra is more than just a capital city. It is a microcosm of Ghana. It is a virtual map of the nation's soul, a complex geographical display of its indigenous presence, the colonial imposition, declarations of freedom, followed by coups d'état, decades of dictatorship, and then, finally, a steady march forward into a promising future.

There is a story in every name, be it of a building or neighborhood such as Christiansborg Castle, Jamestown, Cantonments, Flagstaff House. Many roads and landmarks are dedicated to the architects of independence, not just Kwame Nkrumah, J.B. Danquah, William Ofori Atta, Edward Akufo-Addo, Ebenezer Ako-Adjei, and Emmanuel Obetsebi-Lamptey, the six men who are recognized as Ghana's founding fathers, but other leaders as well, including those of the Non-Aligned Movement like Egypt's Gamal Abdel Nasser, India's Jawaharlal Nehru, and Yugoslavia's Josip Broz Tito.

Given that Ghana's Independence Day is March 6, one might wonder why there is a street named 28th February Road, situated by Black Star Square and Independence Arch. It commemorates the Accra riots, which began on that date in 1948, and continued for five days in response to the deaths of three protesters, ex-servicemen, at the hands of the colonial police. The riots were considered a clarion call for freedom. It makes sense then that 28th February Road leads directly to the monuments of liberty.

Inside Black Star Square, upon declaring Ghana a free nation, Dr. Kwame Nkrumah, the first president, issued another clarion call: "Our independence is meaningless unless it is linked up with the total liberation of Africa."

This is not intended to be a history lesson, though history is perhaps the most straightforward way to explain how multifaceted the city is, how everything in and about it holds meaning and is sending a message. When in Accra, one learns quickly to look beyond the literal. It is not enough to consider a text; one must also consider the context, beware of a pretext, search for a subtext.

Earlier, I likened Accra to a map. As with most maps, there exists a legend through which one can decode any and all aspects of the place. Legends are merely definitions, commentaries.

Accra is a city of storytellers, people who speak and live and love in parables and aphorisms and proverbs. Sprawled on the back windows of taxis and trotros—the minivans that are used for unregulated public transportation—are sayings such as "cry your own cry," "every day for thief, one day for master," "jealousy will kill you," "haste not in life," and so on.

Admonitions and affirmations are also conveyed in symbols. The Ga people, an ethnic group that has inhabited Accra for over five centuries, have a system of symbols called *samai*. An example is adowa fai, the name of a symbol that translates literally into English as "deer's hat" or "crown."

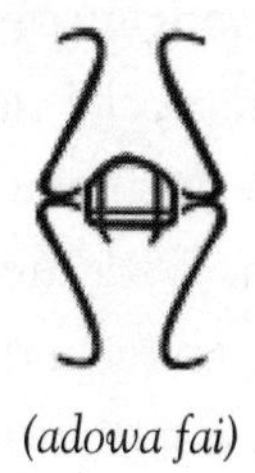

(adowa fai)

The message of this symbol is that the most admirable traits of the deer—such as its cunning, agility, wisdom, and swiftness—are also evident in a great ruler.

The tribes of the Akan clan also utilize a similar system of symbols called *adinkra*. An example is sesa wo suban, the symbol of transformation. The literal translation of the words is "change your character." This symbol is actually made up of two other adinkra symbols, the morning star, which represents the dawn of a new day, and the wheel, which represents rotation or independent movement.

(sesa wo suban)

These symbols, from both the samai and adinkra, are ever present. They are used in the design of cloth, jewelry, and home decor. They are utilized in the creation of visual art and referenced in music and literature. They are an essential part of the culture that shapes life in Accra.

The use of proverbs is not limited to the windows of vehicles and a set of symbols belonging to a specific tribe. Far from it. When an individual dies, a special cloth is designed for mourners to wear at the funeral. Each cloth design has a name, and each name is an aphorism. Weddings and naming ceremonies are rife with parables. Everything in the culture revolves around story, and every story has a moral or theme, one that can be encapsulated in a pithy phrase. We are born into this tradition.

There is one name that every child in Accra who is able to walk and talk definitely knows—Kwaku Ananse. He is the closest thing we have to a mascot or superhero. Ananse is a trickster, capable of assuming any form, though his usual appearance is half man, half spider. The stories of his adventures and misdeeds are called Anansesem, or spider stories.

Before Kwaku Ananse won the right to have all stories bear his name, those stories belonged to Nyankopon, the sun god, and were called Nyankonsem. There are many different tales about how and why Nyankonsem became Anansesem; the one I will share with you happens to be my favorite.

Legend has it that Nyankopon issued a challenge. He wanted to teach Death, a taker, a lesson about loss. Anyone who could bring Nyankopon the golden broom, golden pipe, and golden sandals that belonged to Death would have all the stories renamed after them.

Everybody wanted the stories, but they feared Death. (Whenever my grandmother would tell me this story, she would pause after this observation and say, "That's the way it is, Nana-Ama. Everyone wants to go to heaven but nobody wants to die to get there.")

Only Kwaku Ananse, a slick and wily creature, was foolish enough to take Nyankopon up on the challenge. With the help of a few other creatures, whom he'd promised to feature in the stories once they became his, Ananse entered the Kingdom of Death, a place from which no one had ever managed to return. But Ananse did return—with the items he'd been challenged to retrieve. He also returned with Death hot on his heels. Ananse had planned for this turn of events. He and the creatures who'd helped him enter the kingdom had even laid out a trap. Once they successfully captured Death, they chopped it up into a thousand tiny pieces, which they then scattered all across the land. That is why Death now exists everywhere.

Nyankopon kept his word and turned the stories over to Ananse, making them Anansesem. The stories, particularly the ones that specifically feature Kwaku Ananse, attempt to prove the truth of a proverb by showing what happens when one does not heed its inherent wisdom.

One thing that people, too easily seduced by the city's charm and history and beauty, forget about Accra is that it is a major metropolis. Accra is New York; it is Los Angeles; it is Shanghai, Mexico City, Santiago, Caracas, and Cape Town. It is an urban area, with poverty, desperation, and the inevitable result of a marriage between the two—crime.

In his book *The Coming Anarchy: Shattering the Dreams of the Post Cold War*, Robert D. Kaplan, an expert on global affairs, writes: "Crime is what makes West Africa a natural point of departure for my report on what the political character of our planet is likely to be in the twenty-first century. The cities of West Africa at night are some of the unsafest places in the world. Streets are unlit; the police often lack gasoline for their vehicles; armed burglars, carjackers, and muggers proliferate."

The stories that you will read in this collection will highlight all things Accra, everything that the city was and is—the remaining vestiges of colonialism, the pride of independence, the nexus of indigenous tribes and other groups from all over the world, the tension between modernity and traditionalism, the symbolism and storytelling both obvious and coded, the moral high ground, the duplicity and deceit, the most basic human failings laid bare alongside fear and love and pain, and the corrupting desire to have the very things you are not meant to have.

Much like Accra, these stories are not always what they seem. The contributors who penned them know too well how to spin a story into a web, elaborate with a geometrical arrangement of lines and a beautiful network of fractals. Read them carefully; read between those lines. Consider the context, beware of a pretext, search for a subtext. Remember that in the culture that defines this city, everything holds meaning and is sending a message. Kwaku Ananse exists in each story, in different forms.

It is an honor and a pleasure to share these stories—classic Anansesem, spider stories, in the guise of noir fiction—and all they reveal about Accra, a city of allegories, one of the most dynamic and diverse places in the world.

Nana-Ama Danquah
Accra, Ghana
September 2020

PART I

One Day for Master

CHOP MONEY

BY NANA EKUA BREW-HAMMOND

Mallam Atta Market

Limah abruptly lifted her head from the sticky valley of Charles's chest, stretching to light the wick.

"My time up already?"

Limah ignored him, hurriedly reaching for her T-shirt and skirt. Self-consciously, she checked that her head tie was still in place before bending to hand him his uniform and boots. The flame made shadow ghouls of the rubber soles.

"Do you think I will steal your shoes from your feet?" she half teased, noting his name crudely etched on their inner tongues. Charles thought everyone was out to take something from him. She handed him the boots now, needing him out so she could return the stall to her friend Asana. "I know you have to go back. And I have to clean this place."

He wore his rifle like a handbag before retrieving a five-cedi bill. He held the flaccid note over her head. "You said she's raised the price?"

"From thirty to fifty thousand." The Bank of Ghana had moved the decimal point four places over ten years ago because carrying fistfuls of cash, sometimes sacks, in the tens of thousands for groceries or taxi fare had become unwieldy and dangerous. But for Limah, and everyone else who worked in the market, the currency redenomination might as well have never happened. It hadn't changed the cedi's value or stemmed inflation.

"Nothing free in Ghana," Charles said, almost wistful as he handed her the limp legal tender.

"No. Nothing." Limah loosened the padlock at the door, but still Charles lingered.

"I worry about you here, alone." He adjusted his beret. The two chevron stripes on his navy shirt's shoulder band, indicating he was a corporal, were urine yellow in the wick's light.

"Didn't you all catch the rapist?"

"Is there only one?" He shrugged. "You may see me tomorrow night. Munhwɛ is recording a program here with that comedian Ahmed Razak. The MP has requested extra police presence."

She thought of whom she could leave Adama with so she could make more money with Charles. Asana usually watched her son, but tonight her friend wasn't able to. Adama was with Limah's fellow kayayei in the storage sheds outside the market, but Limah didn't like this arrangement: the kayayei were watching the owners' goods they would pile onto their heads and sell at the market during the day, and watching for armed robbers and rapists with the same eyes that monitored her son. But if she kept making an extra fifty thousand a week—forty after she paid Asana—she could start renting her own stall.

The thought softened the edges of her impatience. "The Munhwɛ people were here all day giving out flyers for a competition," she said. "They say the prize is a car and a date with Ahmed Razak."

Charles punched diagonal lines into the air and twisted the toe of his boot like he was extinguishing a cigarette, mimicking the azonto dance Razak opened his variety show with. His rifle swayed with the movement. "I hope you're not entering the contest when you have your own Ahmed Razak right here."

She laughed at his poor attempt at azonto, ushering him out. "They want only fat girls to enter. The show is called *Am I Your Size?*"

"Heavyweights make the best champions." It was only Charles's height that made his massive paunch describable as a boxer's build. "Let me hear the lock."

Limah closed the door and the padlock's shackle, calculating how long it would take Charles to exit the market before she could return the stall key to Asana and get back to Adama.

Limah and Asana had an arrangement. On the nights she met Charles, Asana sublet Limah the stall for ten thousand, from ten p.m. to four a.m. But it was the eve of National Sanitation Day and Auntie Muni, Asana's landlord, would be in early to make a show of cleaning for the Accra Metropolitan Assembly inspectors. They had agreed Limah should be out no later than three a.m. this time.

Limah quickly folded Asana's thin foam mattress and pushed it under Auntie Muni's counter. Then she gathered her pan and the stiff disk of folded cloth she used when carrying it, loaded with customer purchases, on her head. Again, she touched her head tie, feeling through the yellow polyester for the thinning spot in the middle of her pate, remembering how thick her hair had been before she came to Accra last year to kaya.

Checking for the knife she carried in her handbag—the one she had started sleeping with when Joy FM reported that a rapist was targeting kayayei—she unlocked the stall again. Briskly, she stepped out, her senses sharpened to any presence or sound beyond the ambient snarling of dogs in combat and scampering rats.

Limah had walked the length of Mallam Atta Market

so many times in the last year, she could do it in her sleep. Daily, she shadowed aging madams huffing in the heat, and spry young ones who seemed to stop short at every stall, almost capsizing her pan. Often, she carried for house help dispatched by their madams, some auditioning for a bigger role with insults they believed their bosses would hurl, most drifting too slowly through the rush, shove, and side step of the market, glad to be working remotely. Occasionally, tourists looking for places to stage their vacation selfies gave her a gratuity for carting their personal items on her head. Foreigners tipped the best. Once, one had pressed a ten-cedi note into her hand—one hundred thousand! She was lucky to get more than two thousand from anyone else. With about ten customers a day, she averaged seventy to one hundred thousand a week, most of it going to food, phone credit, and her family back home. Since she had been seeing Charles consistently these past four months, Limah had been able to count on an extra twenty thousand—now forty thousand.

As she turned the corner, the Adomi Street exit in sight, Limah remembered she had forgotten to blow out the wick. She sucked her teeth and turned back, doubling her pace. When she reached the corner stall, a hand snaked out.

"You don't rent this stall."

When Limah realized it was Charles who had ambushed her, she had already sunk all but the hilt of her knife into the flesh under his chevrons. With his strong arm, he yanked her by her headscarf. Limah felt the scallop-edged polyester slip past her shoulders as her heart made an uneven rhythm of her breath.

"I saw you last week, and the week before. You switch places with the one who rents it."

Watching Charles pull the knife out of his arm with a

pained gurgle, she felt exhausted by her lie. In the beginning, she had hoped their relationship could progress beyond these market nights, but now she realized she had just been deceiving herself.

Blood spurted from his bicep, surprising them both. "I want the money I've been giving you these last four months. Every pesewa."

Quickly, she inserted the key and yanked the padlock open, pulling him inside. The flame gyrated with the oxygen the opened door brought in.

Limah went for the Dettol behind the counter. The bottle held just a splash. She dragged down one of the many pieces of lace packed on the shelf that lined the wall, tore it free from its plastic casing, and soaked a corner of it with the antiseptic. The chemical stench filled the stall.

Charles whimpered as he struggled to unbutton his shirt. His right sleeve was now dripping rivulets of blood. Limah handed him the Dettol-soaked lace with shaking hands and watched him hurl it across the stall. The wick flickered dangerously.

"I have to go to hospital," he said with the weary sobriety of a child forced to admit misbehavior.

His blood was everywhere. All over his hands. On his trousers. Fat drops on his boots. Smears on Limah's T-shirt and the scarf that had been on her head. The cracked tile floor, a poor man's mosaic, was slippery with it.

"Help me up!" Charles barked.

Limah was a petite girl, slim and slight. The flame watched her futile attempts to hoist him. "Help me help you up!" she ordered finally, both of them alarmed when he couldn't. Then he slumped, his weight pinning her to the ground. She wriggled out from under him, her foot knocking the wick in the process.

She gasped at the sudden blackness and the silence that followed, only her breath and heartbeat in her ears.

"Limah!" Asana whispered sharply. Ah! Limah knew she had to be out before Auntie Muni came. She tapped the metal door insistently, pulling out her phone.

"*The number you have dialed has been switched off,*" reported the British woman who had won the contract to voice all such messages. "*Please try again later.*"

It was almost four a.m. In an hour, Auntie Muni would be at the market or close.

"Limah!"

Banging now, Asana wondered with mounting anxiety whether her friend had forgotten to drop off the key before heading to collect her son. She only had one and had given it to Limah.

Asana sank to the cement incline that rose into the stall. Seething, she rehearsed the curses she would hurl at Limah, and the cluelessness she would perform if Auntie Muni came to meet her locked out.

She rented the stall from Auntie Muni for thirty thousand a week. She only had use of it at night, to sleep in when the market closed. As part of their rental agreement, Asana cleaned the stall before she left in the morning, had her bath at the market shower, and then returned to sell Special Ice water for Auntie Muni, getting five pesewas for every thirty-pesewa sachet she sold, on top of the 2,500 a day Auntie Muni paid her.

The arrangement was a luxury Asana worked hard to keep so she wouldn't have to return to sleeping outside, praying away rain, armed robbers, and rapists. The ten thousand she took from Limah each week enabled her to save some of the roughly 200,000 (twenty cedis in the new money) she earned weekly selling for Auntie Muni. She planned to buy her own Special Ice carton and bring her junior sister from their uncle's farm in Yendi to sell for her until she could one day own a market stall.

But every week, Limah did something to risk Auntie Muni finding out that Asana let her use the stall to sleep with her police officer. She always seemed to forget something—a scarf, a still-smoking mosquito coil, a condom wrapper—and she always left later than their agreed upon four a.m., giving Asana little time to clean up after her. This week, she had not only told Limah to leave at three, but made an excuse not to watch Adama, hoping Limah would finish early to pick him up. Asana regretted this now, realizing she had no guarantee Limah would come straight back to her.

Ready to pound the metal door again, she heard a rustle coming from inside. Her pocket vibrated. She hissed Limah's name into her phone. "Open for me."

Asana listened for the metallic slide of the unlocking door and pushed her way in. Her eyes adjusting to the darkness, she turned toward the sound of two distinct ragged breaths, suddenly afraid she had entered a trap.

"Limah? Gom beni?" she asked in their native Dagbani, hoping the rapist or armed robber who might be holding her friend hostage couldn't understand.

"I am fine." Limah's voice shook.

"Why are you in the dark?" Asana's eyes still adjusting, she moved toward Limah's voice and tripped. Scrimmaging to her elbows, Asana turned to see what had made her fall. It hadn't been Limah's selling pan or some other discarded object. Whatever it was had the mass of an animal. A big one. Like one of the cows the men in Yendi used to pool money to buy and kill for Eid. She pulled herself up, yanking her phone from her pocket.

"Charles," Limah explained as Asana directed the device's light to the body.

Asana gasped. There was a lifeless police officer in Auntie Muni's stall, and there was blood. She put her hands on her head.

"I thought he was an attacker."

Asana nodded understanding. There wasn't a female among them who didn't know the fear that came with night. Whether guarding the wares they sold in the storage sheds, or asleep on the roadside just outside Mal' Atta, they lived with the paranoia of attacks past and recent. Even those who could pay to sleep in padlocked market stalls were vulnerable to armed robbers and rapists who knew they might be inside, easily overpowered.

"We have to get him out of here before Auntie Muni comes."

"He's too heavy." Limah's voice was thin with despair. "We should call the police."

"And tell them what? You thought your married officer was an attacker so you killed him?" Asana turned her phone's light on Limah. Her friend sat defeated, the swatch of fabric she had earlier worn wrapped around her hair now draped around her shoulders and streaked with blood, the balding circle of scalp she was so self-conscious about, exposed. "A police officer is dead. It will be your word—a kayayo—against his family's desire to bury him honorably, his wife's embarrassment, and his fellow officers' fear of crackdown when it's discovered he was with you instead of at his checkpoint. No. We have to remove him and clean this place before the market opens."

More afraid of what Auntie Muni might do to her than the police, Asana turned her phone around, the light searing her eyes. 3:57 a.m. The market opened at six, but proprietors would start arriving by five.

"The AMA inspectors will be here," she reminded Limah. The Accra Metropolitan Assembly often dispatched officials for surprise sanitation checks, but it being National Sanitation Day, they would be in the market in numbers. "And no telling when the Munhwɛ people will start coming. We have to do it now."

"We could take him to the hospital."

"Do you have 150,000 for a taxi to Korle Bu?" Asana sucked her teeth. "He's already dead. Start cleaning up. I'm going to find us some help to clear the body."

Muni accidentally kicked a short stack of plastic buckets as she turned the corner on the path to her stall.

"Who left these here?" she asked the small girl sweeping in front of the first shop in the row. Even though it wasn't her stall, the AMA inspectors would use such infractions to threaten to fine the owner—a pretext for negotiating lesser levies that would bypass the city's coffers for their own pockets. Where the inspectors started, they would linger. "Clear them now."

"Yes, Auntie Muni."

In front of her stall, Muni parted her bag's leather-band-and-gold-link handles to rummage for her keys. She dug past her phone, her face-powder compact, blotting papers, a handkerchief, a Munhwɛ TV flyer, P.K chewing gum wrappers, and magazine perfume strips she collected, always on the hunt for a new scent. Finally, she found her wallet, pulling out the keys that dangled from the ring attached to the zipper.

Muni tugged at the padlock and latched the heavy spinach-green metal door to the loop that moored it to the cement wall. She sniffed compulsively, as she did every morning. To her surprise, her shop smelled good. Fresh even.

Her kayayo and tenant Asana did a good job cleaning the stall, but there was a smell about the girl that always lingered. None of Muni's customers had yet complained about an unpleasant musk, and most of her lace was sheathed in plastic, but she worried nonetheless that the girl's raw odor would pique a sensitive nose like hers or seep into her stock.

This morning, though, the place had a lemony antiseptic smell to it. The shelves looked neater too.

Tank u, ma dear. Outdid urself. D shop is luking gr8, she texted Asana, using the shorthand her son, Abdul, messaged her with.

Abdul and his sister would be coming soon to help her man the shop. She had seen on the Munhwɛ TV flyer that the area MP and his wife, Alice, were planning to welcome Ahmed Razak to the market. Alice had become something of a friend during her husband's campaign, meeting regularly with the market shopkeepers to rally their support. Even after his win, Alice always dropped by Muni's stall and picked up a few yards of lace when she was at Mal' Atta. Muni looked forward to showing her the new pieces that had come in.

Abdul and Mariama were supposed to be at the market by seven a.m., but Asana and the other girls were to report before six to account for yesterday's sales and refill their pans with the supplies they'd be selling. She unlocked the stall's back door, which led to her small storeroom and the deep freezer inside. She switched on the generator.

The power supply had been out for two straight half days, but the cakes of frosty ice in the freezer had kept the water cold enough. The same couldn't be said for the ice cream and frozen yogurt. She felt the plastic sachets of FanIce and Fan-Yogo mixed in with the small water packets and frowned at their mushiness.

As Muni walked away, she noticed a plastic soap bottle on the floor. Instead of the syrupy green Fairy liquid the label advertised, there was a watery yellow solution inside. It was too pale to be urine, she decided, tentatively raising it to her nose. The pungent odor of ammonia and lemons induced her gag reflex. This was the scent that had greeted her when she opened her stall. She recognized it now as the cleaning fluid the market butchers used to disinfect meat, and the oddly pleasing fragrance that clung to Ibrahim. She arched her eyeliner-traced eyebrows and blinked away tears as she jumped to conclusions. *Of course Ibrahim would want to be with someone his own age*, she told herself. Aside from the way she smelled, Asana was a pretty girl.

"Auntie Muni?" The little girl who had been sweeping interrupted her thoughts.

"Yes, my dear?" She put the bottle down, covering her hurt with a smile.

"I have removed the buckets."

But what if it was Mr. Selifu? Muni asked herself, blooming with hope that Asana's visitor had been Ibrahim's boss instead. Resolving to ask Asana point-blank if she had broken their agreement by bringing a man into her stall, Muni dug in her bag and gave the girl the five-pesewa coin she was angling for. She followed the child out to see if Asana or any of her other kayayei were coming. The market would be open in twenty minutes.

Morning light was diluting the sky, and now, as far down the row as Muni could see, small girls were sweeping. The sound of the dried-reed brooms swiping rock-studded earth and cement was almost orchestral, accompanied by the creaks of traders dragging wood tables and benches into arrangement, and shopkeepers freeing heavy metal doors from their locks. The shrill of a loudspeaker suddenly disrupted this market symphony—a prelude to the more guttural beats of transaction that would come when the shops opened.

"*Testing,*" a man's voice announced, his breath heavy in the distant microphone. "*Munhwɛ TV test.*"

Muni pulled her handbag open to retrieve the Munhwɛ flyer. A sinewy young man with a dimpled grin had pressed it into her hand yesterday, on her way to the fifty-pesewa toilets.

"There's still time to enter, madam," he had said.

She looked up at him, noting his Munhwɛ TV T-shirt.

"Am I your size?" she flirted, reading the title of the show.

"Fat-ulous," he answered.

Muni had giggled at his unblinking recitation of Ahmed Razak's catchphrase.

"You should enter and try for the car."

She winked at him. "I have cars already."

The Munhwɛ boy had reminded her of Ibrahim, rangy and brimming with the muscular energy of youth. Now, she tucked the flyer back in her bag, feeling fresh pain at the prospect of her lover having been in her stall, with Asana.

"My guy never show?"

Ken shook his head at his supervisor.

"Those Mal' Atta girls have Charles under a spell. What kind of chook go for four hours?" Sergeant Duah joked about Charles's longer-than-usual absence.

The two men were moving the pair of metal barricades that made up their checkpoint on the neighborhood border between Tesano and Abeka. They leaned them against a tree off the road along with the plastic chairs they—really Ken—had been keeping watch in all night.

Ken suppressed a growl. He didn't care what kind of sex Charles was having, or why he was traveling twenty minutes by road to have it when there were girls much closer to home. He was sick of doing Charles's job and Sergeant Duah's too.

Both men exploited Ken's freshman rank, one of them usually disappearing for hours from whatever checkpoint they were assigned, or cutting him out of whatever "something small" they coaxed from midnight drivers.

How he longed to report them. But he knew retaliation would be swift. The old guard viewed any attempt at reform by younger officers as a "breach of discipline."

There were forty-four breaches listed in the Ghana Police Service handbook, but only two were consistently punished. The first: "Disobedience of a lawful order given him by his senior in rank, whether verbally or in writing, or by authorized signal on parade." The second: "Communicating to any unauthorized person matters connected with the Service without permission from the Senior Police Officer under whom he serves."

Ken was not so naive that he hadn't expected some form of hazing on the job. His uncle, now a chief inspector, had prepared him with tales of his first-year constable days. But even if he hadn't, Ken knew his people. Ghanaians acquired power three ways: money, position, and age. And when they had it, they wielded it with a hammer's blunt force.

Fitting his helmet over his head, he seated himself behind Duah on the senior officer's motorcycle. Taking advantage of the relatively open, pre–rush hour Nsawam Road, Duah zipped to their Munhwɛ assignment at Mal' Atta Market.

When they arrived, Duah stayed on the bike. "I'm coming, eh."

With gritted teeth, Ken watched Duah rev away, reminding himself that when the new class of academy graduates entered, he would move up a rung. He had received high commendations from his senior officers, and his uncle was friendly with the inspector general of police. He had hope that he would be considered for early promotion. Advancing from constable to lance corporal would mean a little more power and a little less abuse.

He yawned, wiping away a tear of exhaustion as he strode past the sign announcing Mallam Atta Market. Located in Kokomlemle, the central Accra neighborhood built in the early 1950s to accommodate the city's population spike, Mal' Atta served 1,800 customers daily, including workers in the now mostly commercial district and residents in neighboring New Town. From fresh vegetables to hair-braiding services, one could find almost anything among the stalls and stands spread across the market's 57,499 square yards. Stepping over a slim gutter, Ken braced himself as he passed through the entry partition between Mal' Atta's cement walls.

When Ken was a child, his mother sold cloth in Kumasi's Kejetia market. Growing up, he'd felt claustrophobic in the stadium-size crush laureled as West Africa's largest open-air bazaar. His childhood had been populated by men wielding crates and sacks filled with everything from water sachets to ground millet, and women stationed behind tables topped with pyramids of tomatoes, student math sets, or pans brimming with all manner of powdered condiments—all incessantly haggling.

When he reached his teens, and his mother made him roam the market for customers, balancing folded fabric stacks on his head, his aversion to market hustle hardened. He couldn't remember a happier day than when his uncle offered to pay his way through the police academy. Now, as he followed the traffic ambling toward the blaring Munhwɛ TV speakers, he resented his first-year rank all the more.

Mal' Atta attacked with a slew of sensory assaults. While the morning sun overexposed Vodafone-red and MTN-yellow umbrellas, massive wooden sheds roofed with corrugated-iron sheets made shadowy figures of those transacting inside. Between the sheds and umbrellas, the narrow paths were choked. Suppliers squeezed through, carting boxes or plastic containers. Preachers outfitted with microphones and portable speakers admonished anyone within earshot. Itinerant chickens avoided children free from their caretakers' backs who were chasing each other in dusty circles, urinating, or shitting within spitting distance of guardians skinning oranges or hacking sugarcane stalks. Patrons punctuated the chaos, rushing, dawdling, picking, poking, bargaining.

Threading through it all: the kayayei.

The mostly teenage kaya girls either balanced on their heads metal "China" pans coated in chipping plastic, weighted with the purchases of patrons they were muling for, or scanned for customers with pouncing eyes. Some worked with babies strapped to their backs with faded cloth. Ken noticed AMA inspectors chatting some kayayei up, grazing them, patting them, blocking their paths.

Maneuvering through the walkways like the reluctant market boy he once was, Ken found the Munhwɛ setup with relative ease. Four rows of pink plastic chairs faced a wooden stage, and the clipboard-wielding woman on it was directing a camera crew into position. Ken moved behind the platform, hoping to find a supervisor to note his punctuality.

He quickened his gait when he saw Inspector Quarcoo. The senior officer was engaged in what looked like a serious discussion with another uniform. Ken slowed his steps, surprised to see Duah with him, holding a pair of boots.

"I found someone on the roadside trying to sell them," Duah said. He placed the boots on a table and peeled back one tongue, revealing Charles's name.

"Maybe he gave them to the seller?" Ken said. "Charles is too big for someone to steal them off his feet." He turned to Inspector Quarcoo to see if he agreed.

"Look at them," Duah said.

Then Ken saw the blood.

Returning to her stall after a brief walk down the row, Muni dabbed her trickling hairline. A musky odor was aloft, and she knew Asana was now in the tight confines of the storeroom. She used her Munhwɛ flyer to wave away the smell, then dipped her nose in her handbag, inhaling the mingled notes of used perfumed strips.

"You've been using the deodorant I gave you?"

Asana looked up from the pan she was hurriedly filling with water sachets. "Yes, Auntie Muni."

Then why your foul smell? Muni didn't ask because she wanted to know instead if Asana had entertained Ibrahim in her stall. With impatience, she squinted at her employee and tenant. "Your pan will be too heavy."

The girl, still packing on her knees, looked up again. "Sorry?"

"Asana, did you have someone in my shop overnight?"

Muni watched Asana spread her arms, fasten each hand on either side of the pan, and raise it to her head in one motion.

"Never, Auntie Muni," she said almost too coolly. "Please, can I go? I saw that the Munhwɛ people brought bottled water for the crowd, but the sun is growing hot. People will need more."

"You cleaned this place very well, Asana. You used a different soap. Where did you get it?"

"Mr. Selifu."

"The butcher? Or one of his assistants?"

"I knew the AMA people would be here this morning so I couldn't just sweep. I had to scrub. But the Dettol was finished. I'm always seeing Mr. Selifu's boy scrubbing, so I asked him for some cleaning solution."

"Which boy?"

Asana's eyes bored into Muni's. "Jonathan."

Muni watched her kaya girl stagger slightly under the weight of the pan as she reached for the bottle.

"I'll take it back to him."

"You go and sell. I will return it to Mr. Selifu."

Asana stepped out of the stall into the bright hot chaos, before turning her head gingerly to face her landlady. "Oh, Auntie Muni, I have to go home for a few days. Someone has died."

Muni hated to lose Asana even for a short while. "Maybe your friend can step in while you're gone?"

"I'll ask."

As Asana retreated, Muni's phone lit up with her son's picture. "Abdul, where are you?"

Background noise answered.

"Did I tell you and your sister to come here for Munhwɛ TV? Come at once!" She would go to Ibrahim when the children relieved her. She resumed fanning herself as a woman walked into her shop.

"Hello, madam," Muni sang the greeting, hawking the customer's hesitation at a diamanté-studded bolt of teal and fuchsia fabric cut into connected leaves. "Swiss lace. Authentic."

When the woman walked out, Muni took out her phone and opened WhatsApp.

Where r u?! She shook the soap bottle impatiently until her son and daughter startled her.

Muni immediately left the kids to watch the shop, bounding outside. Her hairline sprouted more sweat with the exertion, the trickles streaking her foundation, beading under her chin. She mopped the drops, stopping absently to finger a pack of plastic-wrapped yaki weave dangling from the hair-braiding stall she passed. Her profuse sweating cost her so much in hair and blotting papers, she lamented as she walked on, fluffing her synthetic curls.

She took the long way to Mr. Selifu's, asking herself why she was so shaken by the prospect of Asana lying; that Ibrahim, not Jonathan, had given her the cleaning solution, and perhaps something more. If Ibrahim had done something with Asana, he was free to. Muni was a married woman with children close to his age. And if he hadn't done anything with Asana—her heart beat with hope—then it was just as Asana had said.

When she reached the butcher's, Muni's eyes immediately sought Ibrahim.

"Mr. Selifu!" She projected for Ibrahim's benefit.

"Auntie Muni?" The old man looked up from the warped wooden table he was carefully slicing goat flesh on. Ibrahim and Jonathan stood at opposite sides of the table behind him.

It seemed impossible to Muni that Ibrahim was the same age as his fellow apprentice. At seventeen, Jonathan looked like a child playing doctor in his blood-spattered butcher's coat as he scrubbed a shaved lamb. But Ibrahim made her slick with longing, even under a cloud of flies, hacking at a mountain of meat.

It wasn't just his nearly two-meter height—tall even for the taller northern people—it was his carriage. He never slouched. Meanwhile, Jonathan stood half-folded into an almost fetal stance, practically begging for permission to exist.

"How can I help you, Auntie Muni?"

She retrieved the bottle from her bag. "I wanted to return the detergent your boy Jonathan loaned my tenant Asana." Her eyes darted to Ibrahim's face, to see if he showed any emotion. She exhaled when he didn't. "I ran out of Dettol and she needed to clean. National Sanitation Day and all."

Mr. Selifu nodded dismissal, taking the bottle.

"Isn't that an awful lot of meat you have these boys taking care of, Mr. Selifu?" she said, her eyes still on Ibrahim and the meat he was methodically chopping.

"These days people like smaller cuts. They're cheaper." He turned back to his work.

Ibrahim winked at Auntie Muni.

Can I c u 2night? she texted him when she left. *Asana has traveled.*

Asana squeezed her throat and raised her pitch as she milled through the crowd of onlookers who hadn't been able to afford tickets to the live episode of Munhwɛ TV's new reality dating competition, *Am I Your Size?*

"Pyoooor water!" she cried, passing a group of dusty boys performing an elaborate sideshow of dance moves to beats blaring from the sound system.

"Ma me nsuo mmienu," a man ordered.

She traded him two sachets for sixty pesewas and called again, her voice wavering slightly as she passed a huddle of police officers. Her eyes nearly jumped from their sockets when she saw Charles's boots. She locked eyes with one of the policemen, the single jagged stripe on his shoulder conjuring the bloodied stripes on the dead man's shirt.

The officer signaled to her with a sharp whistle, but Asana hastened away with tangled legs, pretending she didn't hear. He ran to catch her and plucked three sachets from her pan.

"Ken, there's bottled water here," another uniform called after him.

"Wonim mpaboa yi?" the officer named Ken asked, pointing to the table where the boots rested.

"Do I know boots?" she repeated, dumbly.

"Do you know *these* boots? There's a name on them. Charles Gyampoh."

She swallowed her panic. "No."

"We know he was seeing a few of you kayayei."

Asana's knees trembled as a kayayo coming from Mr. Selifu's passed them, her pan heavy with meat. Another followed two paces behind.

"I don't know the boots."

Walking away, her ears pricked at the officer's words to his colleagues: "We have to turn this market upside down. Charles is too big to just disappear. It would take several strong men to overpower him or move him somewhere if he is dead. If he died in Mal' Atta last night, his body is in this market or close by."

Limah stopped at the butcher's stall behind the madam who had hired her. The woman momentarily removed the sugarcane cob from her jaw to order oxtail.

When the meat was weighed, wrapped, and placed in

Limah's pan, she announced playfully, "Mr. Selifu, that's it. You've taken all my money."

The butcher chuckled. "You and your mountains of money? Madam, how can I take all?"

The madam tipped her head at Limah in a *let's go* gesture, and resumed sucking the cob she had long drained.

Limah trailed her, her head heavy with meat, yam tubers, tomatoes, onions, ginger, okra, and garden eggs, and her neck straining as Adama drooped with sleep on her back. Her body was ready to drop, but her mind was awake. She could still see Charles's blood caked under her nails, could still hear Ibrahim chopping him into steaks.

"We can't let anyone buy this thinking this is goat or cow," Limah had said.

"I will drop small bits to the floor, add it to the slop people request for their dogs, maybe add some when someone orders a lot of meat," Ibrahim conceded.

"The main thing is, there will be no body," Asana had said. "While they are watching Ahmed Razak, while they are giving us meat to kaya, one by one, we—they—will be removing Officer Charles."

Limah almost dropped her pan when the madam stopped short.

"This Munhwɛ thing is blocking everything. Look at this nonsense."

A corpulent woman on all fours was onstage. Her buttocks facing the crowd, she jerked to the rhythm the deejay spliced. Ahmed Razak was on his feet on the dais. Praises, insults, and howls erupted through the assembly of two hundred or so packed on the pink chairs, and from those watching from the periphery.

When she finished displaying her gluteal muscle control,

lifting and dropping each cheek to the staccato track, the contestant leaned into the microphone and asked coyly, "Am I your size?"

Razak raised two thumbs and the crowd roared. "FAT-ULOUS!"

Limah followed the madam around the stage, passing the public toilets and a man urinating against a wall dripping red with the painted directive, *Do Not Urinate Here, by Order of* AMA.

It was now nine a.m. and National Sanitation Day was effectively over, AMA inspectors conceding the mess inherent in human exchange and the special case of the Munhwɛ event. Limah felt discarded water sachets crunch under her chale wote as she stepped gingerly over gutters oozing with runoff from washed hands, cups, and hair.

When they reached the market exit on Adomi Street, Limah motioned for help. Two small girls ran up as she lowered herself carefully so they could lift the pan and put it on the ground. The madam yelled into her phone—"Peter, ah! Where are you?"—as an ancient bottle-green Mercedes slowed in front of them.

Limah and her helpers unloaded into the Benz's trunk.

When they were done, the madam, now seated in the vehicle, searched her bag. "One for you, you, and you."

Limah glared at the coin in her hand.

"Hwɛ! You won't be grateful?" The madam threw her desiccated sugarcane cob through her open window.

Clutching her pan at her side, Limah watched the madam roll up her window, a hairline fracture tracing an arc in the glass that separated them. A small smile surprised Limah as she imagined the madam preparing the meat she'd just bought. She retreated as the car slowly pulled away.

SHAPE-SHIFTERS

BY ADJOA TWUM

Pig Farm

The hawker points wildly toward a crowd forming on the other side of the road. Intrigued, I find myself joining the throngs of people from the night market who have abandoned their stations to investigate the source of the commotion. I elbow my way through the sea of onlookers, too entranced by the hum of suspense to protest. I end up at the entrance of a large storm drain. Children love rummaging through the sewage for discarded tires to play with, more often emerging with used condoms that they gleefully blow up like balloons.

In the belly of the drain, two uniformed men intensely dig through its rotten contents. They heave something out of its crevices and deposit it gracelessly onto the road. The crowd steps back, permitting the headlights of a passing car to illuminate the object—a corpse. Its throat has been slashed, the blood coagulated around its neck like a grotesque pendant. Its coarse hair shrouds its face. Its body is bloated from marinating in the dank water. Some spectators clasp their hands on their heads and wail. Others kneel in prayer against whatever evil is responsible.

I disengage. I cautiously approach the body. I nudge its shoulder with my toe, the force causing it to roll back slightly, exposing its face.

"No . . . no . . . no . . ." I moan softly, recoiling from those familiar vacant eyes. I let out a guttural cry. I scream until I'm hoarse, until I have no air left to form another sound. "Help! Somebody help me, please!"

No one does.

A firework rocket announces its launch, rousing me from a violent sleep. I sit up, perspiration binding my thick coils to my forehead. I do not recall my dream, but the terror lingers. Disoriented, I tilt my head toward the dusty screened window. Outside, the starless sky bursts in breathtaking hues of crimson, sapphire, and gold. A typical Pig Farm New Year's Eve celebration rages on. Melodic highlife music blares from one of the many open-air bars. From the raucous laughter and effusive banter that occasionally cut through the musician's nasal vibrato, I can tell that libations are flowing. A prophet clangs a bell up and down the street. His voice quaking with urgency, he warns of the end of days and calls for all to repent. His premonitions are met with indifference by people too consumed with the night's shenanigans to worry about the Rapture.

I know how it feels to be unacknowledged. I have gotten used to reintroducing myself to people I have already met. I no longer take it personally. My own parents admit they did not enroll me in nursery school on time because they had simply forgotten. This particular transgression broke my heart. These days, I use my lack of presence to study people intimately in plain sight; their fears and inspirations. I come alive when I embody their greatest desires.

I have parlayed this skill into a career as a "good-time girl." But like all other mistresses, sycophants, and bottom-feeders, during the holidays I am without purpose. I spend most days languishing on my mattress, comforted only by the scent of past lovers trapped within its fibers.

A sudden coughing fit breaks my sober reflections. I wheeze until my throat is raw. I decide to stop by the local drugstore.

As soon as I cross the threshold of my rented chamber and hall, I am greeted by the overpowering stench of sunbaked feces. I wrinkle my nose in disgust. Although I've been living here for the past three years, I refuse to accept the inhumane conditions that force tenants to empty their chamber pots directly onto the streets. I hopscotch around the dark puddles staining the red earth and turn westward into a narrow alley. I amble past rows of aging compound homes nearly identical to the one I just left. Same leaky corrugated-tin roofs; same adinkra symbols welded imperfectly onto rusting wrought-iron gates; same urine-splashed walls. I run my hands gently along their cool, grainy exterior in appreciation of their sturdiness despite the degradation they endure daily. These structures are probably no different from the people who inhabit them, devalued yet resilient. Many of them labor thanklessly as factory hands, petty traders, and mechanics, yet they persist, determined to make it.

A thin piece of beached wood precariously balancing over a wide uncovered manhole grants me safe passage onto Kotobabi Main Road. I take a moment to savor the town's unbridled energy.

The bushy eyebrows of a kebab seller furrow as he carefully places his meat skewers on top of a scorching coal grill, the crackling fat shooting sparks into the air.

A resounding "GOAL!" erupts from a cracked television propped in the doorway of an electronics repair shop where a group of men are gathered. The announcement is met with cheering and dancing from supporters of the winning team, mixed with objections, jeers, and curses from the sore losers. A fight will soon break out. I move on.

Three young boys, dressed only in shorts made from repurposed flour sacks, zigzag between the legs of the stalls, squealing with excitement. Nearby, their mother molds fermented corn into kenkey, the embers from her coal pot casting a haunting glow on her worn face. I pause briefly here, hypnotized by the smoke dancing out of her crude kerosene lamp.

This is Pig Farm.

This neighborhood is an outcast's haven, dating back to the days of the swineherds who inhabited the land before finding themselves on the wrong side of industrialization. Their livelihood threatened by the introduction of industrial abattoirs, they morphed into the backbone of Ghana's burgeoning economy; making, selling, and fixing things. Today, migrants converge here from across the country to exploit its cheap rent and proximity to business hubs.

A police truck roars past me, its side-view mirror grazing my elbow. I cry out, but it thunders onward, leaving in its wake a cloud of soot that triggers my cough again.

I look up just as a street hawker sprints past me, yelling, "Hurry, hurry!" A crowd follows him, their interest piqued. I change course and join them.

I must have dozed off. I quickly scan the hall. Everything appears as it was. The TV is still airing telenovela reruns. My screen door is still ajar to let in the harmattan breeze. On my coffee table lies an envelope stuffed with cash—enough to sustain me for another eighteen months. Each grimy note is intact. However, I can't shake the feeling that I am not alone. In two determined strides, I'm standing outside my dark bedroom. Nothing looks out of place there either, but my intuition tells me otherwise. I enter.

I smell her before I see her. Cocoa butter lotion mixed with

CK One perfume. "Salome," I utter in disbelief. At the sound of her name, she steps out of the shadows, where she had been camouflaged by the billowing tan curtains that frame the small window. I reach nervously for the light switch and flick it on. I drink her in. She stands still, an onyx idol. Her jumbo braids cascade neatly down the small of her back. She tucks one behind her ear, then speaks.

"Hello, Saman."

Saman. Ghost. She's the only one who calls me that. Upon hearing her voice, I free-fall head over heels into our past.

The ride to the airport is uncharacteristically quiet. Normally, Salome would be reenacting outrageous scenes from our favorite Bollywood movies, complete with neck rolls and a Hindi accent; and I would be applauding and cackling, her constant cheerleader. But today, she just grips my fingers between hers, forehead creased. The taxi driver also says nothing, but from the rearview mirror he glares at the jezebels spooning in his backseat. We lock eyes, my defiance matching his revulsion. He looks away and concentrates on the pothole-ridden road.

We enter the leafy suburb of Airport Residential Area. The smell of freshly cut grass wafts into the car. It reminds me of those brief yet painful days of my youth, when I sought rest atop their sharp blades. I roll up the window.

"You don't have to do this, you know," Salome says.

I tense up. This plan is Salome's brainchild. It's all she's been raving about for the past month. This deal, she has explained, is a game changer for Oga, her big boss, an unseen but revered criminal mastermind.

Then I understand.

I pull her in closer. I, too, ache just thinking about us being apart. Salome found me a year ago and breathed new life into me. But this mission is too lucrative to pass up.

"I want in," I admit. "Besides," I add, tracing her clenched jawline with my finger, "who else can you trust?"

The taxi rolls to a stop. We're here. Salome reluctantly peels herself off me. She retrieves the luggage from the boot. It's an old black suitcase, secured by a brass padlock. Its plain appearance belies the intricate network of hidden compartments which we have dutifully filled with cocaine. She plants travel documents in my palm.

"Our associate will contact you once you get to London." We hug. She gives me a quick peck on the cheek and chews her lip. "You know what to do next."

This hurts, but I'm in too deep to change my mind now.

"Hurry back, okay?" she sniffles. Then she is gone.

I march into Kotoka International Airport, a massive rectangular ark.

The departure hall is a madhouse, congested with people in motion.

A woman with the brightest fire-engine red weave I've ever seen quarrels with an airline agent, shaking her meaty fist.

A porter in an ill-fitting lime-green uniform pushes a trolley up a sloping walkway, the wheels squeaking with every strained step.

And then there are the bɔgas strutting around the terminal, reeking of cologne.

I can't pull this off.

The air conditioner above me is on full blast, causing the back of my neck to break out in goose pimples; yet I fan myself madly with the plane ticket.

I won't get away with it.

I can't breathe. I claw at the collar of my dress shirt but

can't find the button. I feel my chest tightening. I am hyperventilating. I sink to the tiled floor, its black-and-white squares like a giant crossword puzzle swimming before my eyes.

She'll never forgive me.

A white man with wispy auburn dreadlocks and scuffed hiking boots squats in front of me, his head cocked to the side. He speaks with a gentle baritone in a language I do not understand, then offers me a bottle of water with an outstretched tanned hand. I swat it away. He hesitates, then leaves.

What am I doing?

I rise.

I exhale; pick up the suitcase.

I exit the airport into the merciless Accra heat, pulling my bounty behind me.

There's no coming back from this.

My eyes dart between the intruder and the rusty cutlass leaning against my dresser. Salome raises her hands in surrender. She's trembling.

"Please, Saman, I need your help." She inches closer. "Oga wants me dead."

My body turns into lead. "But . . . but you are his best employee," I sputter.

"Was," she corrects me. "When you were a no-show, Oga thought I was in on it. I . . ." She shudders. "I was tortured. Then demoted, doing all sorts of donkeywork to get back into Oga's good graces. But it's no use now. There's a price on my head."

I'm overcome with guilt. No doubt there would have been consequences. I just never thought Salome would be the one to pay the ultimate price.

Salome paces my room, invading every inch of my sanctuary. Her voice scales with each hurried sentence, like fingers gliding across a keyboard. "You were supposed to be dead three years ago, but here you still are. That makes you the only person to cross Oga and live to tell the tale. That's why I tracked you down. I need to know how you did it. I need to get away before his thugs find me. I can't keep running. I need you to help me disappear! I need to start over. Like you did. Go somewhere else. Be someone else." She pauses before striking the final chord. "I need you to make this right, Saman."

Sighing, she takes my hand in hers and implores me with those captivating eyes. "Please give me the stuff you took. I have a kilo on me, but I need more to make a clean break."

"I . . . I . . . sold it," I mumble, head bowed.

Salome stiffens and lets go of my hand. "You . . . sold it," she repeats, choking on the words.

I confess everything.

How I sold what I now know to be a small fortune for a tenth of its value. How I met my buyer, Latif, at an auto-body shop that was also a warehouse for smuggled goods in transit—weapons, precious minerals, even children. How we bonded over life on the fringes. How he clucked in sympathy when I disclosed my dangerous assignment. How he suggested—casually at first, growing bolder with every unanswered probe—that perhaps I was getting a raw deal. How he promised to pay me double while eliminating any chance of incarceration.

Zero risk. Double reward. I liked those odds. I was all in.

Salome mulls over this revelation in pained silence, then lowers herself onto my thin mattress. I drop to my knees before her, weighed down with remorse.

"This changes everything," she says flatly, breaking the heavy stillness enveloping us.

I search those dark eyes, desperate to uncover what she's

thinking, how she's feeling. Instead, there's a hollowness there that didn't exist before.

"I know what I did was wrong," I croak. "But I can fix this. I'll get you the money. Whatever you need. Just give me one more chance. Please. Let me make it better for you."

And I do.

I have not kept in touch with Latif since our rushed exchange outside a mosque three years ago, but tracking him down is easy. I slip the auto-body shop's attendant a twenty-cedi bill and walk away with Latif's number. Once I get him on the phone, he leaps at the opportunity to purchase the kilo. We agree to meet at Club 1000 Hotel to complete the transaction.

I patrol the entrance of the run-down hotel, kicking up clouds of copper dust and obsessing about Salome.

Last night, she asked me to leave with her once the present threat has been extinguished. This time not as a drug mule and her handler but as soul mates taking another shot at their happily-ever-after. With Latif's funds, we should be airborne within the next week, putting all the rancor behind us for good.

I steal another look at my watch. Salome and Latif should have been here by now. I stick my head inside the lobby. A statuesque woman wearing a hijab sits at the reception desk, studying me suspiciously through kohl-rimmed eyes. She chews loudly on a kola nut as I shuffle toward her.

"Good evening, madam," I greet.

She just glowers at me.

"Please, I am looking for my friends, a man and a woman."

She snorts, the force of which sends nut-infused spittle all over the desk. "At this time of the night? Take your pick!"

"She's not a prostitute," I shoot back, a bit too defensively.

The woman shrugs. "Try room 211."

After stumbling along a dimly lit, seemingly endless corridor, I finally find room 211. I knock. "Salome?"

No answer.

"Latif?"

Still nothing.

I turn the handle, but the door is wedged shut from the inside. I shove it repeatedly until it swings wide open, revealing Latif's lifeless torso. I clamp my hand over my mouth and stagger backward in horror. My heart thumps against my rib cage so aggressively that I fear it might shatter. I let out a strangled cry as someone grabs the front of my T-shirt, pulling me fully back into the room. I thrash at my assailant, but my uncoordinated jabs fail to connect.

"Heh! Stop that!" the person hisses.

It's Salome, but my relief is short-lived when I digest my new surroundings. It's a modest-sized, sparsely furnished room, unremarkable really, save a few features.

A claw-foot bed devoid of sheets or pillows.

A wardrobe missing a wooden panel.

A framed portrait of Jesus in a green pasture, bearing a staff in one hand and a lamb in the other.

And blood.

So much blood.

Splattered on the dirty peach walls.

Soaking the shaggy carpet.

Squishing under the soles of my flip-flops.

I retch. "Salome! What happened?" I demand, in between gulps of air.

She slams the door shut and wags a finger at me. "Why are you asking me? Don't you remember? You did this." She sneers.

"Are you mad? How can you joke at a time like this?" I shriek. "Latif is dead!"

Her face contorts into a terrifying mask. "So what?" she explodes. "Did you really think that after you guys stole from me, I would just pretend it never happened and run off into the sunset with you?"

A chill creeps into my bones, like a bucket of iced water has been dunked on me. I back away from her slowly, shaking my head to ward off the frightening thoughts forming in my mind. "You set me up." I gasp.

"And I got my money back." She motions toward a woven red, white, and blue plastic *Ghana Must Go* bag flung carelessly in the corner.

Just then the door flies open and a tall, muscular man enters. He wildly surveys the room, from the man bleeding out on the floor to the two women standing before him. Nostrils flared, he roars in thick Nigerian pidgin, "Oga, wetin happen now?"

I whirl around, expecting Oga to materialize out of thin air. But all I see is Salome. My eyes widen as the final puzzle piece locks into place.

I bolt toward the door, but the man blocks my path, his face transformed into a menacing scowl.

"Seize her!" Salome barks. Instantly, the Nigerian tackles me, covering my mouth with a large calloused hand and pinning my arms to my sides.

Salome sidles up to me, eyes narrowed to slits. "You know what? You are much smarter than I ever gave you credit for. To hide right under my nose while I tore Europe apart looking for you these past three years. I always knew you had potential. That's why I was grooming you. But this." She laughs humorlessly, clapping slowly. "This is almost genius. You had me fooled. A whole me. The leader of the only woman-run criminal enterprise in Ghana. Maybe all of Africa. You cost me a lot. Not just money. No, worse than that. You made me a laughingstock. You already know how hard it is for women to be taken seriously in this society. How much more in the underworld? They said I couldn't do it. That I couldn't run my own organization. That women are emotional, too unstable. Because of you I proved them right. And for what?"

Her voice softens. "I risked it all for you." Her voice is now scarcely above a whisper. "I thought you would do the same for me." She leans in, so close that I can feel her hot breath against my neck.

A sharp pain sears through my abdomen. The Nigerian's rough palm stifles my screams as Salome plunges, then twists a small hunting knife deep into my core. I flail like a broken marionette, but that only seems to galvanize her more. Then she stops.

She yanks my head back and watches me with mild amusement.

And with one flick of her wrist, Salome slits my throat. Blood squirts out of my severed windpipe. The Nigerian releases me, and I land on the soiled carpet with a loud thud. Before everything fades to black, I watch the queenpin pick up Latif's money and strut toward the door.

As I take my final protracted breath, the Nigerian speaks up: "Oga, wetin make I do plus the bodies?"

"Leave them to rot," she snaps, then pauses. "Wait. As for the girl, there's a gutter near the market. Dump her there."

Suro nnipa na gyae saman.

(Fear man, not ghosts.)

—Paapa Yankson

MOON OVER ABURI

BY KWAME DAWES

Aburi

1

A Man, a Woman, and a Boy

—Is it always damp like this?

—You haven't been here before?

—No. Funny, eh? I always said I would visit . . . I would pass it all the time. Everybody at school used to come here. This is where the girls would meet the boys.

—Oh, so you are an Achimota boy.

—It is not the only school here.

—You look like an Achimota boy.

—Well, you should know.

—So you live in Accra, yes?

—I do.

—And never came before . . .

—Never had cause. I am sure . . .

—What?

—No, it is fine. Do you have fish?

—Oh finish what you were saying.

—I don't want to keep you from your work.

—You mean my thriving business.

—Well, when it stops raining.

—Oh no, it is Tuesday. The crowd has come and gone. One or two might come, but we are not expecting anybody. If you buy some fish now, then we will have done well . . .

—So you won't close up?

—One or two might come.

—Right, of course, like me . . .

—Like you. How far in did you go?

—I drove around. I walked a little. The air is so wet—heavy.

—Rain forest.

—Yes, but everything is thick, green. The leaves, the grass.

—Late in the night, if you stop and listen, it is as if the world has arrived here as it always has been.

—Hey.

—I am a poet, eh?

—I know things about you, but not that.

—You know things about me?

—I am a prophet.

—Oh, is that right? I knew you looked like a minister.

—I do?

—So what kind of minister?

—A hungry one. You have fish, fried fish?

—No, just red-red.

—With gari?

—I think there is some. But no plantain. So Baptist, Pentecostal, Anglican? I know you are not a Catholic . . .

—How do you know that?

—Well, you carry your piety like a badge of honor. Catholics are casual about it.

—Maybe that is an insult.

—No, no, just a fact. I think you speak in tongues.

—You can tell that by looking at me?

—Perhaps.

—Anyway, I want red-red, but I need it with plantain.

—You can have it without plantain.

—But how can that work?

—It is finished. So what can I do?

—I can't eat it without plantain.

—Are you a chief? Your stomach makes demands like that.

—I am a prophet.

—That is right. Okay. Wait. Kwaku? Kwaku!

—Yes, Ma?

—Go down to the road and get some kelewele. Plenty. And run and come back now.

—Yes, Ma.

—But you didn't have to do that.

—Well, I read my Bible. You might be an angel, not so?

—No, no, no. But you didn't have to, I was teasing you.

—Oh, you will pay for it now.

—Of course, of course I will pay. I will pay extra. So is that your son?

—What if it is?

—Oh, why are you so touchy? I was just asking . . .

—I can tell what kind of minister you are. It is like you are trained by police. You know, the kind who will ask you questions and you don't even know they are asking you questions, and then the next thing you know, they are telling you things you have already said but didn't know you had said, and next thing you are confessing and thinking, *But only God could have told this man these things about me*, and you fall down and shake and say hallelujah. Salvation. That is the kind of minister you are now, isn't it?

—I don't know if you know police more or preacher more.

—I don't know either. I am a cook. I cook and I feed you.

—But you were not always a cook, now.

—Who told you that?

—You are educated.

—Oh, so a cook can't be educated?

—Maybe. A cook can be anything, but an educated cook was something before she became a cook.

—Yes, I was. Detective Deacon.

—You are a joker.

—Maybe, maybe. The rain is coming down now. That boy better hurry.

—Maybe he went home.

—He went home, yes?

—No, because home is with you . . .

—I didn't say he was my son.

—I didn't say he was your son.

—Well then we are agreed.

—But he looks like you. Yes, I know he is mixed, but one part could be you.

—That is prophecy now?

—I have eyes to see.

—Well, not everything you see is what is there.

—That is true.

2
A Woman

—Let me tell you a story. It is about my grandmother. The Colonial Office had well-trained officers who had to make sure that the sanitation situation was fine in the towns. They lived in constant fear of malaria and sickness, and they were not worried about us, but about themselves. But since they had to live with us, they had to be sure that we were not sick. My grandmother hated them, and she did not like people telling her what to do. She was a tall woman, very strong, and she made her living as a seamstress. They used to come to the road and investigate. They would open the water barrels where we stored drinking water, and if they found larvae, they would turn it over. Well, she wouldn't have it. So one day they came and she moved the wood covering of a barrel, and she could see that there were larvae. She took her dipper and pulled up some water. They said look, "Look, there is larvae." She looked at them and said, "I don't see larvae." They insisted. And so she took the dipper and drank all the water in five gulps. Then she opened her mouth and said, "See?" They called her a madwoman, but they walked away. One day I asked her what would she do if someone hurt me. She said women have killed before. Sometimes a life must not be allowed to continue to make more mistakes. She did not smile. I was very afraid of her. And yet I felt safe with her. When I was bullied, I feared for the bullies. I had to force myself to not tell her. I wasn't afraid of them. I was afraid *for* them.

3

A Woman and a Man

—Sometimes we mourn alone. Sometimes we have no right to mourn. My grandmother told me to be merciful to sad women who we want to call mad. She said everybody has a reason when they are mad. Sometimes they are allowed to tell why and many times they are not. She asked me if I remember when she was always singing and crying when I was growing up. I said yes. I remember because for years she was sad. So sad. So she told me that she was not mad. She said her boyfriend was murdered. I was frightened by this. I said, "How could you have a boyfriend?" She said it was before she met my grandfather. He was her age. When she was studying at the University of Science and Technology in Kumasi, he was at school in Achimota. And he would come and visit her. She looked in my face and said, "Sometimes a touch leaves a scar you always touch," and I knew she was telling me that they slept together. Then they broke up because she thought she was pregnant and told him and it did not make him happy, and he thought she was too familiar with one of her teachers. They grew angry and he left. Then he had to hurry to Lomé where there was a new political time. He became one of the leaders and married a girl from Togo. My grandmother went with my grandfather. Then this boyfriend was killed in a coup. He was apparently hiding in his home while they took his wife from the house. And then she looked back and saw him on the roof and maybe her face betrayed her and the soldiers looked. They found him. They shot him. My grandmother said the woman was a fool. I could not understand her anger. And so she cried, she said, and was sick for five years. She told nobody. It was her only love. She said, "Be merciful to women." We love ghosts. We women love ghosts. They stay with us for a long time. She told me that, you know? She saw me and she could tell that I was living with a ghost.

—A man?

—It is not always like that.

—People die.

—Yes, but sometimes you feel if it wasn't for you . . .

—But she wasn't responsible for the coup.

—No, but she still loved him, and so she couldn't mourn, even though she mourned.

—So you are mourning.

—I am a cook.

—I think we are in agreement that everybody is more than they say they are.

4

A Man and a Woman

—This stew is good.

—Uhhmmm, the plantain is fresh, that is why . . .

—Pepper, it's good, you can cook.

—I am a woman.

—But it is not a given.

—Oh, your wife, she can't cook?

—A lot of assuming.

—So she can cook.

—Who said I have a wife?

—Because you are asking me that question.

—I think *you* are the detective.

—Well, you said I was educated, so . . .

—Where is the boy's mother?

—She left.

—She left him?

—She left all of us. She left everything.

—What does that mean?

—Sometimes the heaviness of life is so much that you have to leave. Some of us leave one place and go to another. Some of us stay in one place but go away. She stayed in one place, but she left. You understand that, I know you do.

—And his father?

—Men are always leaving. That one is not very remarkable.

5

A Woman and a Man

—If there is nobody waiting for you . . .

—Who said there was nobody?

—You have not looked at your phone since you came here. It is late.

—It would be impolite.

—Then maybe somebody is waiting for you.

—So you think there is?

—You are a man with a satisfied body. Clean-shaven, starched shirt, clean socks, and polished shoes, but not too polished, and there is neglect, as if somebody forgot to iron the trousers, and you are not worried about impressing somebody that you are cared for. A maid does not forget to iron your clothes. A wife will smile and say sorry, and quarrel with you about doing it yourself. You sit like a satisfied man.

—You mean I am fat.

—I mean you are satisfied.

—Can I be honest?

—We are alone now.

—Does that not worry you?

—Now why would you do that? Why say something like that . . .

—I am sorry, I did not mean . . .

—Look, I can tell you are here for a reason, I don't believe you . . .

—I did not mean to suggest . . .

—You meant to frighten me a little. Or a lot. If you did not know this, if you say it was accidental, then you don't even know how this power of threat of violence is deep inside you. You think you are a threat by being yourself, but it does not frighten you because you are so arrogant and so sure of your power that you do not fear that I might be afraid of you.

—You are making too much of it.

—And you are not a minister, not a prophet.

—As I drove here, I saw you standing in this place with all

these trees. I have never been here before. I saw the blue cloth you had around you. The shirt you are wearing—a tailored men's shirt, unbuttoned low enough for me to see the filigree of your black brassiere. And I could see your eyes, heavy with knowledge, and your face of carved ebony—and I said, "Beautiful," because that was the easy word. The hard word was *unreachable*. I saw the scarf. I saw you before I got here. This is not to frighten you. It is to frighten *me*.

6

A Man and a Woman

—This was very good.
—Hold your hand out.
—Thank you, thank you.
—Here is the cloth. The ginger and onion will stay on your fingers. You can use soap as soon as you get home.
—I am the prophet, not my wife.
—I forgot that you are the prophet. And now I know you have a wife.
—I suppose, but you knew that. Like you said, I look like a man with a wife. But you don't believe I am a prophet. You have two kinds of prophets. The Bible is clear about that. One will tell you what is to come. That one goes around and says that this and this will happen. That prophet is the one who flames up like fire, and then suddenly, it goes away. That one does not even understand what she is doing. One day she starts to see things, and she knows what is happening. And just like that, it goes away. God goes away. The people who used to live here, Ashanti people, they used to have those prophets. Long before the British people came and built the sanatorium up here, Osei Tutu and his people knew that this place was

special. Some prophet said it. They did not even understand what they were hearing, maybe. That is one kind of prophet. And then there is the one who explains things—that one is like a preacher, but different because she sees things, explains things, shows you things in your heart, shows you who you are. That one is always a surprise to the people who hear her, but never to herself. She is always going to be a prophet. People call them wise. Like how people call *you* wise. Don't they? I know, you tell them they don't know, but you know things and you know people's hearts, and you can tell if they are good or bad. Isn't that it?

—Well, you think you know me well.

—I know *about* you. Yes. I know you were not always cooking. I know if things did not happen you could be an . . . inspector.

—So you are a policeman. Are you investigating me?

—No, I am a minister. A prophet.

—But you came to see me.

—I came to see you.

—It is far for you to come.

—Yes, but it is a nice drive. By the time I reached Achimota there was not too much traffic. Then Dome, then through Kwabenya town, then straight through Berekuso. Even down at the T-junction, the people selling fish looked idle, as if somebody had told them that a storm was coming. Anyway, it was nice and cool by the time I started up here. I did not know if I would find you. But God was guiding me.

—You want to know something funny?

—What is it?

—I have no interest in knowing why you are here. Why is that? I am not even curious.

—Maybe you know. Maybe you are a prophet.

—Oh, you know I don't know. But everything is about one

thing, and that thing, it is so normal in my life that it is not even important.

—You are right, it is a strange thing.

—That is what I said. Look, look, look.

—What?

—There, see, the moon. The cloud opened and the moon, look!

—It is beautiful.

—It is very beautiful.

7

A Woman

—Did you know that in Nairobi, if you map all the tweets that happen, most of them are clustered in the zoo? It is white people looking at animals. And all around, there is darkness. But I like to think of my world, which is a lonely world, as a place where our hearts spark light at moments of great trauma or crisis. Think of the map of the world. Everything is black. Then think of sparks, sharp bursts of white and yellow light every time someone says, "Help." Every second would look interesting. It would make it seem like we are not alone. Sometimes I think of what would happen if every time a woman had an orgasm a light flared up. There is something of pained joy there. The world would look like joy. And none of us would be alone. You may be ready to take me with you. And nothing will spark on the map. This is the darkness of what it means to be alone. But I like to think, my brother, that when I went into that room, and I saw the man lying there, and when there was that moment which I see every day but never say, all across the world, a spark of alarm went off, and I was righteous, and I was not alone. I see it like that.

8

A Man

—I will tell you a story. I got a call to go to the home of a family I know. Well, not really their home, but the place where their son lives. It is not far from Legon, a small place in a compound. It was almost dawn when I got there. There were a lot of people around. They led me into the room where he stayed. The half-light came through the louvers. The son was on the bed. There was blood all over it. He was half-naked. Somebody had cut off his member. It was lying on the floor. I might have missed it, but they showed it to me. I asked if the police had come. They said the police had come and then went and were coming back. I asked them who did it. They said the boy was not good. That he was known to rape women in the area. They said people knew, but no one would trouble him because of the family. They said his brother was in the air force, so nobody wanted to trouble them. He would bring girls to the place and then rape them. Usually they were not girls from Accra. They were girls from the north who came to find work. He would promise them things and then he would rape them. Everybody knew that. I asked them who did it. They said they thought it was the police, but they didn't know. I asked why they thought it was the police. They said it was what people were saying. One woman said she heard a girl crying and screaming, and then for a long time she heard nothing. So I went to see the family. They said the boy was bad, but nobody had a right to do that to him. They wanted to know who was responsible. I told them I would look into it. Then I prayed for them and went to the station. The officers said they had heard, and it was they who told the family, and maybe they

point she went out into the front yard and sat on the steps. Sometimes she liked to do that, just to think and plan her life. And when she was sitting there, a girl limped into the yard. She was crying. The light from the station showed her face as she came closer. Her face was broken. Her head was bleeding. And she was trying to hold together the blouse she had on, but it was torn. The officer could tell by the way she held her body what had happened. The pain was in her center. She asked if she could stay in the station for the night because she was afraid. The officer asked her what she was afraid of. She said there was a man who was looking for her, and she wanted to rest a little bit and then would leave before first light. The officer asked what the man did. The girl did not say, but slowly, the officer got her to talk. The girl said he beat her. The girl said he raped her. The girl said he spat on her. The girl said he beat her some more. By now she was shaking, but she had stopped crying. The officer asked where the man was. She said he was in his place. The officer asked how she got away. She said he fell asleep after he was finished with her, and she sneaked out. The officer asked if she could find her way back to the place. The girl said she could but did not want to go. But the officer convinced her and called one of the constables to come with them. The girl led them to the place. It was in darkness and quiet. The girl pointed to the door. The officer told the constable to take the girl back to the station and wait. The constable did not want to leave the officer, but he followed orders. The officer went into the room, and the man was there sleeping, just like the girl said. He had on a singlet and a pair of jeans, but he was on his back, and his jeans were zipped open and he was exposed. He slept with his mouth in a sneer. Maybe it was this or the white panties near the man's hand that made her do what she did. She found what she was looking for under the bed. She did not even bother to wake him up.

11

A Woman

—I never even bothered to wake him up.

12

A Woman

—You know there was a riot, right? They attacked the police station and then I was officially asked to take leave. I have not been back. They have not written to me or maybe they have. I think somebody told me that they wanted to place me at the police college because I could be helpful there. I was there when the man's brother, an air force officer, brought his men to the station. Big men in their fatigues. From flight lieutenant up, every air force person feels he is a big man. And they beat up the small constable at the gate. But then of course, the rest of them took out rifles and stood there quarreling, and maybe there was a punch. But the man's brother was crying too, because he said that people make mistakes, so why would we do him like that? I know my brothers wanted to be firm and hard, but because of what I did to him, well, every man would feel that I went too far, because I know that when they said it they wanted to hold themselves too, and I understand that, but I told them that they should understand that that is what my vagina felt like when the girl was telling me what happened to her, what he did to her, and when I saw her breasts with the slash, and when I saw the lacerations on her vagina, and when I saw how her eyes were so deeply wounded, well, it was me, and it was the same thing. Why must a woman have to suffer without revenge? I know in their heads they knew I was correct, but they could still only think of themselves with their penises. That is why nobody asked questions. I know that. A woman who does that to a man, and then leaves him to die like that, bleeding . . . Well, she is dangerous. But you know what I kept asking myself? The whole time, I kept asking myself, *Where is this man's mother?* Maybe she was there, but I had this idea that if she was with him, if she was looking after him, I don't know, maybe he wouldn't . . . Isn't it terrible how even we women take the blame for what our boys do? Even as I was thinking this, I was ashamed of my thoughts. But I had a son, and I could not say where he was that night. This is what a woman in my position must ask. I was a dangerous woman. Is that why you are here, now? Are you his brother?

13

A Man, a Woman, and a Boy

—They want you back on the force.

—Is that what they told you?

—We need strong officers. You know that. They want you back.

—You are here to ask me to leave my perfect life to go back to that life?

—I am.

—I left because I knew after I did it that I was dangerous. I did not even breathe heavily. I found the cutlass, looked at the blade. Then I took his pillow and put it over his head. I climbed on the bed and put my knee on the pillow, and I was amazed at how few chops it took for the thing to fall away. He was jumping, and there was blood. So much blood. But I held him down until he stopped. People do not want to die. And yet, I just walked out of the room and back to the station, just slightly straining my muscles from the labor, but in no time, I was washed and at my desk. I gave the girl some money and told her to go back home. I was too cool. At first, I hoped it was shock. But I stayed cool. Even now, I feel the same way. And because I know I can do that . . .

—Sometimes that is what it is like.

—I don't think so.

—But we still want you back.

—We?

—Yes, the church.

—Oh, Pastor, I believe I have backslidden too far.

—It is never too late.

—Ma, it is late, we should go now.

—Yes, Kwaku, get the baskets.

—I can give you a lift down to the junction.

—You see that boy? That is why I have not tried to go back. The problem with the woman officer is that unless she can find a wife, her family will suffer. I do not have a wife. You have a wife, I know. You look satisfied. That night, while I sat there waiting for morning, I started to wonder where my boy was. He was sleeping, I thought. But I did not know for sure. We make these connections. I knew I could not continue. I did not want another officer to be slicing off another young man's penis and wondering where his mother is. I did not even bother to wake him up . . .

—Ah! There it is again. Look!

—Yes, yes. Oh. It is very big tonight.

—Look how the place is shining. My goodness.

—It is beautiful.

—It is.

After "Advantage" by Colin Channer, from Providential *(Akashic Books, 2015)*

FANTASIA IN FANS AND FLAT SCREENS

BY KOFI BLANKSON OCANSEY
Jamestown

The joke about doors in Jamestown was that each carpenter measured differently. No two doors looked alike. Not only did the carpenters measure differently, they even built the doors wrong and would have to plane them down on-site to fit them in the frames. It was not uncommon to see doors whose lower edge slanted to accommodate the unevenness of the concrete floor.

On the other hand, it meant that the rooms always had a draft. You could sort of catch some sleep after midnight when the day's heat had finally dissipated and the cooling breezes blew in from the ocean.

Naa stirred. Her dress had shifted in the night, bunched up around her thighs, and nestled within her considerable cleavage. The little beads of sweat that formed no matter what she did—turn the fan on or turn it off—had made a line that traced the seam of the garment. She breathed in the scent of her body, just awakened, before a shower and the daily application of powder and fragrances. It was a dark, heavy scent, particularly around her armpits. She felt the prick of stubble and sniffed at the coating of sweaty musk that had formed overnight.

Her home was part of a series of "chamber and hall" apartments—two-room apartments consisting of a bed and a hall—that were a step up from the communal rooms that most of the residents of Jamestown shared. Everyone who lived in a compound house, for that's what these arrangements were called, entered their dwellings from a communal yard, and most cooked their meals right in front of the doors leading to their halls.

The chamber was the bedroom, the hall was the sitting room, where Naa received her guests. She could also have her meals there and basically afford to sit around with her blouse either undone or totally off, her bra cradling her breasts, her going-out clothes exchanged for something simpler and lighter. This casualness didn't feel strange in the privacy of her home; once she stepped outside she could see many of her neighbors similarly partly uncovered. Men of all ages hung out bare-chested. Naa herself understood that this was not erotic. Not much could be read into accommodating oneself to the humid tropical climate.

Overall, her life suited her, given the liberal outlook on coupling she grew up in and the indulgences she allowed herself from time to time. Well, really, more like those she lived in *all* the time. She was a frequent presence in the culture of heavy partying in Accra; those in the know took it for granted that on most weekends, at funerals, ironically, the after-parties could turn into combinations of impromptu partnerships.

It was the still of the night. Naa heard the sound of a man's voice; it came from just outside her window, from the alley that led to yet another alley that led to the water's edge. It was a familiar voice. In fact, it belonged to Nii Teiko, a man she knew well. His voice, as she knew it, was level, relaxed with a deep timbre. She was accustomed to listening to it in steady conversation. The voice she was hearing now was rushed, out of rhythm, wavering.

The neighborhood's streets and alleys were agnostic. The piety of children and matrons heading to church was cheerfully balanced by the evening traffic of the drunk, the pickpocket, the trick turner, the odd civil servant, or the errant lawyer persuaded to risk career and limb on some wild delight. The more fanciful of the people who thronged the streets this late in the day believed they were breathing some heady old scent from a time when white men, soaked in whiskey and gin, with their mottled skin and scurvy-blasted mouths, plied these grounds, avid participants in the trade of black humans destined for a damned existence in the land beyond the oceans.

Naa heard the blows, gut punches in rapid succession. They were the sounds made by hard fists banging against yielding skin stretched over bone. A moment of sympathetic feeling had her believe the blows were landing on her. It made her cringe. Her entire being had entered into a heightened sense of alertness. This suddenly allowed her to make out what he was saying.

"Kwɛ! Kwɛ!!" Look, look. "You are killing me," the muffled groans came out. Nii Teiko was trying to draw out a measure of mercy.

"Feemɔ diŋŋ." Shut up. The response was severe and merciless, imposing an eerie silence.

The second voice was also familiar to Naa. He was another man she knew, Nii Odoi. This made her even more chilled by its implacability. There was determination in the voice; its owner recognized that at this point the plan that was unfolding this evening had to be carried out. Not a scintilla of doubt could be entertained. He barked, "Kɛjeee nɔ ko kulɛ, wɔbaafo ogbɛi." We'd cut your dick off if we could.

Nii Teiko twisted and lunged against a wall, banging his head against a set of jalousies, slowing down the grimly resolute parade to the rocks. He knew he was in mortal danger. He had grown up in Jamestown. Death was no stranger here, it would leave a little memento mori in these alleyways from time to time. Once a year or so, some really stupid thief, perhaps too desperate to remember that one didn't steal around here, would try his luck and end up stiff and glassy-eyed on a curb, waiting for the city authorities to cart him away to a mortuary. The police really didn't bother to investigate these deaths.

Nii Teiko could guess that if he were to die in the next few minutes, it would happen painfully. And he was correct. He was stabbed in the side, his face bashed in against the outcrop and his body thrown into the waters he had swum in as a child.

Nii Teiko wasted his last lungfuls of air trying to summon help from the sleeping masses. He knew everyone behind each frame of paired windows, he was sure that they could hear his wails. Each cry for help was answered by a buffeting that turned his mouth into a bloody mess. Fifty yards past Naa's window, Nii Teiko braced himself against the ground, uselessly trying to protect his head. Instincts die hard, it seemed. He lifted his head and said, rather incongruously, given the sort of man he had been, "I will lift up my eyes unto the hills."

That prayer was punctuated with a heavy thwack, not unlike a bass drumbeat, a silencing blow and a determined, if nervous, rejoinder: "Onyɛ sɔɔ mli." Your mother's cunt.

Nii Teiko was weakening, using the last reserves of his strength to tie up some of the loose-end thoughts that flitted across his consciousness. He looked Nii Odoi in the face and uttered his last coherent words: "Mibi oo kaaha ohiɛ kpa amɛ nɔ, ni Nyɔŋmɔ aakwɛ onɔ." My children, don't forget them, and may God keep you.

"Fool, you are calling God. Even devils call God. Buuluu. Fool," was Nii Odoi's unshaken response.

Naa shrank back from the window. Had it really come to this? She heard Nii Odoi's tirades about injustice so often that she had considered them part of their evenings together. It often felt that he thrived on this wellspring of energy, and that when it possessed him fully, he had the necessary focus to really be with her.

Naa's mouth didn't work. A gasp caught in her throat, she tried to push it out but couldn't. Her lips were dry, instantly chapped. She had to brace herself against a wall; on it lay the lupine shadow of her arm, cast by the dim bulb hanging from her ceiling.

Naa was trying to come to terms with the fact that she knew both men. The reasons why flooded over her. She couldn't tease apart the strands of memory that tied the three of them together in playful scrapes, in the occasional very bitter divisions, but mostly in the wobbly tug and push of their overlapping lives.

Nii Odoi had bought the fan. It came in a large white box that had the words *Happy Life* over the photograph of a smiling red-lipsticked Asian woman. Nii Odoi, after she'd let him in, had asked her to go into the chamber for a minute. She could hear him knocking about, requesting that something be placed just so and then politely ushering someone out. After a few seconds, the ceiling light went off. Sitting on her bed, Naa saw a peacock's tail of multicolored lights pulse its way under the ill-fitting door that separated the chamber from the hall. The accompanying hum delivered with it a breeze that stirred up dust motes.

When Nii Odoi finally opened the door, she thought he looked a little flushed, but he motioned her out and pointed in the direction of the noise and lights. When she saw the gift, her hands flew upward to cup her face. It was a standing fan, with several speeds and an illuminated middle section—three bulbs that rotated in a vertical plane. There was a button that changed the steady beam into a strobe; the effect of combining that with the highest fan speed was in itself a conversation piece. Certainly, sex that night with Nii Odoi was disorienting, but in a pleasant and enticing way, one that led to an experience that was out of the ordinary.

The other man, Nii Teiko, destined in the by-and-by to be nothing but a liquefying mass of alcohol and putrefaction, had bought the medium-sized flat screen in Naa's hall. Unlike Nii Odoi, Nii Teiko had sent his gift. There'd been a quick call to Naa to alert her that the present was on its way, but that was all. The little bit of propriety he allowed to guide his life suggested that a gentleman didn't shame his family by being seen taking gifts to the homes of single women. That's what he'd told himself, but in truth, there were probably too many single women in his life, and too little time.

When it all came into focus for Naa, the moment she realized that she represented a point of a triangle once jocular and teasing, the savage procession had already passed her window, the fan and blank-faced TV bearing witness. She felt pressed down by a weight and couldn't move her limbs. In her all-too-quiet room, now that the sound from outside had subsided, her stomach rose and fell in difficult contractions, her breath released in gales. She managed the four steps it took to walk into her bedroom, and saw the backlit image of the woman she had just become reflected in the mirror on the dressing table. She almost didn't recognize herself, worn, frightened, looking more like her mother's sister than she cared to admit. She couldn't control the images of warmth and death that flickered on her retinas. Her right hand, thickened and made strong by work, curled into her left palm. She brought both of them to her stomach as she sat on her bed. Sleep would come no more that night.

Naa spent the rest of the morning hours trapped in bed; her eyes were fixed on the wooden battens of the ceiling. In the middle of the panel directly above her head, a leak had produced a discolored map of a land that was often her secret refuge.

She felt a strong pressure in her bladder but couldn't move. Eventually, unable to hold it any longer, she started to dribble, signaling that the fear of this area that she'd lived in for most of her life was now total. She just didn't know what might happen if her legs carried her past the bolted door into the courtyard, toward the toilet she shared with the three other families in the compound. After tonight, she knew that anything was possible.

Naa had been in her fair share of fights over men. Wives here took it out on the other women, never on their men. Taking it out on a man would lead to questions about one's mental stability. Philandering was what men did, after all. That was what it meant to be one. The fault lay with the ashao, the whore, who would spread her lagbaŋ for him. She was the one who had to be taught a lesson. And, sadly, Naa, who rather naively thought of herself as more of a courtesan than an ashao, got lumped in with the young girls, barely out of their teens, whose initiation into womanhood was to be the pliant, adoring booty call of any man who could drop fifty cedis on them.

Naa knew that it wouldn't take too long for the dots to be connected. Everyone would be talking about how she had been the friend of both men. Actually, she was the friend of a lot of men like them. She was a free woman. She had a little import business that her main lover had set her up with many years before, so she was financially independent. She lived alone; her divorce had happened so long ago that it would often take her a minute to remember the actual year. In Jamestown, women didn't really live alone. A woman stayed home. That is, her bags stayed home. Her personal effects were to remain in the communal house she grew up in until she married and moved out. No single women rented rooms before they got married. It's doubtful that any landlord or landlady would have even given a twenty-year-old with the rent in her hand a room. It would have been like saying that the red-light district had arrived.

Naa was supposed to have gone back home after her husband had returned the drinks to her family, as dictated by custom and tradition, signifying the end of their marriage. The work of the lawyers, as dictated by government, always took a bit longer. Naa hadn't gone back home because she knew how unforgiving the chatter would've been. "Akɛɛ, akɛɛ." They say, they say. The famous opening lines of the rumor mill.

"They say the man found her with another woman in their bedroom."

Eiiisshhh!

"They say when he walked in, she was with two men; she had one of them in her mouth, the other was gyrating behind her."

Eissshhh, eissshhhh!

"They say she was doing styles!"

Eeeiiiiiiiiisssssshhhhh—ooo eish!!!

The first light had yet to fully establish itself; the improvident had made their way to the beach to relieve themselves of the night's production of excreta. You went early enough that the dawn afforded you a measure of privacy, and you were less likely to find the beach dotted with your neighbors' leavings. These quiet ruminative mediations between man—and woman, let's not forget our sisters—and nature that morning were overthrown by the strong, persistent buzzing of a horde of flying insects as they hovered above the rocks in a cruciform over the body of the dead man.

Jamestown police were summoned from their barracks close to the white man's cemetery. At a certain time, the Europeans who succumbed to malaria, and weren't important enough to be pickled and potted for the return trip to Shropshire, were interred in this field, a cozy spot dotted with tombstones, crosses, angels on pedestals, and a monument commemorating the valiant British lost in some campaign. It sat at a long diagonal from the famed lighthouse; it was on the outskirts of Jamestown, close to the Korle—the big lagoon . . . Eventually, though, as the town had grown toward the graveyard, some of these dead had been disinterred and reburied elsewhere; the rest were conveniently tarred over, awaiting, their discovery, perhaps, in some future archaeological dig.

Nii Teiko's corpse was still in the early stages of death, but as grotesque as it looked, with its swollen and split lips, the bruises around its throat, and the blood-encrusted slit on the left side of its rib cage, it still looked somewhat like the fixer he had been. The last time any of the early birds had seen him, he was most likely parading between the neighborhood where his All People's Congress plywood offices had been, on the edge of the busy market, and Maŋtsɛ agbo naa (a Ga phrase rendered loosely, and incomprehensibly, in English, as "the outside of the King"), the huge park in front of the traditional ruler's palace. It was between these two locations that the future of Jamestown, and maybe even Accra, had been decided for a long time, and it was where Nii Teiko plied his trade.

The following week, the neighborhood continued to vibrate with the news of Nii Teiko's death. He really had been a "big man" around there, and it unnerved many to think that such a person could be taken down.

Now that I am effectively *in* the ground, let me tell you what it was like to be *on* the ground, how it worked and why you needed me. This is where I was born. I knew every inch of the area. I knew everyone who lives in these buildings. I even knew their grandparents. I had to: they were my money. I was the person who got the politicians into office—I was never shy about saying that in life, and I'm certainly not shy about saying it now. I was the one who made sure that a grandmother could go to her final rest in a good coffin when her family couldn't afford one. Between these two things, the town moves ahead.

You might walk along these Jamestown streets and see nothing but poverty, but I saw progress. I still see progress. Progress is peace, I would tell my boys. Over and over again I would tell them that if we have peace you can achieve your dreams; we all can. I would say it so often it felt like I'd become possessed by "the voice" of the politicians. To get peace, you need the right member of Parliament to be elected. The right MP knows how to tap into the consolidated fund, how to get the right contractors on board. He knows how to make the right inspectors see double: all of a sudden that two-inch subsurface is a four-inch subsurface, a mile of that is half a million dollars that the right MP can do good with. Scholarships for children of loyal voters, a car for the Maŋtsɛ, a sickly child saved, a woman set up in trade. So what if some of it goes to the boys, or if some of it ends up in the right MP's overseas account. So what? Here, we say everyone eats around their job.

Ours is a historic town in Accra, a town of native stock. Jamestown politics has always been a bare-knuckle affair. Even today, we command the newspeople like *Daily Graphic*, Radio Ghana, and Ghana Broadcasting: each big party starts its national campaign off at Maŋtsɛ agbo naa. That is because Jamestown can make or break presidents. The right MP for us can mollify the president or squeeze his balls small when necessary, at the right time.

And the right time is always election year—but our work is year-round every year. In an election year, we squeeze the balls of the MP extra hard. The situation on the ground is dire, we would tell him. The more money we needed, the more dire the situation on the ground became: the boys who broke the heads of the other party's boys; the girls we sent to spoil the other party's gatherings with loud, vulgar chanting and insults.

Even the "big people," some would call them the "pillars of our society," must eat some. The priests are also inside—discreetly, though; they would look aside, mumble thanks on behalf of widows and orphans, as the envelopes went into the voluminous pockets of their vestments. So, too, are the heads of this or that family association . . . and I haven't forgotten the market women, the fishermen, and the women who buy the day's catch. We just had to make sure that the ground was much better where we were standing than where the other side stood. In fact, we had to make sure that we buried them in quicksand.

I was the spigot, the tap the politicians pissed through. This work was too dirty for my MP to handle directly, and the little schoolboys and schoolgirls who trailed after him, with their foolish university accents, these people were too stupid to be told the truth. Especially today when the newspapers and TV stations are stirring themselves, today when some of them are becoming overzealous, today it takes a dirty man like me, like I was, to handle dirty money that is meant to keep the peace precisely where it should be.

I was expendable, obviously, but I was also wily and I rolled along with it. I made sure the ground was good, I also made sure it was cool, gbɔjɔ—done and with no fuss, as my people like to say. How I did it, I didn't really share with many. The MP certainly didn't care to know, and perhaps he shouldn't. It was all a game of lies and bluffing, this peacemaking campaign of ours. The wife turned her nose up at it, but she liked the estate house on Spintex that we paid for in cash, in the name of a company that our fancy lawyer claimed couldn't be traced to me. I believed him. The kids go to international school. I have a small insurance policy—a fifty-acre fruit farm near Somanya, an old Dangbe town twenty or so miles to the northeast of Jamestown, and three trucks—enough, if looked after well, to last the children through university. This can be a dirty and unforgiving business. You could be up today, and still end up being the dirty piece of shit who didn't bring the votes in. The one they counted on who failed them.

I might have seemed like a big man to the people I passed when I trekked to Maŋtsɛ agbo naa. People see what they want to see. They saw the showy gold ropes around my neck, the Pajero with the shiny wheels, my Friday-night parties where the boys drank free Club beer and local gin and feasted on kebabs. They also feasted on the ladies who showed up. But I knew two things the people didn't. First: the stress I got from their fantasies of unlimited money in my reach, and the strain of kissing ass upward and downward, and the knowledge that

I would stand alone if some of my crimes ever saw the light of day. I would stand alone, and I would fall alone.

The second thing I knew was the distance between me and Peduase, where the leaders—the president and his coterie—a truly sybaritic lot, live a life that wouldn't be believed if I had tried to describe it to the average Jamestown citizen. In my mind, and I'd been abroad once, Jamestown was Ghana, Peduase was the ablotsiri, the land beyond the ocean, of my imagination. With its frosty cold rooms, heavy tapestry, silver trays, and deep hush, the distance between my Jamestown and this transplant was almost an unbridgeable chasm. There, my beer becomes Moët; my kebabs, tough and chewy, become fine small chops; my women give way to women for whom the maintenance of their lustrous skin and hair costs a year's wages in Jamestown.

So, it's not easy, it's not easy at all. I stayed on top by the skin of my teeth. There are always people who want what you have. They see beer, easy sex, violence with impunity, the escape from Jamestown and yet an even deeper immersion into its affairs. Some people saw the ease with which I kept the peace, and they wanted it. Undiluted.

They start to undermine you. They whisper into the ears of your MP.

"See your boy, Honorable?" their sibilance exactly like that of the biblical serpent.

"He's not doing the groundwork, he will make the ground harder."

"See your boy, boss? He spends all his time in rooms with other people's wives, everyone hates him, if you don't get rid of him it might not go well for you, I'm telling you as a friend."

In Jamestown, we call this "chooking." Some call it backstabbing.

And that was all within your own camp.

The guys in the other camp were worse. They were out of power. Out of power meant that they couldn't do jack for the contractors and the other people whose symbiotic relationship with the politicians fattened them both. They were lean and feral. True diehards. Wasn't this the ultimate test? To be true when there was nothing left to feed on but hope? Even I admired the fervency with which they came after me. It ranged from outright insults hurled from the side of the street as I walked by, to nasty side-glances. I would hear, "Thief, thief, you and your thieving government, we will kill you one by one."

I knew these guys. Some of the leaders of the opposition were members of my family. I grew up with them.

Nii Odoi was sitting on the second-floor balcony of the grand old house that overlooked High Street. It had been built by a great-grandfather who had grown rich trading with the English. Over the years, the family's matriarch had become almost permanently ensconced in the living room that opened onto the balcony. She sat in a wide wooden armchair, on plumped-up red cotton cushions filled with kapok. She was usually dressed in a blue and yellow kaba, and her head was covered with a silk scarf, from underneath which poked the ends of her plaited gray hair.

He heard her visitor's heavy footfalls on the wooden staircase. The visitor entered the living room and was received with good feeling and warmth. "O, Nii Teiko, oba?" You've come? the old lady asked. "Ta shi, ta shi." Sit down, sit down. Nii Teiko acknowledged that he was indeed there in the flesh and took a seat at a right angle to his aunt.

"Ma," he started, "you're looking well, paa, have you found yourself some handsome young man?"

"Oh, stop it, you bad boy, since your uncle left us I've flown solo, the bed has been mine alone. If I'm looking well, it's by grace and, of course, your kind gifts."

"Ma," Nii Teiko assured her, "the young guy is bringing this month's provisions. You're so precious to me, I have to take care of you like I would my own mother. In fact, after she died, you were more than a mother to me." He placed a small flat envelope on the side table next to her.

"Oh, stop it." The old lady pretended to be embarrassed by his flattery and gratitude. "You always say that, but your mother, Adjeley, was not just a cousin; she was my closest friend. I always thought that at some point the two of us would spend our remaining days sitting here in this room bossing stories."

There was a short lull in the conversation, each one of them lost for a moment in a reverie about days past, about the woman—mother, cousin, confidant—they had both loved and lost way too soon.

"How are things on the street with your politics?"

"Ma, it's not easy, election year matters. You're my mother, I have to tell you the truth, I don't sleep. The politicians have made our work difficult. The economy has become tough, the market women say no one is buying anything. Our little support we give them has dried up. The foreigners are not bringing in the loans, they say we haven't used the old loans well. We are doing our best, we have to keep the peace, come what may, but it's not easy."

"Mibi." My child. Her voice was as warm and sweet as the milo she used to make for him when he was a boy. "It shall be well. When you're my age, when you've seen Nkrumah, Ankrah, Kotoka, Busia, Acheampong, J.J., and the rest, you know that there are ups and downs. Keep your head, you're smart.

Grace will lead you where you should go. Have faith in Him, and be faithful to the madam. Don't let these small girls turn you against her."

"Mmaa, small girls . . ."

"Oh stop, you think because I'm up here all the time I don't know . . . Nyɛkwɛa nyɛhe nɔ jogbaŋŋ." Look after yourselves well.

He made as to leave, but hesitated and said, "Mmma, I've a small favor to ask . . ."

She looked up at him intently.

"Mmaa, minyɛmi nuu." My brother. "Nii Odoi. He has to know that this is only politics, but he is taking it personal, too personal. I have many enemies, but my cousin . . . my own brother . . . shouldn't be one of them."

The old lady's eyes darkened, she shook her head quickly. "No, you're right," she agreed. "I will see to it."

He said his goodbyes and left the cool breezy room for the hurly-burly of High Street.

A few minutes after the old lady had opened the envelope, examined its contents, and tucked it safely away in her brassiere, her son clomped in from the veranda.

"I hate that fucker," Nii Odoi said plainly. "He shouldn't come here and talk about brother this and brother that. Take it personal? Take it personal? I shouldn't? After all he's done to destroy order around here?"

"Herrrrhhh, Nii Odoi! Watch your mouth! What kind of nonsense ranting is this?" She pointed her right index finger at him. "The man has done what he had to do. Let's face it, he was an orphan who had nothing. Do you remember the scraps I fed him while you ate meat, the mat he slept on while you slept on a mattress? I am sure he has not forgotten, and yet you begrudge him what he has made of himself?"

"Mmaa, please." Nii Odoi waved his hands in the air as if to erase his mother's words. "Don't let me say things that I shouldn't because you're also taking his dirty money. It was you who told me how his grandfather stole my grandfather's property, and how they drank everything away. You are the one who has forgotten, but I have not. You know how we ran this area before J.J. came in and threw everything upside down, how your baking business collapsed, how you were reduced to selling even your gold trinkets so that we could survive. Yes, I ate meat, but that ass deserved the scraps he was given. How dare he think he has the right to throw his weight around? He is the only person standing in the way of the right people coming to power, but it won't be forever, you know."

"Herh, herh," his mother snapped. "Stop it. Enough with these old stories. Are you sure it's not about that stupid two-by-four girl, Naa, who you both seem to like? You . . . you . . . my son, consorting with that reject. Sometimes I think you've lost your mind."

"I have said what I am going to say, it won't be long, things will change with this election." He banged his fist on the dining table. It made the glasses on the runner in the middle shake. He threw his mother an unapologetic and pitying look, then stormed out.

Everywhere Nii Odoi looked, these cadres, these revolutionaries turned politicians, had grown fat. Each day brought more shocking news: the lands they had taken, the state enterprises they had sold to themselves, their homes abroad, their children rubbing their shit in everyone's faces. As far as Nii Odoi could tell, all their shitty boys, Nii Teiko included, were talking about peace while fucking the people in Jamestown over and over again. He had walked up and down those streets and could see that the warehouses, once belonging to them, were now shuttered; his uncle's medical clinic was flyblown; the people who used to be productive were now idling in the doorways of their homes, their daughters' communal property. Nii Odoi had spent the last of his mother's money studying in London, and he had brought that degree back home to Ghana, to Jamestown, thinking that there would be room for him to rebuild, to pay homage to the past and make a difference for the future. But he was nothing there without money, nobody was. Not even the air of ancient entitlement that he wore held meaning. The one and only thing that held meaning anymore was money. And where was it? It was in just one place. Money was in politics.

Nii Teiko may have found his way into a position of power. He may indeed have been the key to change, but Nii Odoi was determined to be the hand to turn that key in the right direction, for all their sakes.

The political boss, deep in conversation with his close associates, one of whom was a carpenter, a true-to-goodness, fly-by-the-seat-of-his-trousers Jamestown carpenter, looked up. A small girl, no more than ten years old, had come into the bar to find him. She tugged at his sleeve, as children do, and he bent his head toward her.

"Please," she whispered, her words barely audible. "Auntie Naa sent me. She said she hasn't seen you in a long time, and would like to see you. She wants you to come tomorrow night at about eleven."

Nii Teiko smiled. He handed the small girl a ten-cedi note and patted her on the head. He'd been so busy with this election business, he'd not paid Naa a visit in a while. He liked her independence. She was the sort of woman who knew what

PART II

Heaven Gate, No Bribe

THE LABADI SUNSHINE BAR

BY BILLIE MCTERNAN

Labadi

The Labadi bɔɔla collectors drive around town from as early as four or five a.m. during the week, bandannas covering their noses and mouths, barely keeping the smell of days-old bean stew from being caught in the back of their throats. Their tinny music rings from the wagon, piercing through the area, attracting customers, an alarm for those who have yet to rise and begin their day. As the minitruck circles around, residents, like dutiful ants, scuttle to the roadside to hail the crew with bags of refuse. After a few hours the truck is full. Often the driver dumps the waste at a landfill site on Mortuary Road, close to the Korle Lagoon. Everything from fridges and mattresses to car parts and cholera can be found in it. After paying a fee to the minders of the landfill, they drive off. And as one job ends, another begins. The salvagers take charge of the refuse. They wade through the junk to make sure there is nothing of value left to rot away, then set the junk alight; flames burn through the rot, licking the stench-filled air around them.

It's not uncommon to find dead bodies there: men and women, young and old, surface. The blowflies and maggots always find them first, crawling around lips and poking out of nostrils. The salvagers groan, hand on head. What happened to these people for their bodies to have ended up in this fill? Bankruptcy? Divorce? Depression? Betrayal? A makeshift burial is given, a short prayer spoken: *In life, in death, O Lord, abide with me.*

But they end it there. No need to get the authorities involved. After all, no one wants to be suspected of a crime they didn't commit.

When Priscilla arrived in Circle, along with all the other travelers venturing into the city, Accra became real. It was loud and obnoxious with cars, commuters, and hawkers vying for space. As the passengers from across the country poured out into the bus station from vehicles big and small, layers of the city's stress settled onto their skin.

Before leaving Aflao, the busy border town between Ghana and Togo, some of the girls had advised Priscilla to look for work in Labadi.

"Osu busy o. Dey get plenty Liberian girls for there," Gifty said, gnawing on a chewing stick. "Dem fill de place."

"Abeg no go East Legon. Too much police wahala," Yomi added.

"Labadi town dey between Osu and Labadi beach," Gifty continued. She spat out wooden splinters from her chewing stick. "You go still find obroni for dat place."

By way of Ghanaian beaches, Labadi is fairly unremarkable. In fact it was quite dirty, the ocean gray with accumulated filth.

Priscilla was directed to Madam Joanna, one of those older women with a perpetual *I am not amused* face, the mouth poised ever ready with a quip should you step out of line. Her darkened knuckles were a telltale sign of regular skin-bleaching rituals. Her hair was shaved low and she wore large gold-hoop earrings, gold bangles, and a collection of necklaces. Her chest heaved in the tight midlength floral dress she wore. More was more for Madam Joanna.

"Good afternoon, ma," Priscilla greeted.

Madam Joanna, while in repose on a sun lounger, shifted her eyes from her diary toward Priscilla. She peered at her over her sunglasses. The young woman was tall, and she wore her hair in long braids that fell down her back. Her eyes shone.

"Yes?"

"Please, my name is Cici. I am looking for work. I was told you can help me."

Madam Joanna raised herself from the sun lounger in a bid to create balance between her and the towering Priscilla, who, she noticed, made no attempt to reorder the space between them. "What can you do?"

"Well, I have experience, ma." Priscilla adjusted the bag so the strap sat firmly on her right shoulder, then ran her hands down her midriff and adjusted the waistband of her skirt where it dug into her skin.

Madam Joanna understood.

During the day, Madam Joanna set up her kebab stand on the beach in front of her bar. All her servers were girls and roughly the same age. Some were slim, others were thick and round. There were short girls and a few taller ones. All were fairly attractive.

Cici would fit right in, Madam Joanna concluded. Madam Joanna offered to set her up. She could live with the others and pay Madam Joanna a portion of her earnings. There was space at the house since one of the girls had recently moved on.

While washing plates at the beach a week later, Cici asked a girl she came to know as Kukua what happened to the previous tenant; she received a shrug in reply. Then a few minutes later, the girl said: "Sometimes it happens like that, a girl just leaves." Kukua sighed, her shoulders rose then fell. "And that girl, Chrissie, she was my friend. She didn't even say bye."

* * *

Of all the chores involved in her work, it was cutting onions that Priscilla hated most. As a child she would often get scolded by her mother for her haphazard chopping skills. The pieces would be all different sizes, as if she were waging a fight with the onion and the chopping board, the knife her weapon. And then her eyes would sting, as though bees had planted themselves in her sockets. But she would continue to chop and slice, averting her gaze, using only her sense of touch. When it was all over, the onion would be in pieces, but in a way, so would she, with tears streaming down her face. She could never tell who came out as the victor of these confrontations.

When customers arrived, Cici's fingers would still be stained with the odor of onions. Madam Joanna said some of them liked that. One regular would give her ten cedis just to sniff her fingers and that would be it. It wasn't too much to ask, she supposed, but some days she resented the work, feeling as though she'd taken a step backward. These new customers were really no different from those she used to receive at the border: truckers with slabs of cement on their trailers and crates of dollars, euros, and pounds hidden between them; travelers with just one bag in tow searching for work along the coast, looking for some comfort for a night; and immigration officers. The pay was a pittance and she'd gotten tired of that life, particularly the officers, the pretend "big men" with false bravado, who were always answering to someone else. Although now she was getting better pay, she was eager to reach higher heights. A nice apartment, a car, trips to Dubai. She wanted more.

It was Wednesday, the day Mr. Boakye would almost always come to the beach with two or three of his employees, usually the younger ones, to drink a couple rounds of Club beer. He would then order some kebabs for the "boys" to chew on, before heading off to the nearby Labadi Beach Hotel where Madam Joanna would be waiting for him in their regular room, cleaned up from the day's beach debris.

This had been their routine for over fifteen years. They were much younger then. Those were the days before the hair at his temples completely gave way to his balding scalp, admittedly later than most men. She would tease him about it, but secretly enjoyed watching the granules of sweat cling to his last remaining follicles during sex. She told him that once. Soon after, he began shaving the whole thing off.

Having Mr. Boakye as a client was a smart move that saw her open the bar in the first place. She prided herself on that move, on him. She had specially imported sun loungers and umbrellas—the type you see on beaches in the south of France, the supplier told her—and a regular stock of the most popular foreign brands. Mr Boakye's connections rarely failed. She called her place the Labadi Sunshine Bar.

The business had changed since Madam Joanna first started working and then taking in girls. In those days it was mostly the Ghanaians who used her services, but in the last ten years there were so many more Europeans, Americans, and Arabs that came to Ghana with all kinds of demands. But Madam Joanna liked to think of herself as a flexible person, able to change with the times to keep her head above water. And like any good businessperson, she learned how to keep the police at bay.

On any given day the crowd at Jokers built up quickly. Priscilla and the other girls spent late nights at the club. Men came to meet women, and women came to make money. Couples sat outside smoking and people-watching over beer and Smirnoff Ice. You could always tell the new girls. The ones who were more used to wearing slippers than stilettos, knees knocking as they walked. Inside, Jamaican dancehall had women bent over, legs straight, the strobe lights catching the twists and turns of bum-shaking on the dance floor. Groups of young men would shout in chorus to American hip-hop anthems, hands tightly gripped around bottles of liquor.

The Brits and the Europeans, who prided themselves on the fact that they worked on the country's oil rigs, were often drunk and obnoxious. The Indians would sit quietly by the pool tables, watching intently as scenes unfolded before them. The Lebanese were also seated, but with a confidence the Indians lacked; after all, this small space in Labadi belonged to them. And of course there were the Africans. Besides the regular Ghanaians there would be businessmen from Nigeria, Côte d'Ivoire, Cameroon, South Africa, Kenya, and others too.

Priscilla quickly discovered that learning a few words in a prospective client's language helped him warm up quicker, and earned her a few extra cedis for the effort. The other girls had advised that she stick with the whites; they were usually only in town for a short while so were prepared to spend more. Best to find the ones who were on their own too. Avoid large groups.

Madam Joanna warned the girls not to get too close to the clients. "Love can be dangerous," she'd say. But love was never an option for Priscilla. Why have love when you could have freedom? Love was what kept her mother pregnant; recycled promises and pleas for forgiveness always inevitably led to a new baby. Love was what made her grandmother, who'd lived her whole life in the village, keep a decades-long hope that her childhood sweetheart would return to her after his studies in Accra, and then later Europe as a young graduate, to make "an honest woman" of her. Love was what kept her aunties serving Sunday after-church akple and soup to their drunken, hot-tempered husbands who left them with Saturday-night bruises. If there was one thing Priscilla had learned in her short time on this earth, it was that love can slow a woman down and hold her back.

That's why she had left home for Aflao, and then Aflao for Accra. Labadi was a good step for her, closer to the life she felt she deserved.

Priscilla took her time getting ready for the night. She wanted a hot bath, so she boiled two pots of water on the stove to fill up her bucket. She lathered her sponge so thoroughly it became a cloud in her hand. This was her time. She allowed herself to feel her body with all its dips and crevices and folds. It was hers. It was important to affirm this daily, to make herself remember. Because, before long, some man might attempt to make her forget.

It was Friday. The sun had just laid itself to rest and Labadi was easing into the night's life. The sounds of Afrobeats, hiplife, and reggae blasted through the neighborhood, sliding through the louvers, filling the room, and bending the walls until the entire space became a bubble.

Two girls from the beach ambled into the house. "Good evening," they said in unison.

"Evening," she mumbled back. Now that they were here they would disturb her.

"You hear say dem deh find annuda person for Dansoman? Weh dey cut am up. Commot ein breasts and tinz."

"Kai! All dese sakawa boys, na demma rituals b dat."

Priscilla had heard stories about women going missing after picking up customers on the roadside. The rumors went that groups of young men would abduct these women and make sacrifices for their online fraud activities. The connection didn't really make sense to Priscilla. They were cutting up people? What did they do with their body parts?

"I need some girls for a party," Mr. Boakye said as he got up and reached for the checkered shirt he'd laid carefully on the office chair by the desk. It was the type of shirt afforded to CEOs; those lower on the chain of command tended to opt for a safe white or blue. "I have a new group of guys coming into town," he added, pushing his arms into the sleeves of the shirt. "I need to make sure they are comfortable as they settle in." Mr. Boakye left the top button undone. He had remained slim after all these years, rebuking the bulk of the "big man."

"Okay, how many?" It was Madam Joanna's turn to dress. Unlike Mr. Boakye, time had settled on her stomach, molded by the loss of babies that weren't permitted to stay.

"Ten should work. And Jojo, they should be fine too. Strong. Healthy."

It had been awhile since Mr. Boakye had called her Jojo. She hadn't realized how much she'd missed it.

"This one is serious business. A lot of money can come."

"Of course, darling. I will arrange for it."

"And you will come. To keep an eye on them. Nothing can go wrong."

"I will make sure everything runs smoothly for you," she purred.

"For us," Mr. Boakye corrected. He put on his suit jacket and kissed the crown of her head.

"For us," Madam Joanna repeated.

* * *

"Give me a Savanna," Priscilla said to the barman at Jokers, who silently obliged. She generally had a rapport with the waitstaff and often got free drinks until someone offered to buy her one. But this was not her guy, so she'd probably have to pay for this one.

"Eight cedis."

She reluctantly handed over the money, picked up the bottle of cider, and took a sip. After a quick scan of the room, Priscilla observed a few regular faces. Tina, the po-faced girl who came to her aid last week after an altercation with a taxi driver; long-legged Hawa, who swore that her incense was a sure way to get clients up and out in less than ten minutes; and Serwaa, the girl who never came out on Saturday nights, because she needed to be up early for church the next morning.

She didn't want to get too close to the other girls. Yomi and Gifty had told her that Accra was not like Aflao. "Na so everybody dey carry dem matter," one of them had said. She nodded at Tina before returning to her drink, tapping her white acrylic nail on the side of the bottle, tracing lines between the sweaty droplets.

"Can I take this seat?" a voice from behind asked.

Priscilla turned to face a tall white man. His hair was gray and spiky; she imagined it might prick her if she ran her hands through it. His mustache looked just as sharp. His skin was blotchy, not yet used to the sun, she assessed. He wore cargo trousers and a pastel-green shirt, tucked in and belted. She put him in his fifties.

"Oh, yes. Of course," she replied.

"So what's your name, pretty lady?"

"Cici. Yours?"

"Stuart."

"Akwaaba, Stuart," Priscilla welcomed.

"Medaase," he responded in Twi. "Do you like to dance, Cici?"

"Yes, I like to."

"Let's dance."

Cici dreaded dancing with the white customers. Their arms and legs were never in sync. But this guy smelled expensive, even if he didn't look it. So Cici took the lead, leaning herself into him, guiding his hands around her hips and thighs.

"We don't have to stay here, you know."

Priscilla didn't like going to her customers' hotels. Most of the time it was obvious she was working and she preferred to be more discreet. Now, anyone who knows of the Grace Jones Hotel knows that it is a place for short times. Priscilla frequented it often enough for management to keep a room reserved for her—room 102.

"What would you like to do first?" Priscilla asked.

Cici was getting too comfortable, Madam Joanna thought. Once they start to get comfortable they start to lose respect. And that was one thing she would not stand for.

"Cici!" Madam Joanna yelled from her front porch, clipping her toenails with concentration and precision.

"Yes, ma?" Priscilla rushed to her side. Although she was getting tired of living under Madam Joanna's roof, she was still far from being able to live in an executive apartment in Labone. The ones with the preinstalled kitchens with glossy cabinets and counters, and floor tiles you could see yourself in. For the time being, she had to do as she was told.

"So you've been with that same man every day this week again, ehn?"

"Oh. Yes, ma."

"Don't forget what I told you. You are here to work."

"Yes, ma."

"And Cici, your rent and repayment will soon be due."

Priscilla was growing accustomed to Stuart's company. She'd not had such close contact with one customer so intensely before. He was actually quite polite and kind, not something she was used to. This had to mean something. If she was smart she could get some good money from him, enough to rent a nice apartment and maybe even start her own boutique for women's clothing. She'd always felt she had a good eye for fashion. She could travel to Dubai and China to buy bags and shoes and dresses; it would be a good business. This could be her chance. And if he was smart, she could be his forever.

"She reminds me of you, Jojo," Mr. Boakye reminisced. "From back in those early days." He took a sip of the translucent brown liquid, whiskey probably. The ice was melting in the tumbler. His eyes followed Priscilla as she poured glasses of nondescript alcohol for a group of guests. She made a joke and they all laughed. The man with the mustache, laughing longer and harder than the rest, placed his hand on her back and kept it there a moment.

"She's sharp, like you were." He leaned in and placed a hand on her shoulder. "Ambitious. I want her."

Madam Joanna's skin pulled to a tautness. The time had come again, she thought, mistaking Mr. Boakye's intentions.

Madam Joanna hadn't received any clients for several years, not since she started taking in other girls. Mr. Boakye was all she had left. He was more than a client. He was all she had.

"Hmm?" Mr. Boakye pushed.

"I can arrange it for you," she whispered. "You don't worry."

"Wonderful." Mr. Boakye got up and walked over to speak with the crowd that was being entertained by Priscilla. Madam Joanna felt her stomach contort into a hollow cave.

In room 102, Priscilla and Stuart were wrapped in each other's arms. It had been like this for weeks. Sometimes they would go for a drink at a spot on one of the other beaches in town. They'd even eaten dinner together a few times; it was Priscilla's first time tasting Chinese food.

Stuart lifted himself from the pillow and rested the side of his head on his hand. He poked his chin over Priscilla's shoulder. "Cici baby, I might be able to stay here with you for longer. My time is getting extended," he said gleefully.

"Stuart, I need to get out of here." She turned to face him.

"What's going on, baby? Talk to me." His wet breath on her lips made her nauseous.

"I just have some trouble, that's all. And I need to fix it quick."

Stuart sat up. "Okay, okay, what do you need? What can I do?"

Madam Joanna sat by her bedroom window listening to the praise and worship songs her church neighbors would carry for over an hour. Their haunting voices always filled her with melancholy and memory.

Hold Thou Thy cross before my closing eyes;
Shine through the gloom and point me to the skies.
Heaven's morning breaks, and earth's vain shadows flee;
In life, in death, O Lord, abide with me . . .

As the singing came to an end she picked up her diary and flipped through it. Three months. Tomorrow it would be three months since Cici arrived, and she was still waiting for her money. Madam Joanna didn't like to feel as though the wool was being pulled over her eyes. She would not be made a fool of, she affirmed. She provided a good service in this business. There had been enough waiting around. Madam Joanna stuffed her feet into her slippers and marched to the Grace Jones.

"Where is Cici?" Madam Joanna barked at the receptionist.

"Erm," the receptionist held his breath, "I'm not sure, madam."

"What of the white man? Have you seen them? Where are they?"

"Maybe check her room, madam."

"Her room?"

Madam Joanna rushed down the corridor to number 102, her will moving faster than her body would allow. She banged her fist against the door, her bangles clanking with every thump. "Cici, open this door! If you're not careful I will deal with you, ehn!"

After several moments, Cici opened the door.

"So you people are together again."

Madam Joanna regained her composure and looked past Cici to Stuart, who sat on the bed with his pale legs poking out from the cover. As he stood up, Priscilla backed into the room and sat on the bed. Madam Joanna and Stuart locked eyes, then both turned to Priscilla. The air shifted.

Madam Joanna had noticed Priscilla when she first arrived at Labadi Beach. A lonely, pretty little thing who walked with a slight air of arrogance afforded to the young. She seemed plain, but that was good, she'd be easy to work with. Before Priscilla had even approached, Madam Joanna could tell she wasn't new to this game. She would keep an eye on her if she was going to work. A girl like that could bring in good money, and there were high-bidding customers to appease.

The day after Madam Joanna went to the Grace Jones Hotel to look for Priscilla, it was almost business as usual. The kebab stand had been set up. The bar was stocked. The girls were chopping up slivers of gizzard and goat meat. But Madam Joanna wasn't there. Cici was. Making directives, as the body of the previous owner of the Labadi Sunshine Bar washed up into the Korle Lagoon.

THE DRIVER

BY ERNEST KWAME NKRUMAH ADDO

Weija

Joojo arrived home in a rush. His wife, Angel, had sounded incoherent on the telephone. Now she was blabbing like an insane person, each heaving sob racking her small frame. Her eyes were red and her face was puffy.

"He has stopped breathing," she cried. "I didn't do anything to him."

It took some time for Joojo to notice that there was someone slumped in their well-worn living room couch, its upholstery covered with the adinkra design "gye nyame." The name of the symbol translates literally as "except God," its message being that there is nothing greater than God. The adinkra symbols are a collection of proverbs believed to reflect aspects of the worldview and philosophy of Ghanaians who believe that they are incapable of achieving anything of worth without God's intervention. It's no wonder, then, that gye nyame is the most recognizable symbol, the nation's obvious favorite, used to adorn everything from jewelry and clothing to furniture.

And, in Joojo's home, today was as good a time as any to call on God.

The occasion was certainly a big one. It had been ten years since Abrebrese had died following a short illness.

The old man had been a person of great wealth and standing in the community. After the death of his pregnant wife during labor, he had buried himself in his work and soon became one of the biggest farmers in the region. He owned several acres of land on which he grew cash crops like cocoa, coffee, and cashews. He reared livestock—including cattle, goats, sheep, pigs, rabbits, and grasscutters—and had won the regional Best Farmer prize on two occasions. A known philanthropist, he always donated large sums at church harvests, funerals, festivals, and other important social activities in the community.

Unfortunately, Abrebrese had died intestate. As is determined by the traditional system of inheritance in such a situation, one of his nephews, a young man he had hardly even known, a factory hand in another town, was endorsed by the family. The young man became Abrebrese's heir and took over all of his property. Yet, after taking charge of the wealth, the young man refused to look after the dead man's two teenage children, so they were left to begin a new life of struggle.

The two—a girl and a boy—were close and so alike that many mistook them for twins, though the visual resemblance was not particularly striking. Ama was a year older than her brother, but it was Susu, at the age of eighteen, who decided to brave the city in search of a better life for them. Ama only discovered the plan he'd hatched sub-rosa when she woke to find him gone, along with a framed family portrait, his favorite memento of the life they'd once had.

Ama, now known by her Christian name, Angel, currently lived in Accra, but her hometown, Kumasi, was never far from her mind. Lately, she'd been thinking about it constantly.

Within many Ghanaian tribes, it is believed that the dead superintend the affairs of the living. Honoring the ancestors is, therefore, a vital custom. On the tenth anniversary of Abrebese's death, the extended family had planned a grand memorial to celebrate his life and legacy. The event was advertised in the newspapers, on radio, on TV, and on the Internet. Those expected to attend included politicians, wealthy cocoa farmers, civil servants, doctors, and traders.

The commemoration was to be held in Kumasi. The second largest city in Ghana, Kumasi is the unofficial center for funeral celebrations. A funeral there is not just an opportunity to bring the community together to bury the dead; it is also an opportunity to display the art and culture of the bereaved peoples. From dawn to dusk, there is unceasing drumming and dancing among the milling crowd, many of whom have traveled from near and far to partake in the communal ritual. Mourners clad in red and black, Ghana's colors of mourning, are seen cloistered in small groups eating, drinking, and generally making merry. Funerals are also excellent opportunities for dating. Indeed, many people have confessed to meeting their spouse in this way, and many people attend specifically for this reason.

The pallbearers are always a key highlight. Well dressed in uniform or designer suits, they put on a show for all in attendance by displaying a variety of dance moves, such as Michael Jackson's moonwalk, with the coffin perched precariously on their shoulders. Another highlight is the presence of professional mourners, people who have been hired for the sole purpose of crying, loudly and dramatically. They sit and weep for hours on end at the funerals of important people, high-ranking members of the community whom they'd probably only heard about but never met, let alone knew well enough to be so heartbroken by their death. There is a saying in the Akan language: *Ɔhohoɔ a osu dennen sen nea ade no ayɛ no.* The outsider weeps louder than the bereaved. In Kumasi, this saying is actually a reality.

There was no way Angel was going to miss her father's funeral anniversary. She'd left Kumasi eight years earlier to live in Accra after meeting then marrying her husband. There hadn't been any reason to return. She'd not maintained a relationship with her extended family, especially given how they'd so handily taken her father's money yet neglected to care for either her or her brother. Susu had left home shortly after their dad's death and no one had heard from him since. Everyone just assumed he was dead, that some tragedy had befallen him in Accra. Angel was inclined to believe otherwise. She believed that her brother had found his way to Accra and, from there, to aburokyire (overseas). Angel often imagined him happily living his life somewhere in America or Europe with a wife and children. It pained her to think of him being sick or dying alone someplace so far away from home, so far away from her. At the same time, it also pained her to think of Susu having a full, joyous life and not wanting to share it with her, so she'd taught herself to not think of him at all, which was hard now with the upcoming funeral.

Angel, along with her daughter, Kukua, left the house early in order not to miss the traders. They came from the rural areas, like Techiman and Kintampo, which are noted for their yams, plantains, and tomatoes; Dormaa Ahenkro, for their poultry and eggs; and Anloga, for their production of onions. They arrived at dawn to off-load their produce. The merchants who received this produce would turn around and sell them at exorbitant prices later in the day at the various markets in town. Angel wanted to be there early not only to buy cheap but also to have the benefit of handpicking the best of the goods.

Long after the traders were gone from Makola, the main downtown market, Angel sat on one of the discarded crates that had only recently contained juicy-looking red tomatoes, and watched as the sun gradually rose, generously dispensing warmth and light, like a veil slowly lifted to reveal the secrets it had been shielding. The sounds of increased human activity and motor traffic signaled daybreak. As if to also announce that morning in downtown Accra was officially underway, the pleasant smell of vegetables was quickly overtaken by the pungent smell of rot from the choked gutters. Angel stayed put with Kukua until the stores opened. She wanted to purchase some supplies and provisions to present as an offering, a token, a requisite show of respect for the extended family back in Kumasi, even though she did not respect them at all. They hadn't done a single thing for her since her father's passing. Even so, it was unheard of for a traveler to return home empty-handed.

By midmorning, after going from store to store, comparing and haggling over prices, she had all she would need for the long journey to Kumasi the following day. As it was well over 270 kilometers from Accra, Angel and her husband, Joojo, would be on the road for hours. Whenever she'd complain about the length of the journey, Joojo would laugh at her. To him, that was a short trip. He enjoyed driving, especially long distances. It was, for him, all in a day's work.

Since they'd be gone, Angel had given their house help several days off to go to her village and spend time with her family. Joojo usually preferred for Angel to prepare the evening meal herself anyway, but it was nice to have the help around for the rinsing, chopping, stirring, and, of course, dishwashing. Angel was running late, yet she still didn't rush to get back home. Joojo would understand how emotional this anniversary business was for her; besides, he was not always home in time to join her for dinner. Lately he'd been working longer and longer hours, sometimes not even making it home until the wee hours of the morning. She assumed it was to make up for the extra money she'd been spending in preparation for the funeral and trip to Kumasi.

Angel smiled at the thought of Joojo. He was the one thing in her life that had turned out right. She'd married a good man, somebody sensitive and dependable. She often thanked the heavens for bringing him to her. She remembered how easy and pleasant their first meeting had been. It was her second day as a waitress at the McDonald's that had newly opened in Kumasi.

"Ei! Why are you so beautiful, awuraa?" he had asked when she served him a chicken sandwich and a bottle of Coke. She was startled, but happy to receive the compliment. Joojo waited until her shift ended and then walked her to the single-room apartment where she stayed. The next evening after her shift ended she had gone home to find him waiting—with a gas cooker, a refrigerator, and a television. These were things she did not have and, of course, had not asked him to buy. He must have noticed when she'd quickly shown him around the night before. His consideration made her weep. That night she slept in his arms. By morning, she knew that he was the man she wanted to spend the rest of her life with.

Kotoka International Airport is always a place of confusion. There'd been a long, slow-moving queue at the Immigration stop where people entering the country have their passports stamped. Owusu was one of the last passengers to complete his arrival formalities. He couldn't help but wonder if the queue in Germany would have been that long and disorganized. He didn't know because he'd never formally entered Germany. Like so many refugees, he'd sneaked into the country. That was nearly seven years ago, and since then he'd called Germany home. Now that he was back in Accra, he realized that Ghana would always be home. His heart and soul would always belong to the Black Star nation.

"Good evening, sir," a voice broke through his reverie. He turned and looked up into the face of a smiling, smartly dressed man. His white shirt looked well ironed and was tucked in. A *man who pays attention to detail*, Owusu thought.

"May I help you with your luggage?" the man asked.

The area around the luggage carousels was filled with unofficial porters, men who'd bribed their way into the airport so they could offer passengers help with their bags, a taxi ride to their hotels, or currency exchange. Many of them were too aggressive, attempting to take hold of your bags before you'd even agreed to their assistance or understood what fee they'd be charging. This made Owusu suspicious, so he usually held on tightly to the handles of his baggage and firmly refused whenever anyone approached him with an offer of help. There was something about this one man, however, that made Owusu feel he could trust him. It was more than his attire. It was his calm demeanor, his impeccable manners. He was polite and seemed educated, trained to interact with foreigners and "big men." Owusu quickly agreed to the man's offer of assistance, sliding his bags toward him.

When they exited the arrivals hall and stepped outside, Owusu stopped to look around. Nothing could have prepared him for the scene that greeted him. Accra had changed so much in the decade he'd been gone. It was almost unrecognizable. He needed a few minutes to take in the transformation. He'd been momentarily taken aback by the migration from manual to digital checkout processes at the airport, but given that most of the nation was using mobile phones and accessing the Internet, he quickly figured it wasn't so noteworthy after all. What did surprise him, though, were the tall, modern buildings surrounding the airport. It wasn't the same skyline he'd left.

"That's my car parked right there," the man said, pointing to a Pontiac Vibe.

"Thank you," Owusu replied, following him to the vehicle.

Once in the car, they formally introduced themselves.

"I'm John," Owusu said, using the Western name that everyone in Germany called him. He laughed, dispensed with the affected aburokyire accent, and said, "Actually, you can just call me Owusu."

The driver laughed as well. "You can call me Abraham."

Owusu wanted to ask the man what his real name was, the traditional name he'd been given at birth, but thought that might be too forward and presumptuous, so he stopped himself. What if his parents hadn't given him either a day name or a family name? What if his only name was his English one? Owusu had heard that some Ghanaian families had now stopped giving their children both an English name and a Ghanaian name, that they only gave one or the other.

Abraham shared with Owusu that he was thirty-six years old and unmarried. He said he hadn't yet taken a wife because he wanted to leave Ghana; he hoped to one day be a bɔga like Owusu. Owusu smiled knowingly, thinking that the more things changed, the more they stayed the same. It seemed that every young Ghanaian dreamed of one day becoming a bɔga, a been-to, someone who had traveled to or lived in America or Europe. It had never even occurred to Owusu to leave Ghana until he started living in Accra. He'd been working as a street kid, selling everything from packets of P.K gum to socks at intersections, weaving his way around the vehicles, standing at some driver's window pleading for him or her to buy something, anything. He usually made two or three cedis a day. It was not enough to feed or house him, so he'd sleep on the streets and eat whatever he could steal or beg from the women at the kiosks. This was the great Accra, the place that everyone in the whole of Ghana spoke of as though it were the best of the best, the light of the world, the city upon the hill. When Owusu slept on the streets he always dreamed the same dream, of one day going far, far away from Ghana and all its hardships.

One evening, he was given the opportunity to make that dream come true. He and a few of the friends he'd made, young men like him whose circumstances had also forced them onto the streets, hatched up a plan to walk from Accra to Tangier, Morocco, and then cross the Strait of Gibraltar into Tarifa, Spain. It sounded like a crazy and dangerous thing to do, but no crazier or more dangerous than the life they were already living. After two years in Spain, he had sneaked into Germany through its border with Belgium, one of the most porous entry points for undocumented migrants. There, he was finally living his dream. Owusu wanted the driver to know that anything was possible, no matter how unlikely it seemed.

Owusu took one of his business cards from his wallet and handed it to the driver. He told Abraham to call him should he ever find himself in Germany. He would show him around Hamburg, where he lived, and introduce him to his wife and children. Abraham asked Owusu whether he had any family in Accra.

"No," Owusu answered, thinking of the young men who'd set out on the journey to North Africa and Europe with him. When they left Ghana, they had numbered twelve, a band of high-spirited brothers determined to find their place in the world, a place where life would not be a losing battle. By the time they reached Tangier, they were six. Two of the men, tired and afraid to travel any farther, had stayed in Ouagadougou. As the remaining ten walked on, witnessing their surroundings transform from savanna to the Sahel to desert, their journey to a place with better prospects started to seem more and more like a suicide mission. The heat became so severe it was difficult to move more than a few hours each day. They were forced to travel by night, well after the sun had set, which was extremely dangerous. Three of the men died of dehydration and heat exhaustion. One after the other, they just dropped dead.

It seemed as though Boyo, the one with whom Owusu was closest, might also perish from the desert heat. Fortunately, he made it to Timbuktu, with its formidable mud buildings, and, despite Owusu's pleading, decided to stay.

"No," Owusu repeated, thinking of Boyo, who'd been like a brother. Then he thought of Ama, his sister. He'd not seen or spoken to her since the day he left Kumasi. He hadn't called from Accra because he'd been too ashamed of his circumstances. And by the time he settled in Hamburg, so much time had passed, he didn't know what he could say to bridge it. How could he explain it all? How could she, living in the small bubble that was Kumasi, understand what he'd been through, the things he'd endured, survived?

"I have no family here. My people are from Ashanti," he continued. People sometimes used *Ashanti* and *Kumasi* interchangeably because everyone indigenous to the city belonged to the tribe. Owusu explained to Abraham that he would be headed there the following day. That's why he had booked a hotel online; it was someplace in East Legon, a part of Accra that was unfamiliar to him.

Abraham assured him, again, that he knew the hotel well and would take him there. "It's a fabulous place," he promised. "Executive rooms."

As Owusu eased into the ride and started taking in the sights and sounds of the Accra streets, the car suddenly jolted to a stop.

"Damn it," Abraham said, slapping the steering wheel with the palm of his right hand. "We're out of fuel. That thief!" Apparently the last attendant he'd bought fuel from had cheated him. As of late, he explained, the attendants had been scamming their customers. They adjusted the scales on the fuel dispensers so the readings corresponded with the amounts the customers had requested. And the attendants then pocketed the extra money.

Abraham sighed. "He should just wait; he'll see what I will do to him." And then he laughed a short, sinister laugh, one that cast him in a light that was a complete departure from the warm, polite gentleman Owusu had been chatting with all this while.

Fortunately, the petrol ran out near a station. Abraham, along with a taxi driver who had stopped to offer his help, pushed the vehicle the few meters. As the attendant filled the tank, Abraham received a call and walked away from the vehicle to speak privately. Owusu leaned against the car and observed him. Abraham had the tall, well-muscled build of a bodyguard. He seemed like the sort of person who remained cool under pressure but could easily turn wild and threatening if he needed to. He was definitely the sort of person you'd want on your side in a bad situation.

"Is everything all right?" Owusu asked when Abraham returned. They both got back into the car. "Was that your wife?"

Abraham laughed. He explained that the call was from

his boss, the owner of the vehicle. "These Accra women," he said with a chuckle. "They are too much. But I am sure that soon, God willing, I will meet the right one. His time is the best."

Owusu wasn't sure what to say. *Amen* did not seem like an appropriate response. He had forgotten how religious Ghanaians were, or at least pretended to be. Abrebrese used to scoff at the idea of Ghana as a nation of God-fearing people. "More like a nation of churchgoers," he'd say.

Life on the Accra streets and as a refugee in both Africa and Europe had taught Owusu a lot about the limits of Christian compassion and Muslim tolerance. He decided it was best to stay quiet. He started sipping the complimentary beverage that Abraham had offered him before they drove out of the airport car park. The driver had said it was the latest craze in town. It was good, but Owusu didn't see why the drink would generate any excitement. It tasted like the same sobolo he had grown up drinking. He'd even learned to make it himself in Germany. It was simply two parts hibiscus tea to one part fresh ginger juice and three mint leaves.

Nevertheless, he made a mental note to surprise Abraham with a considerable tip for his kindness. It also occurred to him to make an arrangement with Abraham to be picked up early in the morning from the hotel and taken to the bus station at the Kwame Nkrumah Circle. It was where everyone went to board buses headed to the northern cities, like Kumasi, Tamale, and Bolgatanga. Taxi drivers in Accra were notoriously unreliable, but this one seemed like a hardworking, trustworthy man, someone Owusu could even befriend.

Abraham reminded him of the guys he'd trekked through the Sahara with and, at times, thought he'd die with. The six of them had somehow managed to cheat death. They'd made it to Tangier, where they begged on the streets for two years until they raised enough money to purchase space on a boat headed to Spain. During that time, three of his mates were caught and detained by the Moroccan authorities; he never saw them again. He guessed that they'd been deported and returned to Ghana or, worse, killed.

Another of his mates had accepted an offer from an expat to come and stay with him as a houseboy. They'd each received such offers, and they'd understood that it was a sort of coded invitation to become a full-time servant and part-time boy toy. He and Mensah had refused, still hopeful that they could make it to Europe. Adama had refused several such offers but then, weary from life on the streets, finally accepted one.

"This way," Adama had rationalized, "I can eat and have shelter and still save for a space on the boat." Mensah and Owusu spotted him a few times in the medina, sporting a djellaba and a beard. Each time they'd called out to him, but Adama pretended not to hear them and immediately turned a corner and disappeared down one of the many small alleyways.

Owusu often thought about his band of brothers and how fate had separated them, given each his own destiny. He wanted to tell Abraham about them, about the journey they'd made, completely on foot, from the shores of Accra to the shores of Tangier. He tried to open his mouth to speak, but his lips felt too heavy to part. The last thing he remembered was Abraham's smiling face looking down at him as he surrendered to the darkness all around him.

The baby on Angel's back was asleep when they arrived home. At two years, little Kukua could sleep through an orchestra, once she was well fed. During the bus ride home, Angel had fed her Cerelac, and it had done the trick. Now, as she rushed to start preparing their evening meal, she could do it in peace. This child was indeed a blessing.

Angel and Joojo had endured a great deal in their marriage. When by the fifth year they still had no children, the couple visited several hospitals and churches and even the shrines of medicine men in hopes of a solution, yet none yielded the desired results. After Angel and her husband underwent a number of medical tests, the doctors finally offered a diagnosis: Joojo was sterile. The couple was devastated. What crushed Angel's spirit even more was going to church and overhearing the worshippers gossiping about her, referring to her as a barren woman and wondering when Joojo would leave her for a new wife. She eventually stopped going to church and withdrew into herself. Joojo, distraught watching his beautiful wife wasting away over something that was his fault, decided to find a solution, no matter the cost.

One day Joojo brought home a newborn girl. Angel was both terrified and overjoyed. Joojo assured her that the baby had been abandoned. He said that one of his friends, who knew of their predicament, had found her. Angel wondered what her husband had to give this man in return, but he assured her there were no strings attached. She readily agreed to raise the baby as their own. How she wished she could share the good news with her brother, Susu. When they were children, they'd often imagined their futures. Susu was sure he could walk in Abrebrese's footsteps and become an equally successful farmer. Angel would become a teacher, study to become a nurse. She would marry a doctor and have several children. She and Susu always envisioned themselves living on the same compound, their children being raised more like siblings than cousins. What a terrible blow their father's death had been. To lose him was bad enough; to then lose their home and their financial security was quite painful. Never did she think she would lose her brother as well.

Angel felt a gentle tug of sorrow in her heart and, just then, Kukua started crying. It was a reminder to not take for granted all that was hers now. She had the best man in the world for a husband, and he had given her a daughter to call her own.

When Owusu regained consciousness, he was naked, lying on a bed in a dimly lit room. His hands and legs were bound with twine. His first thought was to bite the twine off his wrists, but there was a gag in his mouth that had been taped firmly in place. He was still groggy but knew he had been kidnapped. He couldn't believe this was happening to him, not in his own country. He willed himself to remember. His mind was racing. What signs had he missed? Was the driver his captor, or had he also been kidnapped? What did they want, ransom? If it was about money, he had some in his bank accounts and all he would need was his Visa card, which they obviously had. He would happily give them his bank access code; his life was all that mattered. Suddenly, the silence of the night was broken by a voice heavy with terror.

"I beg you in the name of God, please don't kill me," a man sobbed. "My people will give you anything you want. Please, spare my life."

He wasn't alone. There was another prisoner. Could it be the driver? Owusu held his breath as he listened intently, praying. A bloodcurdling scream, like that of an animal being slaughtered, broke whatever hope he had of negotiating with his captors, and he began to weep like a baby. He had to escape. He calmed down and listened. Silence. He rolled himself off the bed onto the hard floor. He screamed from the pain but the gag did its job and muffled the noise.

Owusu proceeded to roll in the direction of the door. When he reached the end of the room, he propped himself against the wall and stood upright. He then hopped close to a window and, without pausing, drove both fists into the louver blades, cutting himself in the process and making a crashing noise that was amplified in the still of the night.

Footsteps outside the room rushed toward where he was. He did not waste a minute. He held his wrists to the jagged edge of the broken louver and cut through the twine. He untied his legs and braced himself to face his captors. It would only be a matter of seconds. Suddenly, *bam*, the lights went off. The room and entire compound were thrown into total darkness.

Dumsor! For years, Ghana had been suffering a debilitating power crisis. As it became increasingly industrialized and citizens continued developing the appetite of a new middle-income country, power became a crucial yet scarce commodity. All the air conditioners, microwaves, hot-water heaters, televisions, laptops, mobile phones, and other devices guzzled electricity faster than it could be generated. The systems were outdated. As a means of addressing the issue, the government introduced "load shedding," a power-rationing program.

The outages were scheduled so each region in the nation would bear its share of weight and citizens would suffer only the slightest inconvenience. Unfortunately, outages also occurred at unscheduled times. This unreliability of power, derisively termed dumsor, was the bane of every Ghanaian's existence, especially those who lived in urban areas. When the lights went out it was *dum*—"shut off"—and when they came back, it was *sor*—"turn on."

The captors undoubtedly knew this, but dumsor was well after Owusu's time. He assumed the lights had been switched off to disorient him and facilitate his capture. Owusu heard his abductors slow down, their steps now hesitant, uncertain. He heard the door to the room he was in open. In the absence of visibility, his other senses were heightened. He stood still, ready to spring on cue. In the pitch darkness, he could sense one of them, to his left, inching toward him. He knew this was his opportunity. He ran as he had many times before as a hungry thief in Accra, as a refugee and beggar on the streets of foreign lands. He ran knowing that his life depended on it, that it was either escape or death. He collided with one of the bodies standing close to the doorway. They both fell. Owusu quickly picked himself up and continued running until he was out of the yard and into the chilly night.

He saw no one. The area, secluded, seemed to hold no other houses. The moon was absent and there were no stars, uncharacteristic for an Accra sky. Without a thought about where he was headed, Owusu ran for over half an hour without slowing down, powered by the sheer force of fear. In his blind flight, he'd turned eastward, rather than westward, which would have led him straight to the Weija-Kasoa highway.

As it was, he ran crashing through tall bushes, and his path led him right to the banks of the Weija lagoon. Only then did Owusu pause to catch his breath. The cacophonous, insistent cries of the frogs and crickets seemed to be warning that the danger was not over. But he could not move. He now felt the intense burning from his steep fall onto the concrete floor, the cuts to his hands, lower torso, and soles, the pain magnified by the wetness of the marshy land he'd stumbled upon. Shivering, he slowly retraced his steps to higher ground.

He mustered up the strength to half walk, half run, until he saw ahead of him a small house with what appeared to be light from a lantern flickering inside.

Thank you, God, he breathed a quick prayer of gratitude, and knocked at the door. A woman with an infant child on her back opened the door. Was he delirious? She bore a resemblance to his sister, Ama. He squinted, then opened his eyes as wide as possible to look at her again.

She screamed when she saw him, this grizzly-looking man, completely naked, before her. When he opened his eyes wide until the balls were almost rolling out of their sockets, as though he'd been possessed, she right away shut the door in his face and slid all bolts securely in place.

Owusu was desperate. He begged her to open the door and save him. There were some killers after him, he explained. He pleaded. He could feel himself getting weaker but used what little strength he had to plead some more.

As incredible as the man's story sounded, Angel believed he was telling the truth. She couldn't put a finger on it, but there was something familiar about his voice. Something inside of her trusted it. She opened the door to his shock but utter relief, and profuse gratitude. He quickly entered before she could have a chance to change her mind.

Angel immediately went to find a pair of trousers and a shirt belonging to Joojo and gave them to the man to wear. She explained that her husband had gone to work and would be returning soon. She served him food, which he devoured before falling into a deep and exhausted slumber on the couch. Not long after this the lights came back on.

Joojo bent down to take a closer look at the man on their couch. Now he knew exactly who he was. At least he thought he did. Joojo just had to put on a believable show for his wife. As he was leaning over, a wallet slipped out of Joojo's breast pocket and fell on the floor. Angel bent down to pick it up, as well as the ID and cards that had fallen out. She looked at the ID and saw that the picture was of the man on their couch. Her eyes then scanned the name: *John Owusu Teku.*

Angel gasped. It was her brother, Susu. Only she had called him that, a corruption of Owusu, a name she'd found difficult to pronounce as a young child.

Angel's eyes widened as all the pieces started falling into place: the long hours, random gifts, sudden influx of cash, the baby—oh God, the baby—the naked man, his voice, that sweet familiar voice, her brother, dead. He was dead.

When the truth finally hit her, Angel gasped again. She looked at her husband's expressionless face in horror. She could see no remorse, no sorrow, no guilt. In fact, she couldn't read him at all. Angel screamed. She screamed even louder as Joojo approached her, and then she collapsed.

THE SITUATION

BY PATRICK SMITH

Labone

Scene I

Bad News, Terrible News

It was in that drab light just before dawn when Ato heard an insistent rattling at the front gate. His instinct was to ignore it in the hope that it would go away, especially because his paramour, Ewura Abena, had just let herself in and crawled into bed beside him. The muggy heat was beginning to rise from the red earth surrounding the house. A cock crowed so languidly, Ato suspected it had raided his liquor cabinet.

It must have been around half past five.

Ato had made it to bed less than an hour earlier, his head full of ideas and akpeteshie, after a session with his friends, known self-mockingly as the Labone Choirboys.

In their twenties and thirties, they had cut their moorings amid the mayhem in Accra. Some were university dropouts, others had lost their government jobs. For them it was about the hustle, finding a connection that would make millions or a way out. Inflated contracts, drug dealing, and trading scams—that's what kept the Choirboys going.

Other plans had been derailed following a dawn announcement by military officers after they had seized the state broadcasting corporation. The government was bankrupt.

It was March 1984 and Accra was set in aspic. Driving

across this once wondrous city in a rust-bucket taxi, you'd see the Independence Arch marking a public square second only to Tiananmen, multilane highways holding few cars, factories standing idle, an empty port, and an international airport once meant to be the world's gateway to Africa.

All were monuments to a splurge of energy in the wake of independence just three decades earlier. Now that ambition had fizzled; politics, business, music, journalism, fun had been suspended . . . everything except funerals. Death was a way of life.

Six feet five in his tsalewɔtee sandals, Ato carried his two hundred pounds with a beaming confidence. In the Accra courts as a young advocate, he could pinpoint the strengths in any case. And he could also marshal the arguments against it. Juggling politics, drinking, and dancing, Ato was sure he was heading for the big time but was determined to have fun en route.

The rattling at the front gate continued. Ato released a sigh of surrender. Whoever or whatever was demanding his attention had won.

"Where are you going?" Ewura Abena mumbled as Ato tried to slide out from her grasp without waking her. She'd wrapped one arm around his torso in a half embrace, and rested her hand directly over his heart, as though she'd been checking for the *thump thump* of his heartbeat.

"Shhhh." He placed a finger to his mouth. He could smell the akpeteshie on his own breath. "Go back to sleep, my darling. I'll be right back, just a moment." Ewura Abena's arrivals and departures were sporadic, based on her husband's schedule. He was a "big man" at State Security. Their marriage was enviable in appearance but loveless in reality. Ato, on the other hand, loved Ewura Abena, despite or even because of her serial infidelities.

Ato's house, the Choirboys' de facto headquarters, was on

Ndabaningi Sithole Road, the main artery of Labone. It was a rambling whitewashed building set back from the road, partly hidden behind a parade of royal palms. Paint was peeling off in places, some of the cracked window louvers were hanging like jagged teeth. The guttering was linked to a network of pipes leading to an eccentric water-storage system. At the front, a wide veranda was crowded with cane chairs, batik cushions, and enough wine and whiskey bottles, strewn across the glass-topped table, to supply the bar of the Ambassador Hotel. Most of the business of the house was done there.

A glance at the place suggested the owner had once lived in considerable style but had fallen on hard times. Like the country itself.

From the other side of the house, Ato could now hear this voice shouting, almost screaming. And an ever more insistent rattling of the front gate. "Mr. Adjei, Mr. Adjei!"

"Oooooh, you too," Ato growled, shaking his head. "Exercise patience." He quickened his pace.

"Mr. Adjei . . . Mr. Adjei, I have bad news, terrible news . . ."

Through the akpeteshie-perfumed haze, Ato could make out the words. The last thing he wanted was bad, let alone terrible, news.

"Mr. Adjei . . . Mr. Adjei," the voice said once more. Ato was now able to place it. It belonged to Kwame Owusu, Thierry's driver.

Ato stopped. He lit a cigarette and drew heavily on it before finally making his way to the gate.

Close didn't begin to cover the friendship between Ato and Thierry Tobler. Brothers, not by blood but by a force that felt equally as binding. Two young men in a hurry to change their fate in a country that had been hijacked by armed robbers, politicians, and soldiers.

Yet they were opposites. Ato was an extrovert, a trickster lawyer who believed his charisma would let him escape from any imbroglio. Thierry was an introvert, a banker and discreet businessman bordering on reclusive.

Somehow their differences had driven them together. The two had stumbled upon a scheme to make a large amount of money. They'd decided to work it themselves, not sharing it with the rest of the Choirboys.

"What the hell, Kwame! What is it?" Ato finally reached the gate. "I had just turned in."

When he opened it, Kwame couldn't hold back. "Mr. Tobler, Mr. Tobler, gone," he blurted tearfully. "Drowned, sir, drowned! Fishermen found him body for Labadi Beach . . . washed up. No clothes. Naked like a baby, a little baby!"

Ato stood at the gate, staring straight ahead. It was as if he were looking straight through Kwame. "Whaaat? Whaaat!" he raged against the shock. "You don't mean it! You dey lie!"

"Na true, I dey tell you, sah. He lef am Jagua on beach road with portmanteau for back . . ."

"Whaaat? . . . Who dey for beach now?"

"Soldiers dey, police dey . . . dem go chase us away o." Kwame, skinny and standing at a schoolboyish five feet six, was tottering.

"Come," Ato beckoned, closing the gate and walking toward the veranda. "Sit down. Tell me the whole story." He directed the driver to a wicker seat before going into the house to get cigarettes.

Inside, the shock hit again, harder. Legs wobbling, Ato sat at the kitchen table, then slumped across it, hitting his forehead on the Formica. Thierry was dead. A shiver of guilt ran down his spine, his eyes started tearing. For a few moments, he kept shaking his head, agonizing over his friend.

"I'm sorry," he cried out. "I'm so sorry." Even as he was saying this, he saw the absurdity of it. He had nothing to do with Thierry's drowning. Yet he had other things to apologize for. "Oh my God, my God, my God!" Ato held a cigarette to his mouth, slid it between his quivering lips, then, with an unsteady hand, struck a match.

Shuffling back to the veranda, he stopped in the hallway, gazing at his favorite painting. It was a portrait of a gangly boy in an indigo-blue tunic and trousers, his head resting, exhausted, on his forearms, a mournful resignation in his eyes. It felt surreal, like looking in a mirror. A long-ago premonition that had been revealing itself to him every single day, for years.

"Onua," he cried, reaching his hand out and gently touching the young man's sad, tired face. *Brother*. "Onua, I am sorry."

Ato meandered through the hallway and stepped out onto the veranda, where Kwame sat hunched over in the wicker chair. His eyes were an odd pink color, almost peach—a combination of the red that came from crying and his usual yellow, the result of jaundice, perhaps a symptom of cirrhosis. He looked like a villain from a low-budget film.

As soon as Kwame saw Ato, he started weeping again. "It was murder, Mr. Adjei. Murder. But why? Wetin they want?"

Another shiver of guilt coursed through Ato. He pulled out a new cigarette, tamping the end on the table. "We don't know that yet, Kwame," he said, squeezing the man's wrists like an encouraging father, even though the two weren't very far apart in age. "But I promise you that we will find out what happened to Thierry."

"Sah, I know what happened. They kill am," Kwame said, pulling his hands free and using them to cover his face. He moaned into his palms, then placed them neatly on his lap. "He say he go speak with the big man. I sabby somet'in' don happened when Mr. Tobler no dey for hotel. I go waka-waka for Labone, Cantonments too."

Kwame told Ato that he had gone to all of Tobler's favorite spots. He said he then ran into a man who claimed to have just seen Tobler's Jaguar at Labadi Beach.

"E be so," Kwame continued. "I don find him Jagua but somet'in' no be correct. I ask fishermen." He looked hard at Ato. "We take boat to look for am. Not'in'. Not'in'. Then we hear somebody cry . . . he don find Mr. Tobler body."

Ato was trying to make sense of it, to create some kind of timeline. Tobler had come to his house in the early evening. He'd told the group that he had to go because someone was waiting for him.

"Why not have her come here?" one of the guys had teased.

Thierry had been involved with the same woman for over a year but had not yet introduced her to all the Choirboys. The only one who'd met her was Ato, and he wasn't spilling the beans.

When the guys kept pressing him, Tobler had said, "Patience, patience. Timing is everything." He laughed. "Every man who meets her wants her for himself. Isn't that right, Adj?" That was his nickname for Ato. Everyone else called him Ato Nii, adding a Ga name even though he was Fante. It was a play on his legal background—attorney.

Thierry winked at Ato, and that had immediately made him feel uneasy. The feeling stayed with him for the night, long after Tobler had left. It was only after he heard Ewura Abena tiptoeing into the room and then sliding into bed with him that it fell away.

"You drove Mr. Tobler when he left here?" Ato was trying to map out the evening.

Kwame nodded.

"To where?"

"Home, home to Mr. Tobler house," Kwame started, "and then he say . . . Madam, madam . . ." He suddenly jumped up. Ato turned to see Ewura Abena walking out onto the veranda with a tray full of freshly cut papaya, orange juice, and a pot of steaming coffee.

"Me wura," she said to Ato, making him blush. *My lord and master*. Long ago, women addressed their husbands that way. She used it as a pet name for him. He was surprised to hear her say it in the presence of another.

In fact, he was surprised she'd come out to the veranda. No one had ever seen them together, not even his house girl or night watchman. Ewura Abena set the tray down and kissed Ato on the lips before taking a seat beside him. She placed her hand on Ato's thigh, the way a wife would, to offer support. Ato wasn't sure what to do so he placed his hand directly on top of hers.

"Good morning, madam," Kwame greeted her. He'd stopped crying. His eyes had returned to their normal urine-yellow tint, the blood had drained from his cheeks. He refused to sit down again when Ato pointed to the wicker chair. "I go, go . . . go now," he stammered.

"What's happened?" asked Ewura Abena. "Something with your friend Tobler?" She turned her head and looked straight at Kwame, even though she was talking to Ato. "So, is there anything more that the driver can tell us?"

"I go," Kwame said again. "I dey fear o, sah. I don see a t'ing, madam. I don't know no'tin'. I go, I go now."

He crossed the veranda then ran to the gate, opening it with such force that it swung wide on its hinges, crashing against the fence. He sped up, didn't look back, didn't stop, leaving the gate swinging in his wake.

As Kwame ran down the road, Ewura Abena grabbed a

slice of papaya from the plate, held the crescent-shaped fruit to her mouth, and took a bite. "Mmmm," she mouthed, licking her lips. She ate the rest of that piece and then took another. "Don't you want some? It's so good, it's almost sinful."

Scene II

Richer Than Croesus

It was meant to be quick and clean, this secret scheme to make untold amounts of money. When Ato Adjei first heard the gory details from Thierry, he didn't believe it. Nor did he quite understand it.

They had arranged to meet in the garden bar at the Star Hotel in Labone, where Tobler had set up residence since returning to Ghana after six long years in investment banking. Not as sumptuous as the sprawling Ambassador Hotel or as central as the Continental, the Star had cachet as a place for a discreet rendezvous.

Resplendent in a pale-blue grand boubou, Tobler embraced his bulky friend. Hugging Ato tighter, Tobler's face beamed with manic elation. "My brother, this is our big break. We will be richer than Croesus!" He patted a fat wad of notes in his trouser pocket. "So, let's celebrate!"

Ato broke free of the clinch and stared at his friend. Tobler's willowy six-foot frame was filling out, and he had doused himself in expensive cologne. High living was taking its toll. A weird condition in a country where many struggled to eat.

Ato saw the creases around Tobler's eyes. Lighter skinned than Ato, he had always had a world-weary look that certain women found irresistible. Now it was just weary; no backstory. His stickman movements had slowed; no longer the killer competitor on the tennis court.

For sure, a bottle a day of hard liquor and several nostrils full of cocaine played their part. Tobler was just five years older than Ato, in his late thirties, but already he looked middle-aged. Once one of the sharpest minds in the locale, an investment banker who read Dostoyevsky and could explain Einstein's relativity theory in plain language, he was losing his edge.

As a precocious child in his father's house, Tobler had met the independence generation of African leaders. A top adviser to founding president Kwame Nkrumah, the Tobler patriarch saw himself as a citizen of Africa, and almost every leader would take his calls—no matter which crackly phone line they came through on.

After a coup ousted Nkrumah, Tobler's father felt a terrible betrayal from which he never recovered. He passed on that lesson to his son, who vowed to stay out of politics and make money instead. Those days were long gone. Now Ato and Tobler were orphans. Their common loss had made them tighter. Somehow, Tobler, loner intellectual and quiet schemer, became a great friend to Ato, everyone's favorite scoundrel lawyer.

As Tobler planted his elbows on the table, surveying the bar as if looking for spies, his sleeves gathered to reveal a hefty Omega watch on his right wrist and a trio of gold bracelets on his left. "Kojo, my man!" he called out to the bartender, like a gambler on a winning streak at Monte Carlo. "A bottle of Rémy Martin VSOP for the table, and charge it to Thierry Tobler, suite 908."

That's strange, thought Ato. Tobler had pulled him in for a discreet chat about a crooked scheme to mint money, yet he was carrying on like a starlet looking for press coverage.

Just then, Tobler grasped his forearms and stared at him. As a stream of Friday-night drinkers eddied into the bar, he lowered his voice. "I can break open a trust fund in Switzerland that holds billions—repeat, billions—of dollars."

"Get real, TT, for Chrissakes."

Like an arrogant professor with an obtuse student, Tobler shook his head in mock despair. "It's about banks, not lawyers, my man. Tricky stuff . . . long numbers."

Kojo, who seemed too interested in their conversation, brought the cognac with a silver ice bucket and two brandy balloons. Taking a hearty swig, Tobler began a convoluted tale about password code sequences and protocol integrity. Ato drummed his fingers on the table.

"Cut to the chase, TT . . . I am just looking for the love of my life."

"Patience, my man. This will help you find that very woman."

At the heart of Tobler's story was his father's ties to President Nkrumah. The two men had set up what they called the national development trust fund with tens of millions of dollars from the treasury.

"Okay, the details are boring. Just know the trust fund started out with millions and is now worth billions. Before he went, the old man gave me a key to unlock the door. I'm the only one left so I'm going to use it."

Ato's skepticism was melting as the cognac coursed through his veins.

"The key is here." Tobler held out his Spanish leather attaché case. "Three files of codes and protocols for the Union de Banques Suisses in Geneva to open this fund."

Tobler poured two more hypermeasures of Rémy Martin, calling for more ice as the din in the bar ratcheted up. He pulled out a bundle of foolscap manila envelopes. "Take these and put them in your safe."

"So I'm part of the plot?"

"If you tell a living soul, you'll have the Brooklyn Mafia after you, and they don't play, even in Labone."

"Brooklyn Mafia? You dey craze, my brother."

"Not Don Corleone. Just a bunch of guys from South Brooklyn. No idea where they got the twenty million dollars."

"Twenty million dollars for what?!"

That piqued the interest of the neighboring tables. Tobler was looking tired and drunk and not making any sense.

"UBS won't open the fund until we flash the cash . . . They want a twenty-million-dollar deposit out of which they gouge their fees and, in any case . . ."

Just then, Kojo the bartender strode over with another bucket of ice, a soda siphon, and a notepad. "You have an urgent call at reception, sir."

"Ah-ha . . . that would be my interlocutor." After Tobler walked over to the concierge, a new kerfuffle erupted at the back of the hotel.

There were two Nigerian men sitting at a nearby table. "Aaah, aaah . . . Fela don come o!" one of them called out to Ato. "The incomparable Afrobeat king is checking into Accra."

They were impresarios, in charge of Fela's long-awaited tour of Ghana. Ato shook their hands, promising to bring some of the country's finest ganja to the great man's room that night.

"And if you need any help spending that twenty million bucks, let us know," suggested the smaller of the two.

Just then, Tobler returned. "We have an assignation, Ato . . . at Cave du Roi." Cave, as everyone called it, was the classiest nightspot in Accra.

Inside the bar at Cave, Accra's beautiful people were getting down to the sounds of Ray Parker Jr. and Lionel Richie pounding from ten-foot speakers. Local stars Teddy Osei and Mac Tontoh were signing autographs at the bar.

Ato, still queasy from the daredevil ride in Tobler's vintage Jaguar, followed his friend as he wove across the dance floor to a private room behind the bar. There, in a white leather armchair, sipping a mojito, was a woman of disarming beauty with intense almond eyes and a broad smile. A younger woman with a low cut was sitting alongside, sipping a cocktail adorned with a parasol. At once Ato was entranced.

"Introductions, first," said Tobler. "This is my alter ego, advocate Ato Adjei. And these stars are the formidable Ewura Abena and her highly talented sister, Amelia."

They both glared at Tobler. Ewura Abena had a day job as the youngest director of the central bank, but her true vocation was counterculture activist, hanging out with artists, musicians, and dissidents. Super-hip but cerebral banker. Something didn't compute as she twisted her plaited hair.

A waiter brought a bottle of Veuve Clicquot in an ice bucket, setting it down on the low table in the center of the room. Ewura Abena smiled at Ato and held out a pack of Benson & Hedges, a scarce but essential commodity in those trying times."You want a jot?"

"Sure," Ato said on autopilot. Instead of cigarettes, there were ten ready-rolled spliffs in the packet. "Well, okaaaay . . ."

Laughing, Ewura Abena threw back her hair, then drew heavily on a spliff. "That's better." Another smile for Ato. "Now Cave makes sense tonight . . . Thierry, will you indulge? But I'll tell you true, my friend, you are looking the worse for wear."

It was a fair comment. Tobler had been drinking shots of Rémy at an alarming pace. He always got boring or stupid when overdrinking. This evening it was a bit of both.

Ewura Abena grabbed Ato's hand. "Let's hit the dance floor." Crowded onto it, she alternately pressed close to Ato then broke away to go freestyle. A slow, smoochy dance to yet another Lionel Richie number convinced Ato that the evening had taken a wondrous turn.

After the song ended, Ewura Abena and Amelia made a diplomatic detour to the ladies' room. Tobler shoved Ato into a corner. "Chale, what the fuck?"

"Whaddya mean, *what the fuck?*"

"There's two fucking things wrong with this," Tobler hissed through gritted teeth. "One, Ewura Abena is married to the head of intelligence, who lacks a sense of humor about this sort of thing. Two, she's *my* woman . . . tonight."

Ato felt like a car tire about to blow out. "If she is married to Colonel Quarshie, what the fuck are you doing with her?"

"For your fucking interest, she is my interlocutor with the government. She will make everything happen."

Ato was about to ask what "everything" covered when he saw the women heading back.

"Permission to fall out," said Ewura Abena sarcastically, beaming at the men's agitated faces.

"Sweetheart, let me run you home," said Tobler protectively.

"Whatever makes you happy, Thierry dear," Ewura Abena whispered in his direction. She turned to her sister. "Amelia, can you drop Ato wherever he's going?"

Five minutes later, Ato was in a car with Amelia on Ndabaningi Sithole Road. He gave her a chaste good-night kiss. A sweet and innocent end to an evening that had been neither.

Clutching Tobler's attaché case, his head reeling, Ato tried to fit the pieces together. Once home, he stashed the folders at the back of the house.

What the hell had he been dragged into? If anyone was

being played, it must be Tobler. But by whom? His woman? His South Brooklyn business partners? Again and again, Ato ran the puzzle through his mind, hoping to discover a clue.

Then the phone rang. It was Ewura Abena. Of course.

Scene III

Picking Up the Pieces

It was unnerving to see a man of Ato's size thrown into convulsions. But on that Sunday morning, the searing aftershock of Tobler's murder had felled him right there on the veranda at the house on Ndabaningi Sithole Road.

His body started shuddering, shaking uncontrollably. Face contorted, sweat pouring down his temples, as the Accra sun beat down. For a few moments, Ato would be still, as if he was summoning the energy for another bout of frenzy. Then the weeping would start: guttural moans, heavy sobs from deep in his chest. Then more juddering. Ewura Abena looked on while eating thick slices of papaya, amazed at the transformation of her towering, confident lover into a trembling wreck.

Even her cool ministrations failed to help. She tried to embrace him, the man with whom she had shared the most intense passions just hours before. He swatted her away.

Ato's implosion had begun well before the driver's terrified exit. Now, he was free to fall apart in his own way.

It was all over. Tobler was over. The big-money plan was over. Trust was over. Everyone was suspect, everyone. Including the woman crouching beside him, pleading, cajoling. Horror, and even desperation, were slowly supplanting her confident default smile.

Rarely troubled by conscience, a sickening mixture of guilt and fear was unhinging Ato as he pondered the lies, betrayals, and crimes that had led to this point. He had not been to church in at least a decade. Suddenly, he felt a desperate need to see Father Dominic, his priest, any priest. In a trance, he ran through a confession, the trembling subsiding with each word.

Father, I have sinned. I have cheated and stolen. I have fornicated. I have taken another man's wife. But I have never killed. I have never tried to kill. I will change after this day. I promise to God, I will change.

He slumped forward and lost consciousness.

When Ato opened his eyes, instead of the rumpled, whiskey-soaked features of Father Dominic through the confession grille, it was Ewura Abena, facing him. Her eyes, lowered, now sought his with compassion.

"Oh, darling Ato. You poor, poor man . . . weeping for your brother. You loved him. You didn't kill him."

Still dazed, Ato blinked, trying to focus. Was this the same Ewura Abena who had been so stonehearted when they had learned of Tobler's death?

"My darling, you feel bad because of us." Those eyes, so penetrating and clear. How could they lie? "Thierry and I were finished. We knew that. He was changing, becoming a bit mad." A wistful sigh. Even a hint of contrition. "I should have tried to save him."

"Huh? You sh-should have w-what?" Ato was stuttering his way into a suspicion. "What do you mean? How the hell could you have saved him?"

A flash of calculation crossed Ewura Abena's eyes. "To save him from himself . . . He was getting out of control. Spending like a billionaire, boasting, drinking, snorting cocaine by the barrel . . . it was like he had already cracked open the fund."

Ato thought of Tobler's attaché case that he'd hidden at

the back of his house and the folders that were inside. "No, Ewura Abena, no, no, no. He was killed for a bigger reason. Someone wanted the money and thought they could get it without TT. Right?"

As Ato was recalibrating his thoughts, Ewura Abena moved closer, wrapping a comforting arm over his shoulder. This time he didn't push her away.

"Where are you going with this, Ato?"

"I'm going to Tobler's killers! Either his South Brooklyn guys or State Security. Maybe both . . ."

That brought it right into Ewura Abena's court. Or rather, the court of her husband, Colonel Kwabena Quarshie, director of State Security. "I hear you, Ato. But what about us?"

"I don't know where it leaves *you*, but I'm the next target if I don't move fast."

"This may sound crazy," she said, looking away from him, "but you should go to my husband."

"Sound crazy?" yelled Ato. "Not sounds, it *is* damn crazy. He'll see through me in a second."

"Trust me, Ato, I know him." She put her arm back around his shoulder. "Offer him something, get him on your side, and then we can pick up the pieces."

Ato wondered which pieces those might be. But it made him see, too, how limited his options were. A meeting with Colonel Quarshie, convened by his wife, may well be a bad move, but right then it seemed the least bad of the ones he could make.

Clearly, a full confession to Colonel Quarshie was out of the question. He would be walking down a track strewn with unintended consequences. But cutting some kind of deal with the colonel might buy him some time to figure out his next steps.

He nodded. "Maybe you're right, Ewura Abena. Organize the meeting."

Before Ato's lover got up to leave on this weirdest of missions, to set up a meeting between him and her husband, she gave him a lingering, reassuring kiss.

Scene IV

A Faustian Pact with Security

When Ewura Abena returned, Ato was chirpier. Back on the veranda, he was devouring a heavy plate of Fante kenkey, Titus sardines, and a mound of freshly ground pepper and tomatoes. He raised a glass of Club beer as she walked across the gravel. "Cheers!"

"Well, Ato, he will hear you out. But no guarantees," she said, lowering her voice as she got nearer. "Right now the regime is on red alert."

Ato grimaced at the absurdity of the situation. To be caught between a military junta and Brooklyn gangsters. "Am I going to end up in the cooler if the meeting with your colonel bombs?"

"It's not by force, Ato. If you don't want to, don't go. But he's one of the few who could help." Ewura Abena looked and sounded brisk. Her mouth set, lips turned down; her earlier tenderness was gone. She wasn't as good an actor as she thought.

Ato grunted, lighting a postprandial cigarette.

"He wants to meet you at the coffee shop, on the side next to the old GNTC store, five o'clock sharp. Don't be late; the soldiers are on a short fuse right now."

Briefing over. Irritated and apprehensive, Ato nodded.

While ironing an orange dashiki in the back of the house,

he could hear Ewura Abena collecting the plates, glasses, and bottles that had been left all about. She seemed to be clearing the stage for the next act. The balance of power between lover and beloved had tilted fully in her favor. He hung up the dashiki and started searching for a clean pair of trousers, all the while running through what he would tell Colonel Quarshie.

Ato's plan was to hand over the sheaves of trust-fund documents and protocols, bartering them for safe passage.

He had already gone halfway down that track, disregarding the strict orders from Tobler, by sharing almost everything with Ewura Abena. That was then, before his friend's murder. Now, Ewura Abena's loyalty felt negotiable.

The worst couldn't be ruled out: do not collect two billion dollars, go straight to jail. A public trial, a national disgrace. Then a lonely death on the beach facing a firing squad. A crooked lawyer, trying to steal the past president's investment fund. Who would miss him?

Bleak thoughts swirling through his mind, Ato finished dressing and set out down Ndabaningi Sithole Road to the coffee shop.

An eerie stillness had descended in the late afternoon. A couple of children clutching a football skipped into a side street; a dilapidated Datsun taxi with faded yellow markings cruised for fares; a young man in a dark suit and starched white shirt, flowers in hand, stood waiting at an imposing steel gate.

Labone was quiet these days. In the 1950s and '60s under Nkrumah, it had grown fast as a domicile for civil servants, hospital doctors, teachers, and journalists. Now, with its palm-fringed streets and whitewashed estate houses, it was on hold. Most people were surviving on the margins between a stake in the official economy and wheeler-dealing. They distrusted the radical pretensions of the new junta, especially the "people's tribunals."

Ato's own loyalties were divided. His father, an ambassador, had amassed a clutch of lucrative directorships; his mother, a high-court judge, had dismissed the people's tribunals as kangaroo courts. They had long ago fled into exile and died there, effectively severing Ato's links with the "old" Ghana.

At first, Ato backed the revolutionaries and their anticorruption purges. Now he had doubts about the policies and the heavy hand of the state, the incessant roundups of dissidents. All that made this meeting with Colonel Quarshie, whose organization had led those purges, a dangerous gamble.

A bulky-muscled guy in green-gray fatigues stood outside the coffee shop scanning the street with a practiced look of unconcern.

Shuttered against the late-afternoon sun, the inside was dark and dingy. At the bar, the manager, nervous and plumpish, was gesturing to a boy lugging a crate of beer. Beyond them sat a few solitary drinkers. Pots were clanking in the kitchen. An aroma of fish being fried wafted out from behind a gaudy plastic curtain.

"Is Colonel Quarshie in?" asked Ato, as though inquiring about an old drinking buddy. The manager, unsmiling, pointed to a battered door at the back of the bar.

Inside the half-furnished room was a bespectacled man in jeans, a polo shirt, and trainers, leafing through a pile of documents on the rickety table before him. Beside them was a full glass of Coca-Cola.

Colonel Quarshie's appearance belied his fearsome reputation. He had last seen active service in Angola a decade earlier, and before that in Congo. Known as the security capo, he had obliterated all manner of threats to the military regime.

"Ah, advocate Adjei," said the colonel with studied politesse, offering his hand. "My condolences for your loss."

"Thanks, and for agreeing to see me," said Ato, putting his hands in his pockets to stop them from shaking. "I have to find out what happened to Thierry Tobler . . . we were close."

"Soooh, Ewura Abena told me." The colonel looked straight across the table, probing for a reaction.

"I'm sure the motive was money, getting into the trust fund. I guess you've heard all about that."

"Not as much as I want," said Quarshie with a hint of a smile.

"I hope I can help." Ato tried to look as sincere as he could. "Tobler briefed me pretty thoroughly, but now it is spinning out of control."

"My office called me down to Labadi Beach this morning to see the body. Your friend was murdered under—" Quarshie broke off. "Let's say the circumstances were embarrassing . . . We were meant to be tracking him."

"He was talking to the government. I know he needed documents from you."

"Let's say there was a trust problem." Quarshie's smile widened. "Perhaps it was mutual . . . Let's see if we can get around that." He fiddled with a pack of cigarettes, then offered a stick to Ato. "All this must be worrying, I suppose? If it's any consolation, we can't afford to lose another one."

It was a remark loaded with ambiguity and threat. Ato wondered if he would leave with a gun to his head. "What do you need to prevent that from happening?"

"That's easy . . . your silence and all the papers that Tobler gave you. My officers will be coming to see you this evening."

Just then, the man in fatigues pushed open the door, his two-way radio active with conversation. He handed it to his boss. Ato heard fragments of the chatter—"blue gate" and "Castle meeting"—before Colonel Quarshie barked orders down the line in Ga. Despite the years he'd lived in Accra, Ato could only understand snippets of Ga. It seemed that some form of security crackdown was going on at the airport. After more commands, Colonel Quarshie handed the radio back and turned to Ato.

"So that's done. Remember, you are now a high-value target."

Ato forced a smile as he and the colonel shook hands. The manager, still nervous, saluted Quarshie as he left. Ato sat at a table and ordered a Guinness. He pulled out his packet of cigarettes and contemplated his new life as a ward of national security.

It took him another hour, and four more bottles of Guinness, before he felt ready to return home. Ato left a hefty wodge of cedis with the barman and shook his sweaty hand.

Outside, he looked into the midevening gloom. Farther up the road, there had been a power cut. He could see candles fluttering in the darkened houses. Strange, he thought, how a country that could not guarantee electricity to its people could have an omnipresent intelligence agency run by graduates of Harvard and West Point.

As he meandered back up Ndabaningi Sithole Road, Ato amused himself by imagining he was under protective surveillance, a high-value asset rather than target.

Then he heard it. It sounded like a motorbike at first. A sedan with a broken muffler, like so many in Accra, coming up behind, rather too close. Just as he turned around, the car skidded to a halt and two men, whites or Arabs, jumped out.

"Hey you!" said one, waving a baseball bat.

"Who? Me?"

The lights went out. Ato's own personal power cut.

Scene V

Suffering at the Star

It was still dark when Ato came around. He felt as if someone had driven several nails into the back of his skull. He blinked, tried to stretch his arms. They were bound tightly behind his back.

More blinking. Ato looked around the room, trying hard to focus. Something about it had an unnerving familiarity. The scuffed blue carpet with faded gold stars. Pale-green walls, and a painting of women gathering around a well in Jamestown. As he realized where he was, he felt the deepest foreboding. It was the suite in the Star Hotel that had been occupied by Thierry Tobler until just twenty-four hours before.

He heard a key turn in the lock. A thickset white man walked in, followed by a slim Ghanaian dragging a large suitcase.

"We're going to keep you here until our boss comes," said the white man in an indeterminate European accent. "You know what we want. Once we get it, we'll decide what to do with you." He glowered at Ato.

The man strode over to the fridge and got two bottles of beer, throwing one to his Ghanaian workmate, who opened it with his teeth, effortlessly.

"You people have given us a lot of trouble. Why?" The white man turned to Ato with another accusatory glare. "Anyway, the boss will decide."

Despite this bravado, the two were uneasy about something going on elsewhere in the hotel. There was shouting down in the bar by the pool, almost drowning out the Fela Kuti tracks the deejay was playing.

"I'll check what's happening," the white man told his Ghanaian accomplice. "You keep an eye on him."

After a few minutes, the shouting seemed to grow nearer, traveling up the stairs. Then, the sound of several people running along the corridor. The white man would have been no match for them. From inside the suite it sounded like he went down very quickly.

In the corridor after that, Ato could hear an animated discussion in Twi about which was the right room. Suddenly, the door burst open and in charged a soldier who must have weighed at least a hundred pounds more than Ato.

"Good evening, gentlemen," the officer greeted Ato and the beer drinker. "You're going to have some company." Inspecting Ato's bloodied head, the soldier untied his arms. "You will be needing some small treatment for that."

The beer drinker nodded, then pulled a bottle of Fanta from the fridge for Ato. Just as Ato was puzzling over the direction of these fluid alliances, in walked Colonel Quarshie, still in the same polo shirt and jeans he had been wearing at the coffee shop.

"You had some sort of accident after we met, Ato?"

Ato rubbed his head. "Someone clobbered me hard."

"Strange that," replied Quarshie, deadpan. "Someone has clobbered me too. It appears my wife flew to Geneva some hours ago. And your house has been ransacked, by the way. I think it's time to talk again, this time about Ewura Abena."

PART III

All Die Be Die

INTENTIONAL CONSEQUENCES

BY ANNE SACKEY

Kanda

A tingling sensation flowed through my body like warm lava, bringing a sense of calm and finality. It was as if I had unknowingly been waiting for this exact moment, a confirmation that over the last four years I had been right to feel constantly uneasy and believe that Alan was not fully invested in our relationship. It was almost an anticlimax.

I replayed the conversation I had just had.

"Serena," my friend Mawuli, a doctor, had said, "I really admire your sense of loyalty."

"Yes, I love him," I'd replied, hoping that it would get him to elaborate on the information he'd just revealed.

"Yes, you must, to stand by him after he stepped out of your relationship to have a child, especially a three-year-old," he went on to say, providing me with a solid number, a *when* to go with the *what*.

"Well, I decided to forgive him," I quickly said, not wanting Mawuli to figure out that this was the first time I was hearing about any of this. It worked; Mawuli went on to tell me about how he'd recognized the child's surname and then confirmed the father. Each word was like a stab to my heart.

I had known Mawuli since we were both in diapers, as our parents were very close friends. We had spent so much time together that he could usually read me like a book. We had gone to the same nursery school, primary school, and secondary school, only going our separate ways when we had to attend different universities to pursue our individual interests. I was glad that an emergency at the hospital had forced him to have this talk over the phone and not in person, as he had originally planned, because it made it easier to hide my emotions.

After the call, I aimlessly drove around. I got onto Switchback Road and had to stop sharply in front of Christ the King Catholic Church for the congregation, which had attended evening mass, to cross the road. I wondered what burden each person had prayed for relief from. This was the church where I occasionally worshipped, even though I was not Catholic, because I enjoyed the consistency of mass. There were so many new churches being built in Accra, but Christ the King was a mainstay. It had been established in 1951, six years before Ghana gained its independence. The parish priest, a man of Irish origin, was known for his compassion as well as his simple yet meaningful sermons.

After all the worshippers had crossed, I drove on. Just after turning off Liberation Road, I pulled over and parked near the presidential residence and office. That building, constructed with a dramatic facade so that it resembled the Ashanti Golden Stool, was forever being named and renamed by various governments. It had first been called Flagstaff House, then it was renamed Jubilee House, then went back to being called Flagstaff House, and now it was Golden Jubilee House, renamed by the current president.

On the opposite side of the road was Afrikiko, a cluster of thatched summer huts featuring restaurants that served a wide range of international cuisines. There was Thai, Spanish, and Ghanaian. There was also a live band on a stage and under the trees that played a mix of highlife and popular European tunes. I contemplated whether to go inside for a drink. Despite the lure of the breezy leisure center, the thought of even reviewing a menu seemed like such a bother. Instead, I called my best friend, Esi.

I met petite, firecracker, blunt, acerbic-but-with-a-heart-of-gold Esi when I started my first job after university. We had both worked for an information technology firm after graduating from the University of Ghana, and she was my constant companion to the many events we attended. Esi had declared herself "single for life." For her it symbolized freedom and untapped potential for growth, and so far she seemed extremely content with her independence.

She didn't sound the least bit surprised when I shared my news with her. "Serena," Esi sighed, "I didn't know how to tell you. Everybody knows, but you seemed so oblivious, I could never figure out the right way to do it. But since you know this now, I have more news. He also has two-year-old twins with Tracey Nartey." Tracey had been a year behind us in uni and now lived in France. I became enraged. Three children?! And two with someone from our school? I had been dating him for eight years. Not once had he ever felt guilty enough to confess? Not once had he been careless enough to somehow let the cat out of the bag? Everybody knew! Everybody! Was I now the laughingstock of Accra?

Part of me didn't want to believe just how deceitful and two-faced Alan had been and was still being, but I knew it was all true. My intuition had been telling me that something in our relationship was very wrong. I was now beginning to understand why. And to think he had always been the one to constantly accuse *me* of cheating on *him*.

I stared hard into the rearview mirror and assessed myself.

Forty-five was kind to me. My café au lait skin was still taut and wrinkle-free. My lips were full, and when I pressed them together, the schoolgirl pout that I perfected in adolescence was still visible. I'd always been told that my best features were my big brown eyes, which slanted gently upward on my roundish face and looked even bigger than they actually were because of my long lashes. My thick hair, though the envy of many, was my nightmare; I was constantly conflicted about it. I could never style it to look sleek and sophisticated. Sometimes I loved its density and natural beauty, the way each part of my head seemed to have a different texture, and how the curls formed and bounced when I moved, especially when it had just dried after a wash. Other times I hated its high maintenance, always having to plait it before bed to prevent tangling, and how the humidity made it frizz no matter how much "taming" hair product I'd used.

This particular day was a hate day. And to top it all, I had noticed a few speckles of gray around my hairline.

I knew I wasn't conventionally pretty. With a dimple in only one cheek and a gap in the front of my upper teeth, some might say my look was merely interesting.

After I had sufficiently analyzed my face, I turned my gaze down onto my body. I was in good shape. At five feet seven, I weighed just sixty kilograms. Even so, despite a reasonable workout regimen, the six-pack I had always coveted remained ever elusive. I suppose the inability to pass up on a good sticky dessert or a juicy burger prevented that. I sat in the car deconstructing myself, criticizing every part of my body and personality.

Why do women pick themselves apart instead of seeing that it's the man they're with who doesn't have his act together? Why do we assign blame to ourselves for someone else's failures? How did I turn into that kind of woman? The kind of woman whom people smile at when she enters but then whisper about when she leaves. The kind of woman who believes that any day now her long-term lover will propose, and they will marry and start a family, when all the while he is having children with other women. The kind of woman who sits in a car and wonders what it is about her, why it is that she wasn't enough.

No, no, no, I thought. *I'm not going to be that kind of woman. That's not how this story will end.*

After sitting in the car for over an hour, I finally took a deep breath and dialed Alan's number. He answered with his deep Barry White voice.

"Do you have something to tell me?" I asked bluntly.

"Not that I know of," he said, returning to his normal speaking voice.

"Not even a three-year-old child?" He was quiet, but the shock and discomfort were palpable. "Wow," I said, "you're good."

"It was a mistake. She tricked me and I didn't know how to tell you." He was convincing. As he spoke, I could almost see him, as though he were standing right in front of me, a well-used look of innocence on his face. Nothing he did was ever wrong. He was always the victim of circumstance, of other people's ill will. "And anyway . . ." Alan went on, "who told you?"

At that point, I lost it and started screaming at him: "What the hell does who told me got to do with this? Is that what is important to you? Why are you not more concerned with telling me about the two additional children you have?" And then I cut the call.

During the drive home—which, thanks to Accra's legendary traffic, took thirty excruciating minutes—Alan kept calling, but I needed time to gather my thoughts and figure out what I wanted to do, so I refused to answer. I just allowed myself to be distracted by the frenzy of rush-hour traffic and all that came with it. Two boys, wearing uniforms that had turned brown from overwashing, rushed to try to clean my windscreen for a tip. The car had been washed yesterday, so I waved them away. I breathed deeply and my nose filled with a familiar mix of petrol fumes, plantain chips, fresh bread from the ladies who wove agilely between the cars, and a hint of the garbage that lay by the side of the road. I didn't need the car radio; there were enough noises coming in from the streets to keep me company.

It took an entire two days before I could sit across the table from Alan, at his house on 7th Estate Road in Kanda, not from the Hilla Limann Highway, one of the busiest thoroughfares in Accra. It was named after Dr. Hilla Limann, the president of Ghana from 1979 to 1981. His term ended as a result of a coup d'état.

It was a quiet neighborhood of medium-sized government-built-but-privately-owned homes. There was also a sprinkling of eating spots and offices, like Fali's Hot Pot at the top of the road. I watched Alan's lips move but I wasn't hearing a word of what he was saying anymore. I was mesmerized by his stark teeth. His lanky frame was draped over the armchair, one long arm flung across its back. Occasionally he would run his hand over his close-cropped hair and down his face. Whenever he did this, I caught a glint of the signet ring on his little finger. It was gold, decorated with a filigree rendition of nkyinkyim, a popular adinkra symbol, whose name was shorthand for a longer proverb: *Ɔbra kwan yɛ nkyinkyimii. Life's road is twisted.*

It was a reminder of the flexibility and perseverance one must have to navigate the journey of life.

Alan had spent the last hour unapologetically justifying why he had not thought it necessary to tell me, his girlfriend, about his three children: first of all, he hadn't even told his family; second, it was a mistake; third, he hadn't felt loved by me; and the last, most annoying excuse was that he wasn't even sure the children those women—Tracey and Akua—had had were his. At that moment I wanted to hurt him so badly; I wanted to see him in pain, the same anguish that his actions had brought into my life. I took a sip of my whiskey sour and, in a flash, it came to me: I knew exactly how I could do just that. I had read in the May issue of *Marie Claire*, while pounding the treadmill, about aconite, also appropriately known as women's bane, devil's helmet, and the queen of poisons. It caused nausea, vomiting, weakness, the inability to move, and, if consumed in large enough quantities, heart problems—also, death.

I tilted my head to one side and looked at Alan, imagining him writhing on the floor in pain begging for relief, totally dependent on me, while I wiped his feverish brow and kept him delicately balanced on that fine line between pain and death.

I took a deep breath and caught a whiff of his ever-present designer cologne—Gucci Guilty, as irony would have it—which jolted me out of my trance. With a sudden burst of energy and purpose, I reached over and grasped his hand, catching him unawares.

"It's okay, I still love you," I told him. "It's a lot to take in and I will need time to process this. But you need to confirm the children are yours with a DNA test. Children are a blessing, whichever way they come into your life."

He looked a little taken aback, and it suddenly crossed

my mind that maybe he didn't want me to be understanding, maybe he had hoped that I would leave him in anger. Well, I was not going to give him the satisfaction. I decided that things were going to go my way from that point on.

Because Alan regularly worked long hours, I often cooked for him so he'd have one less thing to worry about. Surely, if I made him a spectacular meal, he would be convinced that I was sincerely trying to move past this new hurdle in our relationship. So that was precisely what I did the following day.

I hummed a tune under my breath while I put the finishing touches on the lasagna. I even sprinkled an extra layer of cheese on top to make sure there wouldn't be a bitter or acrid aftertaste. When it was done, I called Alan's office, which was in the compound of his home, and spoke with his personal assistant, who must have also been working late.

"Hi, Nelly, I am on my way to drop off dinner for Alan. It seems he is busy so I'll hand it over to you when I get there. Unfortunately, I can't stay to enjoy it with him as I have to attend a school-year group meeting around the corner at the Christ the King Parish."

With the delivery now sorted out, I packed the food in my car and left. I took the Hilla Limann Highway then turned off into Kanda and onto Alan's road. The highway separated the Muslim-populated community of Nima from the Kanda Estates area, which was developed during the regime of Ghana's first president, Dr. Kwame Nkrumah. Nearly all of the houses in the Kanda Estates were built in the sixties and seventies and were in high demand because of the location, the amenities, and the low population. However, the fact that the Nima Zongo was just a street away was an irritant to most of Kanda's residents, including Alan. The word *Zongo* was a variant of *Zango*, a word in Hausa describing a community or area with traders who speak the language. The Zongo in the Nima neighborhood was one of the oldest, dating back to as early as the 1830s. Overpopulation made it look like a slum. This was one of the criticisms raised by the residents of Kanda who were displeased with the proximity of their homes to the Zongo.

I met Nelly, Alan's assistant, in the car park and handed her the foil-covered Pyrex dish. "Tell Alan that the meal will go well with a glass of full-bodied pinot grigio," I said as I got back into my car. I felt a mixture of exhilaration and nervousness as I sped off. I pushed the thoughts away and went straight home because I definitely did not have a school reunion to attend.

Later that night, cocooned in my warm sheets, I grabbed my phone from the bedside table after the second ring. I glanced at the clock; it was two in the morning. Alan was on the line, and he sounded frantic.

"Serena, I don't know what to do. She has collapsed."

"Who? What do you mean collapsed?" I asked, suddenly wide awake.

"It's Akua," he said, gasping as though in the midst of a panic attack. "She came over to talk about our son and then she collapsed. I think she is dead."

A mixture of fear and exhilaration swirled in the pit of my stomach. "I am coming over," I told him.

I jumped out of bed, pushed my feet into a pair of slippers, and rummaged through my bag for the car keys. I sped down the road I had used just a few hours earlier, trying to figure out what had gone wrong with my plan. Even at that hour, the Hilla Limann Highway was full of activity. People were darting back and forth across the road, and I could smell the rich scent of grilled suya meat in the air. I could never determine if that round-the-clock bustle was because the people living in such cramped quarters had to sleep in shifts or if the nightlife was just that great. I tried to play out in my mind what might have happened at Alan's. Had the bastard invited his baby mama to eat the food I'd cooked for him? The dosage of poison that I'd used had been meant to debilitate a larger body. Had whatever she'd ingested been too much for her? Had it killed her? Is that what had happened? Would I be caught? And why was he now turning to me?

I parked haphazardly in his driveway and ran into the house. Alan was crouched over Akua, who was lying on the sofa with one leg at an odd angle. Her clothes were in disarray, as if she had been in the midst of a struggle. I spotted my lasagna dish on the table, joined by two half-empty glasses of wine and a completely empty wine bottle. I panicked a little but, at the same time, felt oddly triumphant.

"We have to get her to the hospital," I said, taking charge of myself and the situation.

He carried her to the car. I jumped in the backseat and cradled her head on my lap as Alan sped onto Presidential Drive behind Golden Jubilee House and then onto Liberation Road. Five minutes later he parked in front of the 37 Military Hospital's emergency room. Alan ran in and returned with a nurse and a gurney and Akua was quickly taken away.

After more than an hour of sitting and waiting, a doctor came out to tell us that Akua was in critical condition; the next few hours would be vital. All we could do was wait. Alan was a wreck. He had a runny stomach and looked peaked, as though he himself was unwell, but he assured me he was fine, all of the worry was just wearing on him.

It was nearly dawn and I had to be at work soon. I told Alan to stay, that I would try to get time off and come back. In the car, I hit my steering wheel. *Damn! Damn! Damn!!!*

It occurred to me that I needed to cover my tracks, so on my way home I made a detour to Alan's house to tidy up and, more importantly, wash the lasagna dish—to remove any traces of my fingerprints or remnants of the poisoned food. Just as I was wiping the countertop, I saw his assistant, Nelly, walk past the big sliding windows. I wondered whether she had seen me standing there washing the dishes or had just gone blindly on about her day as most of us do when repeating the same old routine.

After I was done, I went home, had a shower, changed, and went to work.

I had just settled at my desk when my phone rang.

"She's gone," Alan said in a hoarse voice. "She's gone."

"Gone where?"

"She is dead."

"Shit," I spat out, before I realized what I was saying.

"Huh? What did you say?"

"Um . . . nothing. I am coming over to get you. Stay there."

As I pulled into the hospital's car park, I spotted Alan leaning into a car window, talking to someone. I parked and waited. When they'd finished and Alan stepped away, the car started moving. When it passed by me, I stiffened as I recognized the driver as Tracey, the mother of his twins. What was she doing here from France? Had she and her children, Alan's children, moved to Accra? A flash of anger coursed through me. Akua was only a few hours dead and already he had someone other than me comforting him!

"Well then," I said aloud, shocking myself, "she has got to go too." I couldn't rationalize my train of thought, but all that made sense to me was that I had to punish Alan for his mistakes and hopefully leave him broken. How better to do that than to use the women who had been his accomplices in hurting me?

Two weeks passed. Akua's autopsy showed that she had been taking recreational drugs. The lazy pathologist hadn't bothered to look any further. I had been spending quite a bit of time playing the happy family with Alan and his three-year-old, a charming little girl named Naomi. With a little nudging from me, Alan had now, after the death of Naomi's mother, publicly accepted that she was definitely his child, and was sharing custody with her grandmother. Even so, Alan hadn't completely changed. He continued to deny the paternity of his twins, even though he was still dallying with Tracey. I knew because of all the sneaky phone calls. It wasn't hard to figure out, with the hushed voices and bizarre explanations for needing to leave the room in order to "handle some business" or "sort things out" with some random person or other whose name I'd never heard mentioned before. But I had decided to put an end to all of that. I had managed it once and I'd do it again.

This time, I cooked Alan a batch of meals for the week and labeled them, wearing gloves to avoid leaving behind any fingerprints. Only half of the meals were poisoned, because I would be spending time with him and we'd have to eat together. I wasn't worried about Naomi eating any of the food as she only spent time in Alan's house when I was there; somebody had to tend to her, take care of her meals, baths, and naps, and it wasn't going to be Alan. I knew which meals to avoid; plus, Alan was too lazy to heat up food for any woman, unless there would be a reward at the end of it. I knew that at some point he would have another romantic dinner rendezvous with one of my meals as the pièce de résistance.

One Sunday, a few weeks after Akua's death, I had gone over to Alan's to make brunch for him. He had not been feeling well for a couple of days, so I'd been stopping by to check on him. We'd just finished eating when there was a knock at the door. I smoothed back the bits of hair that had escaped my bun before opening the door. There stood an elegant elderly lady, dressed in a stunning silk boubou. She looked distressed.

"I need to see Alan," she said, her eyes darting frantically around in search of him.

Alan stepped out from the study. "Mrs. Nartey, what are you doing here?" he asked, obviously surprised.

"It's Tracey. She was taken to hospital yesterday and is in a coma. Apparently her kidneys are failing. I needed to tell you because I know she was with you on Friday."

Alan put his head in his hands.

"Who is Tracey?" I asked, pretending I didn't know who they were speaking of.

"My daughter, and the mother of his twin sons," Mrs. Nartey said, looking me up and down. "And you are . . . ?"

"I am his partner, long before his twin sons," I shot back.

"Please let me talk to her alone," Alan said, so I retreated to the kitchen.

After a few minutes, he came in and told me he was going with Mrs. Nartey to the hospital and that he didn't know when he'd be back. He said he would call me later. "We need to talk." Then he solemnly walked out the front door.

As soon as he left I checked the freezer and realized that there was only one Tupperware bowl left. It was marked as not containing poison. I had already eaten the other unmarked ones with him at various mealtimes to divert any possible suspicion. That meant he must have eaten the last poisoned meal with Tracey. I thought about her soon-to-be-motherless children and a wave of regret passed through me. I had already left one of his children without her mother. I quickly shrugged those thoughts aside and reassured myself that given the chance, I'd look after them and love them as though they were my own. After all, I deserved them.

•

When Alan called me that night he was very mellow.

"Tracey didn't make it," he said. We both remained silent for several seconds. "Serena, you've been there for me through all of these strange events. We need to talk. There's a lot I need to tell. Can you come by tomorrow evening? There's also something I want to ask you." In his voice, I could almost hear the sound of resignation, a man about to lift a white flag.

"Of course, I'll be there tomorrow after work."

When I got there, Alan drew me into a hug as soon as I closed the door.

"You're looking really nice," he told me, running his eyes over my black body-con dress, which had a rather high slit up one side.

All the better to reel you in, I thought. I smiled and planted a kiss on his cheek.

"I know I've put you through a lot recently, so I felt that we should talk," he said. I felt triumphant as he ushered me into the sitting room. On the center table were two glasses of red wine that he had already poured for us. He handed me one, like a gentleman, before picking up his own. I took a big sip, looking forward to the evening ahead of us. He set his glass down and caressed the nape of my neck before excusing himself to go to the bathroom.

"Why don't we have something to eat first?" he said when he returned. He had already heated up the last portion of the meal I'd made, a curry, and even boiled some rice to go with it.

I served myself, then immediately ate a huge mouthful. Alan hadn't started eating his plate yet. He continued to drink his wine, looking rather contentedly at me over the rim of his glass with a lopsided smile on his face.

"What?" I asked him playfully, as I ate another mouthful. "I'm hungry."

"You should have just let it be," Alan said. "Yes, I cheated on you, betrayed and lied to you, but you should have left well enough alone."

I had just started eating my third heaping forkful, and I nearly choked on it as I listened to him speak.

"Now," he continued, "my three children have lost their mothers, and I am under suspicion by the police because of the coincidence of how they died."

Oh no, I thought. *He knew! But how?*

"You see," he went on, as though he'd been listening in on my thoughts, "I found it strange that you were being so nice. And then, at a time when you should have been worried, if not about Akua, who we'd just taken to hospital, then at least about me, Nelly saw you here washing the dishes."

Realizing that I'd walked right into a trap, I grabbed a napkin and spit the food I'd been chewing into it.

"So." Alan laughed, absolutely thrilled with himself for having outsmarted me. He poured himself another glass of wine. "Since I will most likely be charged with murder, I decided that I might as well be guilty. I only used half of the portion you brought for the last meal that Tracey had with me. I put the rest into that last Tupperware of food. And that, my darling Serena, is what you have just eaten. I guess we will just sit here and wait to see what happens to you." He took one long gulp of his wine, then poured the remainder of the bottle into his empty glass before finally sitting down next to me.

Tears came to my eyes. I just couldn't bloody win, could I? Why hadn't I simply counted my losses and walked away? Then it occurred to me as I watched Alan guzzling down his glass of wine that even though I wouldn't be the last one standing, I'd still be the one to have the last word, and the last laugh.

"Well, Alan," I said, fighting back tears, "I am pissed off right now that you figured it all out. But you know what? I am not as stupid as you think. When you went to the bathroom, I put a little bit of the poison into your glass of wine, and then poured the last batch into the bottle of wine, for your next romantic dinner. How could I have known you'd drink the rest of the bottle by yourself tonight? So, I guess we are going away together."

He opened his mouth to speak but said nothing. He appeared to be processing what I'd just said. His silence was deafening. Myriad expressions played across his face. First his pupils dilated with fear, then his nostrils narrowed with anger, then tears flooded his eyes before he burst into hysterical laughter, filling the room with an explosion of sound. He started to fall back into his chair. I wanted to help him, I wanted to help myself; I thought to call Mawuli and ask him to rush over and save us, but it took all my effort to lift an arm and stretch it out toward Alan. He returned the gesture, reaching out to me. The poison suddenly took a firm grip of me and everything started going hazy.

"And Alan." I took hold of his hand. "When we get to the other side, you'd better leave those two bitches alone."

TABILO WUƆFƆ

BY GBONTWI ANYETEI

Airport Hills

Anybody could burn down a church.

Anybody could burn the hotel conference room in which a summit of high-finance profiteers was to take place.

That's why the council saved Orange for this kind of job.

The world needed people like him, because he *saw*.

A Tabilo Wuɔfɔ saw not only the big picture but multiple big pictures, like those multidimensional monocular devices children played with.

He saw the world as it was, as it had been, and as it could be. How it could be if Orange didn't do what he did.

More than burning down churches.

Idealism.

Politics.

Science.

Definitely not for revenge because his grandmother had been born in a "camp" thanks to men like the man who "owned" this house—and maybe the man before him and the man before that—so that nobody in Orange's family could even pass the gates.

Not for revenge because his family story, after his great-grandmother gave birth in that detainment camp, had only gotten worse.

And not revenge because the men—and it was always

men—he put down were trying to drag him back into that life. The enemies within, without whom none outside could harm any of them.

Not for revenge, but for justice and balance.

Because he was a Tabilo Wuɔfɔ, a man with the figurative blowgun darts from the past whom they sent to maintain the world's balance of idealism, politics, and science.

Orange huddled in the corner of the room like an orangutan, which is how the stupid dispatcher mispronounced his code name.

Orangutan.

Orange wasn't even his appellation, but he'd gotten used to it. But Orangutan?

They were all supposed to speak Kiswahili, but the grunts who couldn't swing an assegai, let alone flick a Mahdist knife, had to come from somewhere. And from that somewhere came cowards who couldn't learn a new language or pronounce words in the one presently assigned.

Tabilo Wuɔfɔ Orange was simultaneously among the 80 percent of people who hated their job and the 3 percent who loved what they did every day.

He was everybody, was *for* everybody, whether they hated or loved what he did.

Orange looked at the chamber he was in.

It was the product of European designs some African had misinterpreted, as usual. All the space with none of the virtue. Just every expensive feature and convenience the opportunists on all Mepho tiers of the Spintex Road could spin.

There was a big screen they watched nothing on, if they had time.

There was a piece of art by a close nephew, who might

have promise if he delivered on his potential and rejected the lazy opulence he was born into.

This time there was no 3D portrait of the household's large wife, whose hair was bigger than Orange had ever seen.

Orange had been here before. And every time, he asked the same question: why? He had a predictable job dealing with predictable people, so it was no surprise that his mind had become predictable.

It didn't matter where Tabilo Orange was from. He was from everywhere. The tourism app on his phone reminded him of this. Every hundred or hundred thousand cubits, no matter where he was, the app sent him stamps. History, trivia, and the most powerful propaganda.

The stamps detailed battles from the first, second, and third waves of the whites.

Biographies of great women and men.

Summaries of moments that may or may not have been great without the women, men, and battles.

They shouldn't have, but they all blurred into each other.

"History applied."

It was being updated even now, with everything after Alkebulan.

"Hello!"

Finally. Orange had gotten tired of waiting, if waiting was what he was doing. The word she opened with was as mundane as the vision of this house.

"I . . ."

This word had more meaning and promise, he felt.

Orange looked at the body of the man that was her husband or father or sugar daddy.

The man died how he had never tried to live. His face freezing with piety and dignity. The surprised look had gone before his last breath had. His hands and palms were still outstretched in what was a universal gesture of honest intent. In his mud-cloth robe, the dead representative appeared almost righteous.

Orange had used a bullet that guaranteed less blood than normal, leaving less scope for superstitious motives. He had done what he was here for. So why was Orange still here? Of all the thoughts bounding and clambering around the cage his head had become, this was the biggest.

This was the usual job. He had killed the target. *Sanctioned*, the council liked to call it. Orange was permitted to sanction anyone who got in his way, on or off the premises. But the woman hadn't gotten in the way. So why was Orange still here?

All these questions. All this reality.

And the woman in the room beyond that wall had said, "Hello."

Now she said, "I . . ." and, "I . . ." again.

Orange guessed at the words that would follow.

Interesting and potentially lifesaving for her. Another day at the office for him.

"*I'm not involved.*"

"*I won't say anything.*"

"*I'm sorry.*"

For the things that targets did to bring Orange to them, being sorry was never enough. It could never be enough for him. The Tabilo Wuɔfɔ had to be the iron fist inside a dyed batik glove. Orange kept a smile as big as it could get without cracking the ebony mask it was carved into.

Korshie had no idea how safe she was.

Who ever heard of a bathroom that was also a panic room?

With the house's proximity to the old airport, she had thought it might be safe enough here. The representative had thought it was. At least he had said he thought so.

Representative Akoto had almost never seen things the way she did, except when it came to expensive shit. Like this house.

He wasn't a *leader* like his retinue called him, appealing to his ego

Korshie wasn't even sure if the lock was in place. She was scared to walk or even crawl to check, in case doing so alerted the man outside.

Who ever heard of using *guns* anymore? For this kind of thing?

But he *was* a professional. So fast. And his gun was silent.

Scared to die now, Korshie had never had so much regret, and wanted to live long enough to *enjoy* that regret.

She had seen the assassin before today. She called him an assassin and not a killer. Why? If he was a killer and she had seen and not done enough, she was also a criminal. If he was an assassin, then she was something different.

It felt like she had seen him even clearer than she saw him now on the video panel. Him or the dead representative wearing an oversized robe that dwarfed the representative inside it.

The assassin's mistake had been to pointedly not look at her. She was not only used to being looked at by every man but expected it, from those attracted to her or not. Even when it got tiresome, made her feel vulnerable or like she was nothing more than her appearance, she dressed for it in anticipation.

Yes, she had put on weight. She'd been putting it on for over two years now. Between her disinclination to exercise and Representative Akoto's domestic appeals, a part of her knew she had begun her development into the archetypal large African woman.

Even now that she was fat they would look. Her cheeky lips and the refraction of her curves, if not resistant to fat, would remain constant with expansion. They would still look.

Even now, he didn't look into the camera she had trained on him. He hadn't smelled any kind of way in particular. She had known criminals who wore too much or not enough aftershave. He was neither, so something small after his passing had distracted her. Representative Akoto's next words or action would have been that something small.

She was often struck by how different the representative was from leaders before and after Alkebulan she had learned about in class. They'd had so many ideas that overflowed from books, but still enough charisma while they lived to inspire ordinary people and soldiers with guns.

Her collusion with the assassin was like no other, involving what she would have considered suicide if a part of her had indeed known he would come like this. It was an unspoken and unknown agreement

The fact that Korshie had run here instead of falling to the floor like she always did when scared was evidence enough. Korshie felt like she'd gotten a bullet in her back for every millisecond it took her to throw the door closed, sit on the toilet, and clamp her hands over her eyes, nose, and mouth.

"Representative." It's what he had always told her to call him. Or *Representative Akoto* if she could sound natural saying the whole thing.

Dead.

She had tried to warn him, hadn't she?

Had she warned him any more than all the other little things she complained about?

A part of her had to admit . . . She had to admit because maybe the little part of herself she denied became the big part.

This was only a small part of her thinking now. Smaller than her wondering why the assassin hadn't come in here yet. She couldn't imagine that this door she had opened and closed ten times a day for how long had more security than whatever he had broken to get into this house in the first place.

The airport was long gone, and air travel wasn't what it used to be for getaways.

Her thoughts stopped when her son materialized on the video feed. She watched him walk into the room, the one with the assassin in it. The son she had tried not to think of, reasoning that not thinking would keep him away, would keep the assassin from looking for him. Her son looked at the assassin almost matter-of-factly, and the man five times his size looked back.

Her son must have heard her run into this room, curious at the sound of her voice. Was it still a voice when it was a scream?

The man in the corner looked so dangerous. Moments ago he had only been a blur of blue and orange and classic West African sepia, but now he looked so heavy compared to her son. Her son eyed this assassin for longer than she had. Not hearing any words pass between them, she panicked and got up, anxious that she'd miss her son's last words because the microphone was too cheap.

This was the man who shot Representative Akoto asking no questions, placing no threats, offering no chances.

"You wouldn't kill my baby!" After she said it, the sentence was already a blur.

"Why not?" the voice above the blue shirt with the orange stripe said.

"You wouldn't. You just wouldn't!"

His eyes crumpled. Expectant, confused, disappointed. He genuinely wanted a reason.

And she was struggling for one.

A reason.

A reason that came too naturally was that you didn't kill children, not even if you were a child yourself. Not in New Africa. Not anywhere.

She watched her son disappear from the feed as he walked toward the door to this bathroom. She knew her voice sounded like it was coming from everywhere out there, but her son knew where to go. Or maybe this was simply the only room he hadn't yet searched.

She didn't move the camera to watch her son. Instead, she opened the door and, seeing nothing but her boy, pulled him in with one hand and shut the door with the other.

Her son wailed, his finger briefly caught when she closed the door. She'd been trying to move faster than she ever had before. This time she checked the lock.

Korshie covered her son in kisses and watched the man, who was stuck in place as if the feed had frozen. She willed her son to sleep through what was going to happen, like he did after his best cries.

While she kept kissing, she thought she could hear the man repeating a series of questions over and over.

"Why doesn't corruption sicken you?"

"Why don't you automatically see the bodies of children while you spend money meant for the masses?"

"Why is his spending money, meant for hospitals and farms and schools, not a crime as disgusting to you as directly killing your son?"

"What stops your son from growing up to be the same?"

Korshie didn't know if any of that was real, or if that was where maybe the fugue ended, because she could conjure no answers to them. But she did summon the answer to her first question of a few moments ago. She had wondered why this was happening. She now decided she knew why and was part of it.

If Orange had killed the boy and the news had gotten out, people would remember to be sad past breakfast.

People's sadness about the loss of hope. That was what stayed.

It wasn't easy. He disconnected the dispatcher's voice in his ear to make it easier.

Maybe he would kill that dispatcher next.

No more Orange or Orangutan.

Just a Tabilo Wuɔfɔ.

Orange wondered what others agents, soldiers, assassins of the Tabilo Wuɔfɔ division would think if they saw him like this. He did not know if there was more, not for sure. He had never met another in his training or years of experience, but they had to be out there. A secret battalion of them—1,675 was the number that rang out in his head. Shadowy protectors, 1,675 deep, spread out, disconnected, only engaging when called for.

The Tabilo Wuɔfɔ were the kind of soldiers the great leaders hadn't said they would send, but they had to.

Every Tabilo was on his own. The pressure and blood and tactics were theirs, while the council only pointed out the targets and strategy sometimes, maintaining plausible deniability always.

The council felt they only had to answer to children, maybe those not yet born, but a lot of loud and inconvenient people already in existence felt they deserved to be answered *now*.

But a Tabilo was not to talk about their work to anybody not directly approved.

Since Orange had been promoted to this level of interventions, he found his methodology was better suited to sanctioning the smaller people. He could escape in a coachload of bus passengers. There were no Mepho buses through areas this rich.

He used to watch the smaller people for two weeks sometimes . . . learning the ways of the NCM—neocolonial minors. He didn't have that luxury with the neocolonial privileged types.

The more he watched the big men, the more he risked triggering special security measures and a punch in the face. Orange didn't like having his face punched; like a tortured African pugilist who wasn't from Bukom had once said, being punched in the face was bad for the planning process.

This Representative Akoto had been a different kind of big man, maintaining quite a low-key life when not *representing*, and Orange had soon found out why. But with the man here lying dead it hardly mattered now.

Orange spared a thought for the man outside. His patrol had been part of the plan. He would be almost the least severe collateral damage left behind.

Orange had almost smiled at the confusion on the uniformed man's old-fashioned face when Orange rolled through the barrel quickly, making sure he had queued up the right projectile in what was basically a gun. *Is the bullet real? Why the old-fashioned gun?* Orange could *see* him thinking.

Then Orange shot him.

Until now, he hadn't spared him another thought. It was a matter of whether he had gotten the anesthetic content just right, enough to be effective for long but not fatal.

What was the difference between that man and the woman in the bathroom? Orange had had three to five chances to take her down and ask his final questions in his postsanction report.

But he had felt like no anesthetic, natural or otherwise, would suffice for her. He needed the truth serum he was currently testing.

Representative Akoto had had none of the ideas Korshie expected then learned not to expect. He'd also lacked the pomposity of other leaders she knew. They talked and walked like they had the weight of the world on their shoulders. Representative Akoto never did.

"Big-big men and their small-small girls."

She remembered now that that was the song Representative Akoto had been singing when the assassin swung into the room. He'd been wearing a robe matching the one she presently wore. Well, he was still wearing it. Did dead men wear bògòlanfini robes?

The representative had grabbed one of the air-conditioning drones and sang into it, giving his voice an auto-tuned effect like music from the 2010s. She sometimes laughed on the outside, but she hated it when he sang that song. It had been a song she loved that they sang in school to hoot at corruption, yet here she was.

Had she warned him every time she was reminded of the assassin, every time her phone app made its sound? Because she remembered her phone app chiming in unison with his that time he hadn't looked at her, at the Ayawaso Mall.

Great Accra. These hills were along that city's fault lines and were the reason why the metropolis surrounding Ayawaso still had this name and hadn't been retronamed like so many places, titles, and things after Alkebulan. Accra had become great, honoring the city that was then wasn't, not having belonged to its people for too long,

Wuɔfɔ was a Ga word that should have translated as "yellow" for the barely literates who still insisted on using English, but of course the letter *y* didn't exist in most African languages that now organized the thoughts of even the superliterate, so "yellow" became "ellow," which became "orange" to avoid confusion.

Tabilo just meant "soldier."

How Ga had become the lingua Frafra of a sector of African intelligence forces when only the big regional languages became the operating tongue had to be an interesting story.

Wolof for mathematics, Yoruba for stock-market economics, even old Punic for the military.

The Tabilo Wuɔfɔ used the language of a small tribe of the same name that had managed to insert themselves into the great battles and produce moments and people that made Orange's history-application stamp.

What remained of the Ga still clattered and strolled about, shouting around the seven old towns lining the ocean immediately south of these hills. But they showed almost no sign of their propensity to unexpectedly insert themselves into whichever revolution came next.

There was nobody else quite like the small peoples that had somehow made a mark on centuries of the great histories of one of the eventual founding lands of this Pan-African federation. Just like them and their work, what Orange and the others did would be in a few recognized history books, as would the names of those he had sanctioned.

She watched as he rose.

He did it in one slow but smooth movement, as if he were

giving a lesson on how to stand to the inattentive Representative Akoto. He stood without straining; his face carried no surprise or confusion. Then, like the representative always had, he yawned.

The wait was over. His work could be very dark. They trained them never to let hubris delay a legitimate sanctioning, but when the universe lit the way with irony-fueled running lights, Orange was inclined to follow. And his training had informed his inclinations, so he could trust them even when they went against his training.

He had decided what he was going to do next.

Maybe this was always going to be next.

This was the time.

He checked the weapon, readied what he would use to kill her. Kill her son.

She smelled burning. For a second she thought he had already shot her through the door or a wall. The smell was of angry plastics, some burning element—not the odor she expected from the afterlife.

Then he explained. "That's the wiring of the silent alarm you triggered burning against the surveillance circuitry. Cheap distins. Your outfitters didn't respect Representative Akoto over here, or you, Korshie."

Of course he knew her name.

"In twenty-two to twenty-five seconds, after I finish talking, it will explode. Everywhere else in this dwelling will be mostly safe except that panic room you're in." He spoke with that same analysis-of-the-facts tone he'd used to her "*Why not?*"

That stern look. It was how he looked at her before. Hadn't

he? Was that today? Had he looked at her like that before?

That stern look that every man or woman who cared about her used. Not smiling like those who didn't care. The look meant they expected her to do better. Could she?

Korshie's crying was punctuated by telling her whimpering son to be quiet, and what she figured were either pangs of fear or conscience. She tried her level best to convert these to laughs, because she had gone from hoping that the man in blue and orange would not kill her to hoping that he would save her. All the while he stood out there with his weapon trained on where her head would be if she ran . . .

Again, she couldn't tell if she was saying what she thought she was out loud between tears or with any meaningful part of herself. Whether she was saying what she had or hadn't done was a mystery to her, let alone if she was lying to herself with all her negative confessions. She told him she was telling herself for the first time things she'd wanted to tell Representative Akoto but hadn't.

All she knew, when she knew, how she knew, the men who visited him that rarely looked like what they were.

Orange ran.

Love was the difference.

The council knew it could backfire, but if it did, the thinking was that it would backfire in the right way.

Orange jumped, making his escape out of the building with just a second more or a second less than he needed. He wondered why he had done what he had today. And about what he hadn't.

It didn't matter—not even to him, he told himself—how many of her oaths she'd actually stand by. A Tabilo would be back if they weren't real. Maybe even Orange himself.

* * *

Silence. A silence even more portentous than when that man had sat in that corner not saying anything. Even her son showed a reverence for the moment, making her wonder what else he understood about their life in this house.

She didn't know what to make of it, but tried to enjoy the sense of relief that might have been premature.

The first silence had been dangerous but this one, existing where an explosion and fire were supposed to be, had no danger. It was just a silence.

The shooting was the savior.

Obun! OBUN!

The sound of an old weapon mixed with the sounds of the new.

Kutu! Kutu!

Laser fire seared through all materials each weapon's holder had been authorized to dismantle.

OBUN-KUTU!

OBUNKUTU!

A massive disagreement waged with loud fast metals and vicious contortions of faster light and energy.

Just when she thought the shooting would work its way back here with all the mortal uncertainty it carried, it stopped.

Now, she watched the one they called Bumoclo.

Bumoclo was his name, not one of the new force's titles.

He was the most extravagantly dressed. While the rest wore one- or three-piece uniforms, Bumoclo's protective wear seemed to embody infinite diversity in infinite combinations of justice.

Still, she couldn't tell if this peacock was in charge as he led his one-man parade through the house. He strutted in thigh-high waders tucked into boots. His gloves were pinioned to a belt; two additional belts could be seen strapped around his missile-proof breastplate, which featured a digitally inscribed samai symbol that matched his blue shoulder pads and visor.

While they all worked or waited, they made big police talk.

"Time was, people who lived in overconcreted houses like this used to accumulate their money in caves in Europe. They could've eaten the same amount of food, worn clothes just as nice—clothes just as tailored—with a little bit of organization."

"Or reorientation."

"If they could see it."

"I'm glad they haven't given all these over to nationhood departments. After all, how many ideological centers do we need?"

"Everyone I know has been reeducated enough."

Bumoclo watched the surveillance feed and made notes on his Mepho tablet, using a tidy lexicon and diacritics and symbolism he understood even if those he reported to didn't.

One of the cops saw what Bumoclo was doing and explained, "Its control section was damaged by the fire in the panic room–bathroom there, but we've retrieved *some* footage."

"This fits no home-invasion pattern I'm accustomed to seeing."

"Signs indicate he was in here for a while."

"What exactly was he doing?"

"Just sitting here."

"Mhm, I see." Bumoclo tapped his notes where he had written the same before. "He sits like a soldier."

"He's a soldier?!" Korshie spoke for the first time, not having replied to a question since they arrived.

"You needn't worry. Deputy Amartey there got him outside."

Deputy Amartey, standing with both hands on the waist of his utility skirt, turned away when she looked at him, as if to ask whether she would thank him in these circumstances. Proper deferral to a senior officer, or shyness?

But he had just killed a killer.

"The way he's sitting on his haunches," Bumoclo continued, "conserves energy, limits lactic-acid buildup, so he can spring into action." The sentry's squat, almost definitely.

"Were you a soldier?"

"No, but my father was, in the Alkebulan war. A soldier then police. I didn't want to be one, but now I am. Just like my grandfather and my great-grandfather before him. Just a cop."

"Do you believe that township legend that Igbo scientists are injecting pregnant mothers with something to hardwire all their DNA, to make them want careers that best suit their skills and what the nation needs to build?"

Pause.

"No . . . Neither do I."

And just like that they were back to talking about Representative Akoto.

"So you actually live here?" Bumoclo asked her.

"It's a new Africa indeed."

He reduced the lights on the horizontal aerials coming out of his helmet so she didn't squint at him. "What was he to you?"

"He was . . . my client."

"Oh, I thought so."

"Oh . . . you did?" She tried not to make that seem like a question, but she must have, despite herself.

"Here we are living in this socialist utopia, but you're so

good at your job that one of New Africa's council representatives consults with you at this late hour—it stands to reason your rewards will amount to a house like this."

Was he mocking her? He didn't seem the type.

He would discover the truth later. This untruth was the only one she could manage right now.

Bumoclo frowned and stopped searching the room.

He had picked as his adjutant Officer Amartey, who was not conspicuously stupid. With the killing tonight, Amartey had shown more than the usual propensity for future promotion. But he was supposed to protect him from getting into awkward conversations with witnesses, like the one Bumoclo had just endured.

Now Bumoclo was back on the safe ground of standard violent-incident questioning. He could let his attention shift between seeing if her answers were the same as what she'd told his deputies, and watching the surveillance feed of the killer.

Investigator Bumoclo didn't mind that his metro department was one of the least funded by the Pan-African government. He took pride in it. He would take that underfundedness and still solve more crimes than they could expect. If his grandson had no more murders to solve and had to switch territories or become an archaeological or spiritual investigator, that was all right with him.

Bumoclo observed that the man in the video had arms slightly longer than normal. Not wildly out of proportion, but just enough to be easy to see in person, though more difficult to notice on CCTV, unless you were studying it as closely as Bumoclo was.

Now Amartey spoke up: "Identification on the man in the

video, sir!" Amartey was very much in humble mode as he continued, "You were right. He was a soldier, sir."

"Oh! He's an *orange*," Bumoclo said.

"What? What does that mean?" Korshie asked.

"Sorry?" he said virtually to himself. Everybody else seemed to be projecting their voices to let Korshie know how hard they were working and would be working for the good of their citizens. "He was a veteran of the Alkebulan war."

She sighed with disappointment. "Lots of people are."

"Yes, but *yellow* means he was discharged for cowardice . . . *Or* . . ." he drew out the word for longer than the rest of the sentence, "as is the case *here* . . . officers who went absent without leave . . ."

"But *after* the war?" his sergeant asked, feeling stupid, but that was what the report he was reading said.

Korshie interrupted: "Weren't they supposed to get help?" With the settling of grief, shock, loss, fear, new feelings rose up inside her, like indignation and righteousness. "How was this allowed to happen?"

"They were supposed to. Most did. My father did. And this man must have needed a lot. He would have been very young. Records coming in show he was tracked occasionally as a vagrant, institutionalized all over the continent—but never for long. It's a new Africa with no borders." Bumoclo shook his head. "And to die here, in *that* uniform."

Korshie's voice was soft, cautious but stern: "The man you killed coming out of here was a man in uniform?"

"Yes."

"Light blue with an orange stripe down the middle? A uniform? Are you sure?"

Was that disappointment Bumoclo registered? Relief? He couldn't always be sure. Shock was a strange thing. "Yes." He was taken aback by the question. "Short sleeves, you've seen them all around town selling cheap kinds of iced goods. But I'm sure women of your station get their iced dairy goods from the Ethiopian quarters."

She had stopped trying to outthink him and interpret his tone.

"I expect this is not a job a lot of background checking takes place for."

"An ice cream hawker? An ice cream hawker killed my boyfriend—boss! Client?!" she corrected herself. "He had to be a professional. He was so fast."

"Well, he had been a soldier, like I said." Bumoclo put his glove back on. "AWOL though. I'm afraid it seems the inquest will find Representative Akoto—well, in fact all of you have been victims of some kind of post-traumatic syn . . . syn . . . syn-distin!"

WHEN A MAN LOVES A WOMAN

BY NANA-AMA DANQUAH

Cantonments

Every morning for the past five days, Kwame had woken up next to a corpse. Well, technically, Adwoa had not yet become a corpse. She was still a fully breathing, flesh-and-blood human being; but there was no way, in those first few lucid moments, that Kwame could have known this. So each morning he'd lean over, position his lips right next to Adwoa's ear, and whisper in a voice rough and gravelly, an odd mixture of fear and sleep: "Good morning, my love." And then he'd wait, the fear twisting his intestines into a tight bow of pain.

Each morning she'd return the greeting—meaning, of course, that she was not dead.

"Good morning, sweetheart," she'd mumble, turning to face him, her eyes wide open, the hazel pupils shimmering with life. She'd then softly, softly, place her lips on his, making him remember why he loved this woman with all his heart. And making him regret, at least momentarily, his decision to end her life.

Had this been before "the illness," as they still, for some reason, called his bout with cancer, Kwame would have received her kiss as the invitation it was. He would have pulled Adwoa to him and they would have made the sweetest, most tender love. That had always been their way, their ritual. Before breakfast with the kids, before the obligatory daily discussion about the details of each person's day, then the school drop-offs and the long work commutes, before anything else, there had always been that—their love. It was elemental.

He sincerely believed that those lovemaking mornings had kept them together for twenty-five years. It wasn't simply the sex; it was all that informed it, defined it, drove them to it. Some couples observed date nights or planned regular weekend getaways as a means of checking in, making sure they were still in step. For Adwoa and Kwame, their time together each morning did the trick. It confirmed anew that they were still each other's priority, that even with all the things and people vying for their attention they still chose to greet every single day in each other's arms. And it was in that embrace, their passion spent, that they planned and dreamed, declared their commitment to one another. Their mornings brought to the fore a certain vulnerability, one that spilled over into the rest of their interactions, made them more willing to compromise, to forgive.

Kwame desperately missed that intimacy, especially now that they'd returned to Accra. And yet, whenever Adwoa inched her body closer to his and slid her hand inside his pajama bottoms, he immediately recoiled and pulled it away.

Adwoa suffered from hypertension. Hers was not an extreme case. She was thick, about a dozen kilos over the recommended maximum weight in the "normal" range on the chart posted in their doctor's waiting room in America. Kwame had always dismissed that chart, believing those markers were meant for non-African women, those who were built without fleshy thighs and full, round butts. That theory, however, had come crashing down when he'd seen the same chart in one of Dr. Agyekum's examination rooms.

Even though Kwame thought Adwoa looked fine the way she was and didn't need to lose a single kilo, he did think that she could eat a little healthier; they both could. His weight also fell beyond the "normal" range on the male version of that chart. He had a paunch. It was not exceedingly large, the size of a slightly deflated soccer ball, and perhaps would not have been too noticeable on a taller man, but on his five-foot-eight frame it stood out.

They were both fairly sedentary. Before the illness, when Kwame was still working full-time, he met with clients in the mornings then spent the afternoons writing letters and briefs and motions. As a bank executive, Adwoa also spent most of her days at her desk.

"The uneducated live longer," she often joked, "because honest work is corporeal. We should have become farmers. Each degree we've earned has probably taken ten years off our lives."

Before the children arrived, Kwame and Adwoa hadn't been so formal about meals, not during the workweek. They'd eaten heavy breakfasts—kenkey and fish—and packed their lunches. Dinners were more spontaneous. Sometimes they ate out at restaurants. Other times they prepared a bowl of gari, opened a tin of sardines, then threw some habaneros, a tomato, a sliced onion, and a pinch of salt into the blender and made fresh pepper to complete the meal.

On the weekends they ate like royalty. Like most people they knew in the small Ghanaian community of Washington, DC, they ate food from back home. Every other Sunday, they would take their old white cabriolet, the first car they bought in America, and drive to one of the African groceries in Northern Virginia. There, they would stock up on all the ingredients they needed to make jollof, kontommire, tinapa, apɔnkyenkrakra. Then came the kids—Henry and Ama, their oburoni children—one almost immediately after the other.

Try as Adwoa and Kwame did to stay true to their culinary heritage, by the time the kids started school, their home had successfully been assimilated. It became, quite essentially, American. It was pizza on Friday nights; popcorn and double-scoop ice cream cones on Saturday afternoons; and brunch consisting of scrambled eggs, bacon, and pancakes after church on Sundays.

Whereas the excess weight, lack of exercise, and heaping platters of heavily salted french fries did not appear to have any obvious adverse effects on Kwame's health, with Adwoa they contributed to a constantly elevated blood pressure. Whenever she made an effort—started walking daily and eating healthier—her body rewarded her, and their doctor followed suit by reducing the dosage of her medication.

Adwoa made significant progress after Henry and Ama went off to college. They did away with the requisite family dinners on weeknights. Kwame invested the additional time in his law practice. Adwoa did the opposite: she cut back her hours at work and started taking various classes at the local gym—Zumba, Pilates, kickboxing, yoga. Before long, Kwame could tell the difference in her body during their morning lovemaking. She was stronger, had greater endurance, and, above all, showed more confidence. She moved her limbs with the grace and agility of an athlete. It made him self-conscious. He sometimes wondered what she thought of his body, which was still soft and sagging. Was she repelled? He wanted to ask her but couldn't bring himself to display such weakness in the presence of her newfound strength, so instead he'd turned the question into an accusation.

"Pretty soon," he said as he entered her one morning,

"you'll trade me in for a younger model, some fit macho man you'll meet at the gym."

She arched her back, received him with her entire body. "Never," she moaned. "I will always want you. I will always want this. You are my everything." Done with their morning lovemaking, they lay facing each other. She gently took his hand, laced their fingers together, and whispered, "Till death do us part."

Kwame stared at her, and everything he saw brought him joy—her short-cropped hair, mostly pepper with traces of salt scattered throughout; her wide smile and perfectly straight teeth, the result of years of orthodontics; and that smooth butterscotch skin he so loved to caress. He wondered how he'd gotten so lucky. All of his male friends had girlfriends, women other than their wives, women who supplied whatever was missing in their lives—laughter, excitement, romance, attention, sex. He had Adwoa, only her, always her. He didn't want or need anyone else.

Right then, Kwame had a fleeting image of her at his funeral, inconsolable, wailing to whomever would listen that she prayed the Lord would take her too because she could not live without him. Her grief was palpable. It nearly moved him to tears to imagine she loved him that much. He blinked hard to clear the image, then leaned forward and kissed Adwoa's forehead, which was still moist with sweat, and repeated, "Till death do us part."

"Homicide by suicide" is a term that Kwame coined while reading an article in his doctor's waiting room. He didn't even know what magazine it was in because someone had torn the cover and first few pages off. The article was about the number of deaths that occur every year as a result of people inadvertently taking the incorrect medication. It was some ridiculously impressive number that he had since forgotten, though he'd immediately told himself the real number was probably much larger.

According to the article, pharmacies sometimes mislabel prescriptions, giving John the pills that were meant for Jane. Also, with so many new medications, many of which sound similar, there is the issue of simple human error—a patient is handed a prescription bottle containing a month's supply of zolpidem, a sedative, instead of Zoloft, an antidepressant; or Fosamax, which slows bone loss, instead of Flomax, a prostate medication that makes it easier to urinate. Though the names are similar, the medications usually look nothing alike. Still, as noted in the article, that is not the point; most people do not stop to look at what pill they are taking. They just trust that what is in the bottle is what is supposed to be in the bottle.

For the better part of a year, Kwame had been taking Flomax, yet no matter how hard he tried while reading that article, he couldn't picture the pill. Was it round or oval? Was it white, blue, pink? He didn't like to think of himself as average. He was hardworking and exemplary, and the life he'd led reflected that. He'd chosen an intelligent, beautiful, and loyal wife. Their children were bright, award-winning; they attended Ivy League universities.

And yet, in this instance, Kwame had to admit that he'd been as clueless and careless as the average person. Every day, he'd opened his pill bottle, shook a tablet into his palm, popped it in his mouth, and swallowed. He'd done it all by rote, mindlessly. He could have very easily caused his own death. The thought of it made him shudder. Then it occurred to him that this was the perfect way for someone to cause another person's death. "Murder by suicide," he whispered.

My goodness, he thought, *I have to tell Adwoa*. She'd be just as alarmed by the realization that she had also been absent-mindedly swallowing her medication, then she would laugh at what she called his "lawyer brain."

"Why must you always find criminality in everything?" she always asked. "*Ehbeiii!* If I didn't know you were such an honest man, I would fear you!" Then the two of them would laugh.

But he never told Adwoa about the article. By the time he'd arrived home, there'd been more pressing news to share.

For nearly a year, Kwame had been under the impression—the illusion, really—that he suffered from benign prostatic hyperplasia (BPH), more commonly known as an enlarged prostate. That day at his doctor's appointment, after reading the magazine article, he'd learned that he had prostate cancer. That was the news he'd carried home with him.

There were tears. There was anger, confusion, disbelief. There were more trips to the doctor. More tests, more interpretations of the results. A second opinion, a third, and a fourth. They all agreed: it was cancer; it was aggressive; it had most likely not spread, but the gland needed to be removed immediately.

After the diagnosis, they made love every morning with a fervor that was almost bestial, as though they were two feral animals who'd just found one another. She was often late to work. He'd altogether stopped going into the office. They spent every morning making love as if their lives depended on it. They made love in the evenings too. Adwoa no longer went to the gym. After work, she would come straight home. They'd have dinner delivered, eat the food in bed, then tend to another, more primal hunger. He loved that her body was growing softer, that the angles of her face and shoulders and hips were smoothing and rounding, becoming curves again. He dreaded the day when he would no longer be able to enjoy them like this, when he would not be able to explode the whole of his love and joy and longing for her.

"They're going to turn me into a eunuch," he cried the day before his surgery.

"Don't be so dramatic." She laughed. "The doctor said that after you recover, you'll eventually be able to do everything again."

"Not everything," he sighed.

"Everything except ejaculate." She kissed him on the lips. As though it did not matter. As though it were nothing at all. She did not understand.

Kwame wanted to die at home.

He wanted to take his last breath in Accra, surrounded by the sights and sounds that had ushered him into this world.

He knew he wasn't dying. Not yet, at least. But the illness had brought him face-to-face with his mortality. His body had never before failed him, but he knew that while this failure was the first, it would not be the last. It was the beginning. No matter how long it took between that beginning and the inevitable end, Kwame knew that his body would only continue to fail him.

Their time in America was supposed to have been brief, only until they'd completed their education. But then they'd had children and decided to stay, only until the kids started school. And then it was only until the kids reached high school. Only until he'd built the practice up enough to sell it for a mint. Only until they could start collecting Social Security because, after all, they'd paid into the system. Only until they finished building their perfect retirement villa. Only. Only. Only.

It was time. They'd agreed before the surgery. As soon as his wounds were healed, they would go home.

They'd rented a house in a gated community, just behind the new American embassy in Cantonments. "That mighty building," a taxi driver had called the embassy. And he was right, it was. Kwame resented it. He resented America. He had come to associate it, however irrationally, with the illness, the failure of his body, the disappointing state of his manhood.

They'd been building a house in Prampram, about an hour outside of Accra, right by the ocean. There, they could wake up in each other's arms and listen to the roar of the waves. For five years they'd dutifully sent Kwame's younger brother, Fiifi, regular remittances so that he could oversee the construction. He would send them updates, e-mails with detailed descriptions of what the contractors had accomplished. Sometimes he'd include pictures. They'd hoped that once they were on the ground, actually living in Accra, they could speed up the process and be able to move into the house within a year. When they finally repatriated, what they discovered, instead, was that their retirement villa was nothing more than an empty plot of land. Fiifi had been lying. Believing that they would never actually return, he'd been pocketing the monthly remittances. Not even a single brick had been laid. Fiifi's photos were of a nearby home, one that belonged to white expats. This one detail, the fact that the home Kwame had been envisioning himself and Adwoa in actually belonged to white Americans, somehow made his brother's betrayal hurt all the more.

"It'll be all right," Adwoa assured him. "No use getting angry. The plot is still ours. We can still build the house. I'm sure we'll soon realize that there's a blessing in this somewhere. We're alive, we're back home, and we're together. That's all that matters." His wife was ever the optimist. And because he loved her so much, he allowed himself to believe her.

Even so, he couldn't summon optimism. Thankfully, nothing else caught them by surprise. Kwame hated surprises. Their life back home fell easily into place. They'd been smart about their savings and pragmatic with their plans. They maintained a modest existence, one that easily exposed them as the returnees that they were—no full-time driver, no live-in help. They shared one vehicle. If it was gone, the other made do with a taxi. They shopped for their own groceries and prepared their own meals. Once a week, a young woman, Mawusi—an Ewe name meaning "in God's hands"—came to wash their clothing and clean. It was the beginning of a new life, their new life. He sincerely looked forward to living it. Still, he could only feign optimism; he could not yet feel it.

Weeks passed. Months passed. Kwame's body continued to fail him. His American doctor had told him it would take time. His doctor in Accra had echoed the same words. Neither had been able to tell him how long, to give him a concrete number, something that he could hang his hopes on.

The surgery had, predictably, disrupted their morning routine. In the first few weeks of his recovery, he'd slept in late, drowsy from the pain and the medication he'd been given to relieve it. Adwoa took excellent care of him. She tended to his every need while single-handedly organizing their move. By the time they'd settled comfortably into their home in Cantonments, he was feeling much better. The pain was gone, and he was anxious to move forward. But try as he did every morning when Adwoa greeted him with a kiss, those beautiful eyes expressing a specific yearning, he could not rise to meet her desire.

Every morning they tried and tried, and there were many days when, for a few moments, Kwame reached the level of "almost." Half-cocked. Almost ready. Almost able. Almost the man he'd once been.

"Be patient," his doctor advised. "These things take time."

In all other ways, his life was perfect, even idyllic. Kwame had reconnected with Mr. Johnson, his best friend from childhood. His name was Kojo but everyone called him Mr. Johnson in crèche; whenever an adult had asked him his name, he would respond, "My name is Mr. Johnson."

Growing up, Kwame and Mr. Johnson lived in the same compound. They'd spent their entire lives side by side, from crèche to primary and secondary schools. They'd both married their sweethearts, the first girls to whom they'd pledged their hearts. In many ways, Mr. Johnson felt more like a brother than Fiifi.

While Kwame and Adwoa had attended university in America, Mr. Johnson and Naadu stayed in Accra to complete their studies. They'd later moved to London and had three children, all girls. When their children were young, the couples vacationed together once or twice. The men stayed in touch throughout, but as both of them left the logistics of family vacations and such to their wives, and the women did not share as close a bond, those few instances never turned into a tradition.

Naadu was killed in an accident. At the request of her family, Mr. Johnson brought her body home for the funeral and burial. When it was all done, he saw no reason to return to London. The children were busy creating their own lives, and without Naadu, there was nothing there for him. He figured it would be easier to remain in Accra. He'd been living there for nearly a year when Kwame and Adwoa returned.

Several times a week, Kwame would meet Mr. Johnson at +233, a popular jazz club, to talk over drinks and music. On the way home, Kwame would sometimes stop at the Cantonments roundabout. It was a mile or so from the entrance to their housing complex, and a popular gathering spot for prostitutes. He would pick up one of the women and drive her to a secluded spot on a nearby side street. He didn't consider it cheating. It was, in his mind, a therapeutic exercise. What else would he want with a common whore?

When he was with Adwoa, the weight of his inability to perform, to please her as he had for so many years, was crushing. With the whores, there was no tenderness. There was no expectation, no disappointment. There was only a straightforward transaction. Be that as it may, his body still continued to fail him.

Adwoa started going to the gym again. At least that's what she'd told Kwame.

"I feel like I've let myself go," she'd said. "I want to get my body back."

For whom? he wanted to ask, but didn't. "I love you just the way you are," he said instead.

"Our birthdays are coming soon," she whispered, as though revealing a secret. "I want to be able to slip into something sexy." She grinned and winked. He smiled politely, then turned around and walked away.

They'd been born two weeks apart, he in late October and she in early November. This year, they would both turn fifty-three. He imagined that by their birthdays, he'd be back to normal. He hoped that he could whisk her away on a small trip to someplace romantic like Mauritius or the Seychelles. He wanted to reclaim what the illness had taken away from them. But that was nothing more than a fantasy. Already they were in the last days of September, and he was still unable to make love.

"You know, there are many other ways to make love besides penetration," his doctor reminded him when, during his appointment, he complained for the twenty millionth time about his dysfunction. "I've found with my patients that sometimes their attitude makes a huge difference. Positivity can lead to progress." The doctor's comment made him feel ashamed of himself. Right then and there, he decided to try harder, not to change his situation, but to make the best of it.

After he left the doctor's office, he drove to the gym at the Air Force Officers' Mess. It was on the other side of Cantonments, and it was where Adwoa and, it seemed, every other returnee and expat worked out. If she was done, he thought the two of them might go for lunch at the Buka in Osu. As he drove into the complex, he noticed Adwoa and Mr. Johnson sitting together at a table in the outdoor social area. They were talking and laughing, so deeply engrossed in whatever they were discussing that they did not notice him drive in, turn, and drive back out.

When Adwoa came home that afternoon, he asked about her morning, whether her time at the gym had been productive. He assumed that she would tell him about running into Mr. Johnson and fill him in on whatever they'd been discussing.

"Oh, it was good," she said while stripping off her sweaty gear. "I ran into Ama Dadson. We spent some time catching up. She's started an audiobook company." Ama was an old friend of theirs. She'd attended Wesley Girls' Senior High with Adwoa. "I'm going to have a shower; do you want to join me?" she asked.

"No thank you. I'll probably have one later this afternoon,

before I change to meet Mr. Johnson at +233. Would you like to join us?"

"That would be nice," she said, walking toward the bathroom, "but I'm going to let you boys have your fun. Give Mr. Johnson my regards. I'll be out in a minute so we can have lunch."

That evening while having drinks, he asked Mr. Johnson about his day.

"I was in Tema all morning, some small meetings about a project," he told Kwame. And in that moment, Kwame realized that something was going on between his wife and his best friend.

Adwoa and Mr. Johnson met nearly every day. Kwame had started looking at the call logs on her phone and reading her text messages whenever she was in the shower. He knew the times and locations of their meetings.

I can't tell you how much this means to me, she'd texted him one day.

This is just what the doctor ordered, she texted another time.

Does he suspect anything? Mr. Johnson asked once.

Not a thing. He doesn't have a clue.

He was confused by the casual cruelty of this woman he thought he knew so well. How could she press her lips against his every morning, tell him how much she loved and wanted him, and yet sneak around with his best friend and then laugh behind his back about how he didn't even have a clue?

And Mr. Johnson! Of all the women he could have chosen to replace Naadu, why his wife? Why Adwoa? They'd been friends for nearly a half century. Kwame had shared his most intimate secrets with him. He'd even told him how inadequate he'd been feeling since the surgery, how he'd not been able to make love to Adwoa.

During the times when he knew they were meeting, he wondered what Mr. Johnson was doing to her, how he was touching her. He wondered if she'd ever worn her gold and blue waist beads while she was with Mr. Johnson, if she'd ever pleaded with him, in that near-growling voice, to do things to her.

Sometimes when Kwame pictured them together, he would come closer to achieving an erection than he ever had since the surgery. This only confused him more, made him angrier. It hurt to think of the pair.

The pain was unbearable. Kwame simmered in it all day, every day. He thought it might kill him. He even considered killing himself, but he decided, no, he would not give them the satisfaction of his death. He would kill *them* first.

Since Adwoa and Mr. Johnson believed that he was clueless, he saw no reason to let them think otherwise. He continued the charade that was their relationships, greeting Adwoa every morning as though they were still in love, being buddy-buddy and having drinks several nights a week with Mr. Johnson.

He planned to take care of Adwoa first. He remembered that article he'd read at the doctor's office, before his diagnosis. He now believed that it had been an omen, a sign of things to come.

One night, after some drinks at +233 with Mr. Johnson, he stopped at the Cantonments roundabout to speak with the whore who sometimes serviced him. He asked her to buy him several fentanyl tablets. He needed a powerful opioid. And with the influx of counterfeit pharmaceuticals from China and India, it was pretty much guaranteed that any drug purchased in Accra through unregulated sources was lethal.

The following evening, he stopped by the roundabout

again to pick up the fentanyl. He went home and deposited a single tablet in Adwoa's bottle of hypertension medication.

Every evening that week, as they got ready for bed and Kwame watched his wife take her medication, he believed that the tablet she was swallowing could be the one that would end his suffering. He believed that while they slept, that tablet would make its fatal journey from Adwoa's stomach to her small intestine to her liver, which would immediately empty the chemical compound into her bloodstream, sending it to all her other organs, including her heart—her deceptive, ungrateful little heart.

The anticipation was so stress inducing, Kwame could hardly sleep. That whole week, he was a disheveled, bumbling wreck. He was racked with guilt, fear, satisfaction, anger, sorrow, and, more than anything else, sadness. Each morning she survived, it made him regret his decision to kill her even more. He didn't want to do it. It made him sad to think that his marriage, his perfect union, had come to this. But Adwoa had left him no choice.

The morning of his birthday, she'd not woken up easily. He shook her shoulder several times, greeted her loudly, and nothing. He started to cry. He was crying so hard, he looked like he was convulsing.

"What's wrong, sweetheart?" Adwoa asked. At first he thought he was hallucinating, but then she sat up, reached over, and started wiping the tears from his face.

This made him cry even harder. "I'm sorry," he wept. "I'm so, so sorry."

"You have nothing to be sorry for," she said. "We'll get through this. I love you." She leaned over and kissed him on the lips. "Happy birthday," she sang.

"Kiss me again," he insisted. She did. "And again." His

love for her flushed out every other emotion he'd been feeling. What had gotten into him? She meant everything to him. What kind of life could he have without her? How could he ever face their children again? As soon as he was alone, he'd remove the fentanyl from her bottle of blood-pressure medication.

"I love you," he told her. "I love you more than anything." And as he was telling her this, he felt himself becoming aroused. His doctor was right—what guides the pleasure of lovemaking is the love. There are ways to work around whatever is lacking.

"You might hear some commotion downstairs," Adwoa told him as they were getting out of bed. "I asked Mawusi to come this morning to prepare breakfast for us. I was up late last night organizing your gifts and making sure she has everything she needs."

"You didn't have to do that."

"I wanted to. It has been a difficult year for us. I know you've been having some challenges recovering from the surgery, and we're going to have to make some adjustments. But I am so grateful that you are alive and still with me. I thank God for your life, and I want us to celebrate it."

He felt like a terrible human being, the worst on earth. He was so ashamed of himself and his selfishness. He turned and started walking toward the bathroom so that she couldn't see his tears. "I'm going to have a shower. Will you join me? I'll say my thank-yous in there."

"I'm right behind you," she called out to him. "I couldn't fall asleep last night so I took a sedative. I don't like mixing medications, so I didn't take my blood-pressure tablet. Just taking it now." A pause. "Here I come."

He heard her footsteps. Then she stopped.

"I . . . I don't feel . . ." He heard her fall.

"Adwoa!" He ran into the bedroom and picked his wife up from the floor. He carried her in his arms and hurried down the stairs, screaming for Mawusi. When he got to the bottom, he saw Mr. Johnson, then he saw his parents, who lived all the way in Cape Coast. He saw his doctor and Ama Dadson and various other old friends.

"SURPRISE!!!" they yelled at him, blowing bazookas and throwing confetti in the air.

He stood there looking at them, all the people he loved most in the world, staring at him as he held his wife's limp body and listened to her breathing turn shallower and shallower.

PART IV

Sea Never Dry

KWEKU'S HOUSE

BY AYESHA HARRUNA ATTAH

Tesano

It sits on the corner of Eleventh Avenue and Golden Souvenir Lottery Road, a big, dark house with a colonnaded balcony that wraps around the second story. In it is a man who has lost his mind and is now dying, and a woman who thinks the whole thing is going too slowly.

The air of the room in the eastern wing of the house is redolent of disinfectant and urine. There should be books or a vase of flowers on their nightstand, but instead it is topped with a cityscape of medicine bottles. Larabah is unhappy for many reasons, but right now it is because she didn't sign up to live in a hospital at thirty-five. She knows she could move into another room, in the western wing or downstairs, but this one has the best light and doesn't smell like his children, one of whom, almost fifty, still lives downstairs. She fiddles with the cannula of Kweku's drip, hanging coolly on its stand, as if it isn't keeping a man alive. They say you shouldn't let air into the veins. What would happen if she did? Would he die instantly, or would it be a slow, drawn-out expiration? When the bell rings, she is relieved. She wants Kweku to go, but this way doesn't feel right. She doesn't want him to suffer.

Naana is downstairs, present, yet it's become an unspoken rule that it's Larabah who does the housekeeping, cooks the meals, and opens the gate. Glorified housekeeper. It's another grievance against Kweku. But at this point, is it his fault? She descends carpeted stairs, once a deep burgundy, now a drab brown.

The wet heat of outside cloaks her skin, and as she draws the whiny gate open, Grace—or is it Faith?—squeaks in. The only decision she and Kweku's children reached without a single argument was that he'd be taken care of by this rotating pair of nurses. Both nurses are wisps of women, so small that they require Larabah's help to transfer him from bed to wheelchair. His body—which has never been high on the list of why she married him (funny, kind, big house)—is hard to look at. She chokes down the word *repulsive*.

She shifts her gaze from the large urine pouch, bursting to orange fullness, to the tube swallowing his manhood. "I struggled to get him to drink yesterday," she tells the nurse while stuffing her bathing suit into her tote. Imagine living in a house with a pool and paying money to swim elsewhere.

"Ah, yes, his urine is too dark." The nurse pulls her uniform out of her bag. "Okay, Auntie, I'll tell Doc. We might need to put another drip on."

She shouldn't be called *Auntie* at this age. But then, Grace or Faith is in her twenties, and Larabah is married to a seventy-eight-year-old. She supposes she had it coming. She's glad for Grace and Faith. Although they have no weight, physical or otherwise. They once suggested that Kweku be moved downstairs to Naana's room. Naana said no, and that was the end of that.

Both Naana and Larabah spend their days inside the house. Now, Larabah finds that she has to leave to get her work done. What Naana does with her days, Larabah couldn't say. Managing Kweku's pension cannot be called a job.

Larabah slides on her sunglasses and walks out of the house, down a path that should be separating lush green grass but instead splits a patch of laterite. The wall of the house, in outlined brick, is too short. Everyone can see into the garden. Thankfully, the palm trees cover the second floor. Three years ago, when she moved in, Kweku's mind and body were still working, yet he never listened to her suggestions to let in more light; to paint the walls bright white, instead of the pastel peach and blue that dim what the house could be. It wasn't a stubborn refusal. It was comfort with the way things were. He'd lived there for so long, he'd grown used to its imperfections. She saw the cracks, the bad plumbing, the decay. He saw home.

A house with a pool, the bottom of which is split by a large crack, making her think of continents shifting. When she moved in, it was full of water and mosquito larvae. Now, grass is sprouting from between the continents.

Then again, she didn't always listen to him either. She should have continued her driving lessons as Kweku had insisted, but one accident was all it took, falling into the gutter right outside the house. She should have had more sangfroid, but she didn't like looking foolish. "You give up too easily," Kweku had told her. If she'd listened to him, she would now enjoy more range in her roaming; she could leave the neighborhood to think. Taxi drivers annoy her, and a missus like her isn't supposed to be seen in trotros. So walking is all she is left with. As she leans over to latch the gate closed, she hears her name.

"How's Bra Kweku?" asks Maa Rose, always planted outside her liquor store–chop bar, across from Kweku's house.

"Hmmm," Larabah says, hoping that the accompanying shrug makes it clear she's suffering.

"It will be well," says Maa Rose, as Larabah hurries around the bend where taxis double-park, where a woman sits with a pyramid of hard-boiled eggs. *What does she do with the eggs she doesn't sell?* Larabah asks herself, as she does every single day.

Larabah heads toward the Total petrol station, considering whether to turn left or right to get to the club. Right will take her by Karldorf, but it's the route for when she wants to be seen and complimented. Straight ahead is for introspection and plotting. She marches ahead, by Ayrton Drugs, wondering if there isn't a venin being manufactured right now that she could slip into Kweku's drip. Probably best if things can't be traced easily. She continues on past the house where she and Kweku attended a party where the hosts had filled a bathtub with ice and in it bobbed bottles of Club beer and soft drinks. "Classy," Kweku had quipped. When his brain worked, he really was a good time. When she first married him, the whispers on people's lips were that she did it for his money. *But what money?* she wants to ask them now. It was simply that he made her happy. And now she's unhappy.

The tarmac becomes red dust. She makes her way past three adjacent churches and stares at her feet. While she is mostly irreligious these days, these faith matters have a way of letting guilt seep into the brain and heart.

At the Tesano Sports Club, she shows her membership card to the receptionist, a dull man who takes his time entering her details into his ledger. In the changing room, she pulls her braids through a band and wraps them into a chignon, catching her reflection in a mirror. This could be a chance for her to start over again, for that sweet, heady, mad rush of romance. This time, preferably with a body that can match hers. Her body is lean, and on good days she looks about twenty. She slips on the bathing suit.

Her limbs cut through the water and she moves forward, pushing through her breaststrokes. She hangs to the side of the pool, watches the swimming instructor rope a Styrofoam cylinder onto a pool divider. The man has taught everyone in Accra how to swim. Could she start over with someone like him—all brawn? Virile, some might say. But he probably doesn't know how to save money. He should have his own swimming club by now. Probably has women taking care of him. Money that comes that way never sticks. He locks eyes with her.

"Sister Larabah! How's Bra Kweku? It's been too long."

"Not well oh. He fell down and broke his hip."

"No wonder. We'll pray for him."

She's turning into a raisin. She doesn't feel like working. Her deadline isn't till next week. Copy for a new Moringa-based elixir.

She goes down the road where she walks to be seen, makes a left, then a right toward Awo's Boutique. Expensive. She used to be able to buy clothes from places like this. Another reason for her resentment: she had more money before marrying Kweku. All her money has gone into keeping his house from crumbling. Now she's tired of playing nurse and tired of his suffering. And yet, is she allowed to play God? She makes a U-turn and enters Awo's Boutique. At the very least, she should be prepared for the funeral. A voice sneaks into her head, her mother's: *Larabah, that's not how we do things.* But better to be prepared.

The smell of a fruity floral spritz wraps around her. Strong smells give her headaches. Hell for her would not be brimstone. Hospital smell or cloying flowers, more likely.

"Good afternoon, Auntie," says the salesgirl, her skin sloughed of color. "How can I help you today?"

"I need a fascinator," Larabah says. "In black."

"We have a range, Auntie. People really like these." She

displays a festive thing with bows and frills. Rather silly. "Or this hat?"

"It's not the beach I'm going to," says Larabah. "That one, please bring it."

"People call it a hatinator now."

It has enough hat to cover her head and enough drama with its lace detail and enough class with its one chic bow. It's perfect. As she's paying, her phone rings. Kweku's lawyer. What day is it? Wednesday. *Shoot*. She forgot about the family meeting, so caught up in herself and her resentments. She can't fold up the hat and can't let Kweku's children see it. She should have friends in the neighborhood after three years of living there, but trusts no one.

"Please hold on to the hat for me, I'll come back and get it this evening."

She leaves the boutique, passing by the police barracks with its cream concrete banisters, utilitarian facades, and balconies strewn with laundry—all unchanged since the British occupation of the Gold Coast. In front of Sranak Supermarket, a man struggles to reverse and has caused a bottleneck. She weaves between the traffic and comes out close to Alive Chapel International, a church that has left no room for trees or a garden in its compound. Churches these days are just about the numbers. She rounds the most dangerous curve in the world and comes to their street.

Kweku's house is visible from halfway down the street. How long does it take for one to adapt to a place? Three years and she still thinks of it as Kweku's house, not hers. Kweku built it in the seventies, and Larabah imagines it was the dream house for all the children in Tesano at the time. An upstairs and downstairs, a large arboreal garden, a swimming pool.

She waits for a string of trotros to pass by before crossing.

Downstairs, Kwaw and Naana are seated on the velveteen chairs, across from Adjei, who looks like he would rather be drinking a beer.

"Welcome, Larabah," he says, his fingers raking the kinks on his head. "Esi has a meeting, so Naana will update her. Kwaw called me because his condition doesn't seem to be improving, and we have to discuss the possibility of your husband and your father passing on."

"Isn't this premature?" says Naana.

"Naana, let him talk," interjects Kwaw.

Larabah decides she'll just listen.

"Your father already has a will, so you don't have to worry on that front," says Adjei. "But you will need to start thinking of how you want to bury him."

They need to consider which family members they would like to have present, what kind of funeral, all depending on the contents of their father's will. They drone on. Once he's nice and buried, she wants out of the house. His children can squabble all they want over it. She just wants a new life. Where she goes next will arrange itself. Life always sorts itself out, she's found.

"I still say all this is too early," says Naana. "He could also live for a long time, his doctors tell me."

That makes Larabah sit up. *Live long to suffer? Not if I can help it.*

"True," says Adjei. "But it's always good to be prepared."

"Naana, please tell Esi what we talked about," Kwaw says, punching at his cell phone. "I have to head back to Osu now. Adjei, thank you."

What was the point in calling her over?

Larabah goes up to her room, where Faith/Gloria is watching her cell phone with headphones attached.

"Grace?"

"Faith." She pulls the white buds out of her ears.

"Sorry, Faith. How is he?"

"He ate the rice water Auntie Naana made. And he's drinking more now. We'll do everything we can to heal him, in Jesus's name."

Larabah sits on her bed and stares at Kweku. She's surprised Naana made him rice. And all that talk about her father living longer. She's never cared. The truth is, only a few days are good, like this one. But most days, he's a shell of a human being. Doesn't drink, doesn't talk, all pain.

He's staring straight ahead, not saying anything, until Faith lifts his arm and dabs the bedsore on his elbow. Kweku hurls out a scream that forces Larabah's eyes shut. Why is everyone trying to keep a suffering man alive?

"What painkiller did Doc recommend?"

"Paracetamol, Auntie."

Larabah slides the door of their wardrobe open, another contraption that she's sure made anyone who first saw it ooh and aah. A thing from the seventies, now a dust magnet, prone to getting caught in its hinges. It gets jammed and she forces it and the whole door falls out. She places it against the rest of the wardrobe and pulls out a T-shirt, tracksuit, and cap. She changes, steps into sneakers, slips on her shades.

"I'll be back," she says to Faith.

Nosy Maa Rose has a few more clients now, including one who was there in the morning, head bowed on the plastic table, obviously passed out. She's too busy catering to them to waylay Larabah. Making a left, Larabah walks by the woman who has made her corner so black with charcoal that she has nicknamed her Tar Baby. Larabah breaks into a run and turns left, right, then onto the untarred road toward the end of the neighborhood. Assurance Hotel sits in its hidden cove, a place she's never entered because the huge Indian almond tree in its courtyard suggests more seed than assurance. She doesn't stop running until she comes to the border of Tesano and North Kaneshie. A physical border that looks like a gutter but becomes a raging river as soon as the rains start. There, she stands at the concrete edge of the river, next to the footbridge, and watches. A dog with a patchy coat crosses the bridge, digs in the grass, extracts a long bovine-looking bone, and starts gnawing it. More people cross the bridge. A man on a bicycle. A woman and her son. Farther down, she sees Ato and waves him over. His uniform is a T-shirt, camouflage shorts, and a fanny pack. His mask is a constant smile; a scar stretches from his eye down to his jaw. They lean on an unpainted wall.

"Ohemaa, long time no see. Same as last time?"

"No, tramadol."

"Ei, sistren, that one is no joke oh."

"He's in too much pain and the doctors don't care. They want us to check him into the hospital so they can make money off us. His children just want his money."

"Don't play with this one. It's so strong, if you're not careful he'll die."

And he'll be in a better place, she almost says.

"Life is some way. Everyone in the area knows Bra Kweku. You could go to him with all your wahala and he wouldn't turn you away. The day I waved at him and he didn't notice me, it really pained me. I didn't know he was sick then. Bra Kweku paaa. Such a nice man. He knew everyone's names. If you hadn't told me about the dementia, I'd have said something had happened to him. But the Mary J, did it help?"

"He fell before I could give it to him. I still have it. So the tramadol . . . ?"

"I have to order it. Come back tomorrow. Or should I bring it to you?"

"I'll come."

There's a beat, where neither of them says anything and the *whoosh* of water rushing in the gutter fills the silence. There's complicity in the silence. Whatever happens, he's in on it. He won't get her into trouble.

"Ohemaa, whatever you decide, I know you're doing it for him. Walahi, you made the man young again. The two of you on your evening jogs . . . oh, it was so nice to see. You know something?"

"What?"

"I mean it, you're doing it for him. I have two kinds of customers. The people who buy Mary J for themselves, they are serious addicts. Then the people who buy Mary J for other people. Now, *they* are interesting. They do it because they care about the person. Come early tomorrow."

He can't see her eyes, and she's thankful. Who would have thought the neighborhood drug dealer would get philosophical and make her cry?

She was hoping she could slip Kweku the tablets in the space between Faith and Grace's shifts, but she'll have to be patient. She goes back to pick up her hat.

The next day, she meets Ato, who slides her a box of tramadol in a brown envelope. When the nurses take breaks, on days when he's compliant enough to swallow, Larabah gives the pills to Kweku, two at a time. She hopes that slowly his breathing will still, that when he goes it will be peaceful, his cells slowly extinguishing, grinding his organs down to a halt, turning off the lights, giving him the peace he so clearly needs.

Little does she know that two weeks later, when his heart

ticks its last beat and his will is read, she'll be the proud owner of the house on Eleventh Avenue and Golden Souvenir Lottery Road.

THE BOY WHO WASN'T THERE

BY EIBHLÍN NÍ CHLÉIRIGH

East Legon

East Legon, 5:00 p.m.

The sun begins to wane around now. Its light, already weakened by the harmattan, thins.

The world under the pylons takes on a vaguely apocalyptic aspect. Normally overgrown with weeds, plantain palms, or tall maize plants cultivated by opportunistic farmers, this narrow belt provides the only common space in the neighborhood. A space dominated by the wires and metal that bring electricity to the Accra metropolis, dotted between which are kiosks and flimsy lean-tos raised on blocks to protect against sudden rain or unwelcome creatures. No one is supposed to live under the pylons, but in a city where officials see prohibitions as income-generating opportunities, many do.

The young men and older boys are arriving on the sloped football pitch; jogging, stretching, kicking imaginary footballs while they wait for the coach. Their activity accentuates the smell and taste of harmattan: a salty dust with the faint chalky whiff of crisp, cooler evenings. The younger boys are playing on the smaller adjoining strip of ground. In their patchwork football uniforms, they play with an overeagerness and one eye on the larger, lower field, hoping to be noticed. Bare feet skillfully steer the football toward a makeshift goal or skid across the dust to block an opponent.

Today, this normally verdant scene has had its vibrancy

muted by the dryness and dust. Homesteads have lost any semblance of privacy as plants lining the pathways retreat, exposing their most intimate functions and the scale of plastic detritus. Even the pylons are shabbier than normal: skeletal giants marching across the only greenery. In the unfinished buildings beside the lorry park, windows gape at passersby, dark cavities in concrete gray broken by sudden flashes of color as the evening breeze catches the garments drying on makeshift lines.

The football pitches, however lopsided, form the center of the community where neighbors gather to chat, exchange jokes and stories, and organize their youth—young men and women in whom so many hopes are stored, with their swaggering self-consciousness and focus on the future. Hopes of the community seniors have been wiped out over the years by poverty and the casual corruption of Accra's authorities. These are the people forgotten and unseen; briefly unearthed every four years, to be courted by the politicians. The young people of the area attend all the rallies enthusiastically for the T-shirts, excitement, and momentary whiff of promise.

Across the dirt road from the pitch, Rashida's father is guiding his sheep between patches of greenery. They and the goats help keep the grass in check. He is the oldest resident of the community and lives with his wife and children, livestock, and extended family—siblings, cousins, in-laws—in one of the partially constructed buildings that line the road.

This area was so different when he first migrated to the capital from the north. The village where he had stopped and decided to settle was just outside the city boundaries at that time, and his livestock grazed in the empty fields around it. Over the past ten or so years he watched Accra burst its boundaries and sprawl in all directions as families expanded and migrants like himself arrived, in search of fertile pastures and, perhaps, paid employment. Bush was cleared and grasslands replaced as the slow, inexorable combination of sand, blocks, and cement became new estates. His adopted village was gradually subsumed by East Legon, which is now a well-established neighborhood. Indeed, it is touted as one of the up-and-coming areas of the city. Much of its new prosperity is driven by wealthy young Nigerians choosing to invest in, or commute back home from, Accra rather than exist behind fenced walls in the chaos of Lagos.

East Legon is an area of stark contrasts; ostentatious estates exist alongside incomplete buildings and rows of flimsy wooden structures that provide shelter for the urban poor—shelter that is charged for, yet still under constant threat of destruction. With a clockwork inevitability, the city fathers point to slum dwellers in times of flood, drought, and insecurity as the source of the area's problems, and their kiosks are either leveled by the bulldozers of the metropolitan authorities or dismantled by the families themselves to be transported elsewhere once word of the impending demolition filters through.

Rashida's father still has grazing land around the football pitches and untarred roads. He has had complaints from the big houses; they don't like the smell of his goats, his noisy cockerels, or his cattle taking up the road. For now he's all right; houses take time to be completed in a place where neither credit nor cash is readily available. Under the pylons in East Legon, as in so many of Accra's neighborhoods, the first and third worlds exist side by side.

He is fond of accusing neighbors' dogs of eating his chickens, though everyone guesses the missing fowl to be already cooking in Rashida's mother's pot. Most people understand the pressures of a large family and smile at the transgression. For it is a community.

To the left of his dwelling is a line of wooden kiosks that house a number of families, mostly from Togo and Volta to the east of Accra. This is a diverse community where French mingles easily with Hausa, Ewe, Twi, and pidgin, where the predawn high-pitched call to prayer is followed closely by the guttural chants of the roadside evangelical preacher, amplified by his portable microphone and speakers.

As the sun begins to dissolve into the horizon, its subdued, dusty light allows the mosquitoes to emerge from their daytime shade. Children, already returned from school, are out and about until nightfall in an hour and a half. The electricity has been off all day, as it is so often. During "lights off," the neighborhood children are expected to be back safely inside their homes before darkness.

Three of the older girls are fetching water, willowy bodies stretched tall as their arms reach to steady the full metal buckets balanced on their heads. They wear cloth full of bold geometric shapes; contrasting blues, purples, and golds; and fluted tie-dyed patterns wrapped around their waists to protect their uniforms from the dust and the inevitable cascade that happens despite their best efforts to walk steadily on the uneven terra-cotta ground.

The younger children, including Rashida's two brothers, are shrieking in delight as a shredded tire they are pushing, given to them by one of the roadside mechanics, takes off down the slope. Older women, hands on hips, heads leaning toward each other, chat on the corners while keeping an eye on the new generation. A number are in traditional outfits of long skirts with matching fitted tops or boubou of contrasting organic patterns; some flamboyant in vivid oranges, blues, and purples, others using the monochrome palette of a recent celebration or death, the remainder in their westernized workday attire.

Rashida is lying on the grass with her face cupped in her hands, striking an angry pose. Small for her age, she has an open round face with a firm jaw and intelligent eyes, now lit with indignation. Her thick eyebrows furrowed, she is glaring at the boys who refuse to allow her to play football with them though they know she is better than they are. Worse: she has nobody to appeal to. Rashida knows her father, so close by, would be of no help.

She is the oldest child in her family, and learned early on to look after herself and her siblings, who arrived in quick succession. Education is her solace and she excels even in the overcrowded state primary school she attends. Most evenings she joins her friends to play around the green spaces, trees, and roads. Her wiry frame can often be seen darting around the common, racing up and down the dirt paths in those carefree moments between school and darkness.

Rashida has thick raven hair, and today her mother braided it into cornrows with colored plastic beads at the end of each plait. It is Rashida's favorite hairstyle. She loves the rhythmic beat of her braids swinging from side to side, matching her stride.

Unfair, unfair! she thinks as she jumps up suddenly and stomps off toward the thicket on the far side of the football pitch. Despite the trees, this is not a pretty place. Toward the front is an ad hoc dump where most of the community waste is thrown. Farther back is where most residents defecate, despite the best efforts of the plumber (and part-time pastor) who led the construction of a pit latrine close by. He often tries to improve conditions around the community. But this project wasn't helped by its proximity to the Happy Your Self drinking spot, where the rowdier community members spend large parts of each day and, when needs arise, stumble into the bush under the trees to see to nature's call. On warm humid days, the acrid stench of ammonia and decay intensifies as the sun climbs in the sky. The dry cooler air of harmattan tempers the odor, and Rashida knows a spot right at the back where she can sit, undisturbed, in relative comfort, and stew.

The new shoes are the first thing she notices. They are white with three blue stripes on each side. The soles, almost completely unscuffed, are facing her.

Rashida bends down, looking hard at the lean, angular body of a boy lying in the shadow of the trees.

There is something very wrong.

The boy is in his school uniform—the same one worn in all state schools with a golden-yellow shirt and brown shorts—which, though badly ripped and stained, is brand new. Rashida stands up and looks at the boy's body, afraid to touch him. He is facedown and unmoving. The shock of fear, that instant realization of catastrophe, banishes all thoughts of football, all anger. Covering her mouth and turning abruptly, she runs toward her father.

The pounding of her own heartbeat in her ears is deafening.

She knows she should be silent.

"Dada," she whispers, her voice breaking. "Dada!" emphatically. "Something terrible is in there." She points toward the trees with only a slight tremor in her hand.

He asks her what it is but she says nothing. He sees from Rashida's clenched fists, her unblinking eyes, and a small tic in her lower jaw that she is terrified. He decides not to press her. If his oldest child is afraid then this must be serious. "We'll get the pastor and investigate."

Though from very different cultural and religious roots, the pastor is a serious man whom Rashida's father consults on many community-related concerns.

Rashida and her father walk quickly now toward his home.

"Al Hajji, how now?" The greeting of their immediate neighbor who, as usual, is sitting outside his door in sparkling white underpants, is ignored in their focused haste.

The pastor is a short, stocky man with a body that is used to toil. He is wearing his threadbare singlet when they arrive, working with his son. The two of them are placing new concrete blocks at each corner of a wooden kiosk to stabilize it. He looks up at the sound of approaching steps and greets Rashida's father with a half wave, half salute.

"My brother," says Rashida's father, ignoring formalities, "I beg you, come see something."

The herder's urgency, and the lack of his usual smile, gives the pastor pause. He pulls on his *All Praise Jehovah Ministries* T-shirt and follows them, unquestioning.

Rashida is holding her father's hand tightly as she leads them quickly through the cluster of trees toward the body. When they reach the spot, she says nothing but stands looking down with her hand clasped tightly over her mouth.

The herder and the pastor crouch low to examine the boy. In the dappled light they can just make out the bruises around his neck, torn nails on his fingers, and the blood all over his shorts. He has old tribal scars on his face. Rashida's father recognizes the marks—the boy is from one of the northern tribes. He swallows hard and looks at the pastor. Both men are nervous and sad and confused. How could such a young boy have been damaged so badly then discarded in this stinking, filthy place like a bucket of night soil?

Trouble has come.

* * *

Wiamoase, Ashanti Region

In fact, the boy was older than he looked, and he hadn't always been alone, far from it. He had been loved once.

His mother's prince, her hero, her beautiful boy.

He grew up in a small town just outside of Kumasi, Ghana's second city, in the Zongo area where mostly Muslim, Hausa-speaking people from the northern parts of Ghana had settled over the centuries.

He had run around lush fields and forests overflowing with the white noise of chirping insects, the creaking of growing branches, and the distant rustling of the canopy leaves. Wet with humidity, he and his cousins wove through creepers and ferns taller than he was. And the trees, they were taller than anything in the world.

They swam in whirling brooks, diving in quick succession from smooth mossy rocks beside a pool or splashing each other near the grassy banks. He was scrubbed clean from head to foot twice a day by his mother, whose face he knew better than anything; every line that appeared when she smiled at him and the way her eyes closed when she laughed. On some evenings, if his father was home from cattle drives and not too tired, the boy would ask to hear tales of his travels or fables passed down from his grandfather.

Most of all, the boy wanted to go to school like his big cousins who lived in the same compound. His father's parents, siblings, and all their children called the same walled enclosure home. He wondered at their books, their pens, their lined paper on which they worked with such concentration. Every evening he waited outside on the dusty road to see his cousins coming home from school, so grown, so clever.

His mother assured him that he would go to school the

following year when he was seven and that he would certainly be the cleverest boy in the whole school and that he would go to the big university in Kumasi when he finished secondary school and would be the first person ever in their family to be a doctor. "Imagine that! My son the doctor," she'd say, kissing him. He'd run away from her, half laughing, half shrieking at her kiss. He loved hearing her say that. He loved her. Within the protective bounds of his mother's affection he felt indestructible, like he could achieve anything.

Months later, just before his seventh birthday, his grandmother, his mother's mother, came to stay. She had traveled from Ghana's northern savanna, a land of brush and grass close to the border with Burkina Faso, where his father's people had come from many years ago. He had never met her before. She moved slowly toward him when he came into the room to greet her, and bent her curved back to gently touch the side of his face. He looked up at her and smiled, recognizing the warmth and pride in her eyes as she gazed into his. Her lips felt dry when she kissed his forehead. "Grandma is here to help me," his mother explained, placing her hand on her swollen abdomen, "until your little brother arrives." But her smile was fleeting and uncertain; she turned her head toward her mother and back to him, all the while twisting the corner of the patterned wrap, which covered her pregnancy, around her fingers. The ghost of a premonition took form in his head—was his mother sick? If anything happened to her . . . He shook his head to expel the thoughts, unable to even contemplate the possibilities.

As the days and weeks passed, his mother did less and less around the house and began to spend most of her time in bed. Her appearance changed, becoming both thin and bloated. Her ankles were swollen, her face was permanently drawn, and her once silky ebony skin was dry and turning gray.

The boy winced as his grandmother bathed him with much harsher scrubbing than he was used to. He didn't understand why a new brother was wanted at all, and certainly not why he was causing such disruption and distress to his mother. He wished the unborn boy away.

One morning he awoke to hear activity in his mother's room. She and his grandmother had each packed a bag. His father, who had returned home unexpectedly, looked at the boy's confused, troubled face and explained that his mother was going to a hospital in the next town and would come back soon with the new baby. All would be well. As the two women left the house, his grandmother carried both bags. They turned toward the main road and the boy followed, not wanting to let his mother go. They had rarely been apart.

At the corner of the road his mother bent down and kissed his forehead. "Go back to Dada now, I'll be home before you know it." She took off her necklace, removed a silver bead from it, and placed it in his hand. She told him to keep it in his pocket and shine it on his shorts whenever he missed her. She tucked the necklace into the pocket of her housedress, held his face in her hands, and used her thumbs to wipe away his tears.

It was the last time he ever saw his grandmother.

And he never saw his mother again.

East Legon, 5:30 p.m.

The roads crisscrossing the greenway under the pylons are busier now as workers from town, in their starched and pressed office clothes, trickle back home. Heads down, they tread the pockmarked paths, carefully avoiding dust and the motorbike riders who use this route as a shortcut. In the opposite direction, mothers take their children from friends' after-school care and start the long journey home.

The football training session is in full swing now. A and B teams are playing a practice match to an appreciative crowd's delight. The coach is shouting instructions at players while the sideline experts add their own commentary to laughter and exclamation.

Away from the park, birds in the area are striking up the evening chorus of shrill chirps and hooting bass tones. Swallows dart in and out of trees and empty buildings in apparent joy at having escaped the European cold. High up in the pylons, kites' shrieks give warning to small creatures—the field mice, rats, and occasional squirrel that forage in the long grass.

Rashida's father and the pastor are walking back toward the trees, having called in the help of Rashida's uncle and the pastor's oldest son. None of their neighbors have an inkling of the violence that has occurred in the tree grove. An argument between residents or a discovery of theft becomes the talk of the community within seconds; a crowd will gather to watch, comment, and occasionally join in. Even natural deaths give rise to stories of dark practices and months of gossip in the community. The discovery of the boy would create too much noise. The men have told no one.

"We should really call the police," whispers Rashida's uncle, a slight, copper-skinned man, not unlike his brother but at least a decade younger.

"Quiet," says the pastor. "Let's go to the trees to discuss this before we decide what to do. There are too many idle ears around." At the last point he glances toward the drinking spot.

With Rashida still beside them, they are all looking down at the boy's corpse. The men have turned his slight body so he is facing the sky and the fading sun; his cheeks are bloodless and ashen. Kneeling down, Rashida's uncle gently closes the boy's eyes. Rashida still can't quite grasp what she is seeing. This small boy who is about her own age, lying there lifeless. She can sense the disquiet and distress of the adults around her, with their muted speech and agitated postures, shuffling from one foot to another, which multiplies her own fear.

Slowly her uncle looks up at the group. "Please, we must call the police. If we are the ones telling them of this then they can't blame us," he reasons with his older brother. "If we don't tell them, then the person who did this . . ." He can't quite bring himself to name it. "THIS!"—he points toward the boy—"will go unpunished. The police will investigate the murder and children will be safer—all our children will be safer."

"The police are no friends of ours," says Rashida's father. As a northern herder, he is harassed almost daily by constables looking for lunch money. "If they come here to investigate, they will cause trouble for everyone. Think! My brother, once the police come, the city people can come knock our houses, ECG can take away our lights . . . they can even take our animals."

Leaving Wiamoase

Four years after his mother died, the boy was taken to Accra to live with his father's cousin.

Nothing had been the same at home.

The boy had tried asking why his mother never returned. He even asked about the baby brother who was supposed to be coming back with her. But no one, not his father nor his aunties nor cousins, would explain. When he heard them speak about her, it was in riddles that he was too young to decipher. It was as he grew older and witnessed aunties and cousins during pregnancy, emerging from it with tiny bundles of new life wrapped carefully to their back or held tenderly to their breast, that he knew with certainty that his mother and baby brother had died. That knowledge made him sad, and sometimes he would sit outside the compound alone, looking at the corner where he had parted with his mother. Almost instinctively, he took the silver bead from his pocket and rubbed it on his shorts.

His father started staying away for longer periods. The boy was looked after by a young female relative whose attention and patience were limited; she hardly spoke to him beyond issuing instructions, and would beat him if he was slow to move or asked questions. His clothes became ragged and he was often hungry in the evenings. School became a distant dream.

One afternoon the boy was surprised when his father came home with a new wife and a few of her family members. It was a splendid group that entered the compound, the women wearing abaya wrappers with matching V-neck tops, bright grasshopper green, with gold-lace embroidery all over. On their heads were elaborate coverings of shimmering golden material wrapped around and around. His cousins and aunties danced and ululated in celebration, but the boy was silent. He was confused and upset.

As the day wore on, he was called into the house to be formally introduced to his father's new wife. He stood in front of this unfamiliar woman, clenching and unclenching his fists as he stared directly at her face. In his confusion he failed to show her respect or affection, and remained resolutely silent when she asked him questions. He kept glancing around for clues as to what he should do. Looking back at her made-up face, the boy saw her lips purse as offense bloomed into a thorny grimace that never left.

In time he understood that she saw him not only as a surly inconvenience but as a bringer of bad luck. In the mornings his muttered greetings to her were acknowledged with a nod if at all. On more than one occasion he heard his new mother's laughter in another room as she talked gaily to other members of his family. It would stop abruptly on his entrance, whereupon she would scowl slightly while moving toward the door, making some excuse to leave his presence. Once she was with child, she avoided the boy entirely. She even persuaded his father to send him far away, to Accra.

The boy often wondered if it was true that he brought bad luck. He had, after all, wished his unborn brother away. Had he also somehow caused his own mother's death?

Accra was a shock, huge and bustling with people and languages he had never heard before. It felt unknowable. There were no trees; the city was a mass of concrete and steel. And it stank. The filth poured out of the gutters and into the Odaw River, which flowed almost invisibly, beneath a carpet of plastic bags and human waste, into the sea at Korle Lagoon. Cars roared past with drivers shouting out the windows at people in their way, smoke-belching taxis beeped constantly at potential fares and people delaying things at traffic lights, while motorbikes mounted the paths to avoid the gridlock, but not always the pedestrians.

Lost and distraught, the boy drew into himself. His father's cousin was a pinched, mean man who appeared to do little. As far as the boy could see, he just sat on the road outside the house with other men playing checkers all day. His wife, who worked long hours selling vegetables at the main market, treated the boy as an unwanted burden she could ill afford. She offered little in the way of conversation or comfort, and even less in the way of food.

They lived in one room and a hall; part of an overcrowded, unfinished compound house close to Abossey Okai. It was where scrap-metal dealers hawked used car parts and rusting shipping containers of electric rubbish that had been discarded on the open landfill site beside the Odaw River. The bathroom, shared by all who lived in the compound, was disgusting, so most tenants relieved themselves in the large gutter that ran along the back wall.

As the days and weeks went by, the boy began to get used to his new living arrangements. His cousins included him in their games and plans, and he even got an occasional smile from his new aunt when he helped with her market wares. Encouraged by a smile one day, he decided to ask her about school.

"Please, Auntie," he began, and waited for her to look away from her basket. "Please," he said again when he caught her eye. "Auntie, I have always dreamed of going to school like my cousins, and I was wondering . . ."

His voice trailed off as he saw his aunt's eyes narrow and her lips tighten. She shook her head slowly and he caught the sharp hiss as she sucked her teeth in annoyance. School was out of the question for the time being, his new aunt said, but he could help her by selling yams along Graphic Road, a busy route through one of Accra's industrial areas. If he earned enough, she might allow him to start classes. Though he was a bit disappointed by her response, he comforted himself with the thought that at least school wasn't altogether out of reach.

Yams are heavy, the boy knew that all right, but those gray tubers, the length of his arm, were worse than carrying a big concrete block. He tried walking along the center strip of the six-lane Graphic Road with four yams in his arms, the way the other boys did. He just couldn't hold them long enough, and his scrawny legs, unused to the weight, almost buckled when he tried to walk faster. When the traffic lights changed and cars came to a halt, he could not keep up with the other yam sellers running to the stalled vehicles to hawk their goods. He sold none on his first day. He returned to the house despondent. His aunt merely shrugged and said he would have better luck another day.

The boy was twelve now, but being skinny and small for his age, he looked much younger. One of the older boys, who was muscular and had a face hardened by the city streets, with dark sun-ravaged skin and swollen eyes, told him that being young could work for him. "Make yourself look pathetic," he said, chuckling and mimicking a toddler. "Rich people will give you money, they'll buy your yams." All the other boys laughed.

The boy tried that, but it didn't work either. As the days and weeks went by his aunt's patience evaporated. One evening, he arrived back with the stock unsold and she beat him mercilessly as her children and husband watched. Between the pain, the fear, and the hunger, he barely slept that night.

On arriving at his spot the next day, the haunted faces of the other boys showed that they knew what had happened to him. It was as if they could read each bruise and welt. While there was understanding for his plight, there was little they could do to help him. He was, after all, their competition, and their own safety depended on their sales.

When the beatings became more frequent, the boy moved out and started staying with two of the other yam sellers along the railway track near Agbogbloshie, where Accra's most destitute slept in improvised lean-tos close to the lines. He asked some of the market women if he could sell their wares on the road, but they too had small margins and were unable to help. He begged for food and money from drivers in traffic or office workers passing by. If there was nothing else to do, he sat with his group under a bush on the center strip of Graphic Road.

One day while he was idling under a tree, an older boy came and stood in front of him. A good deal older than the other yam sellers, he was a young man really, and had two very odd scars on his blemished face. The boy squinted and bent his head back to get a better view of the newcomer. His gaunt, pockmarked face showed the premature wrinkles of too much time in the sun and the jagged scars of knives or broken bottles. What alarmed the boy most were his eyes; they were expressionless, bloodshot, and tinged yellow. The boy was immediately wary of him. Yet Two-Scars seemed to have come there specifically to see him.

"The boys tell me you don't have luck selling yams," he said loudly, addressing both the boy and his yam mates for added encouragement. "How would you like to make some real cash?"

"Go for it!" egged on the other boys. "Why not, what have you go to lose?"

"Let's go see Madam tomorrow," said Two-Scars through a half smile. "She'll love you."

Later on, he quietly asked his friends who this young man with the two scars was. The other boys told him that he was well known, he used to sell yams like them when he was a young, young boy—but he left some years before and now he was making plenty money! He came occasionally to talk to youngsters, just arrived and sometimes got them work with Madam.

* * *

East Legon 5:45 p.m.

"God will punish the person who did this," says the pastor. "It really has nothing to do with us. This boy was just left here. We can bury him without telling anyone." He looks up and raises a hand. "Vengeance belongs to the Lord!"

Rashida's uncle speaks up again, "But what if we bury the poor child and his body is discovered later?" He pauses. "Remember what happened when they leveled the road here—they broke so many houses? It will be much worse for us then. They will see us like the people of Sodom and Gomorrah, thieves and murderers."

He mentions the name of the notorious slum in central Accra deliberately—it is a place where migrants from the north exist in squalor on top of a landfill site. People demonized by all sides for living lives of poverty and assumed criminality. When the last big floods occurred a few months earlier their houses were demolished by the metropolitan council and the inhabitants cast out of their fragile refuge with hardly a murmur of protest outside their community. The men ponder their dilemma.

A gruff snort alerts the group to an uninvited presence behind them. It is the seamstress who has a container shop on the road perpendicular to the pastor's kiosk. She is a hefty charcoal-brown woman with an imperious walk. In late middle age, she is older than the men and, in truth, the most influential person in the community. She is dressed in a yellow and blue tie-dyed skirt to her ankles and fitted top with a matching wrap around her waist, all of which accentuate her ample figure. A ferocious gossip, the seamstress is feared by transgressors and nontransgressors alike.

The men look at each other quizzically and then at the woman, but they say nothing. The seamstress, her hands on her hips and her feet planted firmly on the uneven ground, gazes with a profound sadness on the boy's lifeless body. She sighs deeply and audibly, but still says nothing.

She gathers her composure, wrapping her cloth tighter around her waist, then she informs the men that the police will do two things. "Precisely nothing to solve the murder, and they will harass every one of us to get money and cause more trouble." She points to the street of walled houses, its hum of generators. "Do you not realize," she asks, "that the big people around here are already starting to complain about the drinking spot and the increasing numbers of young men hanging around, doing nothing—not to mention your cattle?" At that last point she peers squarely at Rashida's father and opens her eyes wide. "This young boy's murder will bring misfortune one way or another." She shakes her head slowly.

The group is silent for some time, each one thinking about the boy and the violence done to him and the problem of how to deal with it, about their own families.

Looking up suddenly, the seamstress says decisively, "Best we bury him now, quickly and quietly."

The pastor, Rashida's father, and the others nod without speaking. They will bury the boy where he lies, right away. Rashida is gripped, almost paralyzed, by the intensity of the events unfolding before her. She moves back a few paces behind the others to avoid looking at the boy. She twists a bead at the end of a braid and stares at the ground as she tries desperately not to think of him.

Madam's House, Asylum Down

The boy was dumbstruck by Madam's house. Bigger than any he had ever seen, it had an upstairs with lots of rooms and gold handles on the doors. There were huge pictures on the walls: young girls in frilly dresses, glittery landscapes, and a particularly large one of Jesus on the cross, hung on the main wall. The picture changed when you looked at it from different sides. On one side the eyes were open, on the other they were closed. The boy was fascinated and moved from side to side to see the face change. The air was kept cool and fresh by air conditioners. He saw a young girl about his own age sitting on the couch watching cartoons on the huge curved TV; the sound was very loud, and she didn't seem to notice him at all. When he sat down beside her and said hello, she started, her eyes widened, and she bit her lower lip while scooting swiftly to the other end of the sofa. The boy was puzzled but didn't have much time to dwell on it as Two-Scars entered the room with Madam.

She stopped a short distance away and looked him up and down excitedly. She clapped her hands and moved forward to hug him, pinching his cheeks and doing a little dance. All the while the girl on the sofa giggled oddly. Madam signaled to a young woman standing in the doorway to take the boy upstairs for a thorough wash and to put him into some new clothes. She then turned to the boy again, and taking his bewildered face in her hands, she repeated, "New clothes!" Madam really did seem to like him.

After he had been cleaned up, Madam came back to look him over once more. She told the boy that he was just perfect. He would be making money for all of them very soon. He really didn't know what she meant, but felt her affection and her care like a tonic, like a ray of sunshine after a long violent storm.

In the house with him were a number of boys and girls his own age. The girls all had their hair done, braided into large plaits with yellow, pink, blue, and green baubles on the ends;

each had a pink plastic hair band. There was another boy there too. He looked to be about fourteen and had the fuzzy upper lip of an adolescent, his hair a reddish tinge and his skin the color of rust. One of the young girls ran over to the adolescent and whispered in his ear. As she did so, she stroked his leg backward and forward. He brushed her off and skulked away slowly with his shoulders drooped and his head bowed.

Over the next few days, the boy met other children at the house who were all a puzzle to him. Most of them had been selling goods on the street, like himself, when they were brought to Madam's place, and were all about the same age. There were sisters there who were younger than he was, who sat together always in a corner of the room as if in their own world, apart from everyone else. A boy his own age was exactly the opposite, talking constantly and insisting on hugging children and grown-ups alike as if scared to be alone. Disturbingly, he had the same yellow and bloodshot eyes as Two-Scars.

A sense of anticipation and trepidation grew in the house. Madam told him that he and the girls were going to a party with some very important people. She had bought him a special new outfit for the occasion. The boy laughed aloud when he saw the new shoes, blue trainers. He was confused, though, when she pulled out a new school uniform for him. Brand-new brown shorts, a yellow shirt, and startlingly white knee socks. "Try them on," she encouraged, "you will look so sweet."

Two-Scars arrived at the house and Madam asked the boy to sit beside him. "He's got something to tell you," she said. "Listen to him carefully."

"Some men like to play with children," Two-Scars told him, "boys or girls. They might be rough and it might hurt. You'll be frightened sometimes. But they like that, you can see in their eyes they like you to be afraid. Never scream, never ever. One of them gets really angry if you do." He looked at the boy and saw he had not understood at all, had no idea what was about to happen. The boy was frightened all right, but of the wrong person. Two-Scars hesitated. He wanted to tell Madam the boy was too young or wasn't ready. But why bother? Any argument was useless, he knew.

Instead, Two-Scars pulled out a bottle of gin and a small bag of white powder. He told the boy to rub some powder onto his gums. The boy did, and his head lightened; he felt a rush of energy, like he used to feel running through the forest in Wiamoase, and the colors around him seemed brighter. Two-Scars then offered the boy some akpeteshie. The boy took it, warily, and immediately felt nauseous. His head spun and he gagged slightly.

"This is horrible," the boy said with a grimace. "Why do you want me to keep drinking it?"

"If you don't quite remember what happened," Two-Scars explained as he poured more gin, "then it's easier to forget."

The boy was sent off on his first assignment. A large black four-wheel drive pulled up to the front of Madam's house, and the boy and three of the girls got in, vanishing from view behind its tinted windows. *He'll get over it, I did*, Two-Scars reasoned to himself. *Look at me, I'm all right. He'll get used to it. When he gets back I'll take him for Papa's pizza and ice cream.* Two-Scars took another swig of akpeteshie and carried on his internal dialogue. By the time he was done, he felt better, and left the house.

East Legon, 6:00 p.m.

The pastor and Rashida's father are standing over the makeshift grave. Leaning on his shovel inside the pit, the pastor's son wipes sweat and dirt from his face. He and Rashida's uncle have been digging with an urgency bred of fear. He thinks it is deep enough now. Rainy season is months away and the ground will have hardened well before that.

"It's getting dark now, we need to get back. Rains won't be here until May, it will be okay," he says, looking around. The seamstress agrees with him.

"It's better to stop now. If we are all away too long, people will wonder." Everyone nods assent as they normally do when the seamstress speaks.

Slowly their heads turn toward the small body lying beneath the trees. The tragic finality of the scene strikes each one; a heaviness built of guilt and gloom descends, but remains unexpressed. Their daily existence takes precedence over sentiment. The men move together to lift the boy into the grave, even though Rashida's uncle can lift him alone. The boy's small body is beginning to stiffen, but they are able to fold his knees as they lay him into the ground. Rashida, still standing well back, watches the events, removed as if watching a TV movie.

Her father asks the pastor if he will say a few words over the boy before they cover the grave.

The pastor looks uncomfortable. "He's one of yours, I think," he says.

"I don't think that matters, do you?" responds Rashida's father, looking at the pastor directly.

"I suppose not," the pastor relents, though, in truth, he believes that a person's faith in death, as in life, matters very much. Still, he bends his head and mutters a few words. Everyone present is keenly aware that these prayers are considerably quieter and more equivocal than his usual rants.

Rashida's father turns his hands to the darkening sky and

his brother does likewise. He prays that the boy will have an afterlife that makes up for the horrific strife visited upon him in this world. Then his mind wanders—he thinks of Rashida and her siblings, his pregnant wife, his next day's work, and how he will keep them all safe. The seamstress prays quietly to herself, thinking of the children she has lost: her week-old boy who was born with jaundice and didn't survive long enough to be named, and her beautiful, funny, kind nine-year-old girl who died in her arms as they waited all day for a doctor at the clinic.

Slowly, the men begin to shovel the dirt onto the body without looking at this last violence. The seamstress tells them to pack the dirt well and to scatter dead leaves on top to disguise the disturbed earth. They nod as she turns away toward her shop, feeling the death like a new emptiness.

Abossey Okai, in Traffic

Some days later, as Two-Scars ambled along near Graphic Road, he saw the car in traffic. It was unmistakable, with the tinted back windows and the party sticker on the bumper. The boy had not been all right. In fact, he had never come home. The girls had arrived the next morning, but there had been no sign of the boy. No one had even bothered to ask the driver what happened, what was the reason for the boy's absence. The longer the absence became, the bigger the pit in Two-Scars's stomach grew. This was their life; over the years he had come to accept that. But the boy was so young.

Two-Scars straightened up. He was going to find out what happened. He jogged over to the SUV and knocked on the back window before he had time to think about what he wanted to say or do. Instead of the back window lowering, the front window went down, and an angry voice shouted, "HEY!

Hey you, move away now! Honorable doesn't have time for the likes of you."

"Boss, Boss," Two-Scars called, trying to look through the opaque glass. "Boss, I'm your man oh!"

The window eased down halfway. Two eyes and a nose revealed themselves. Two-Scars got a jolt at seeing the face again and lurched backward. Did he see a flash of recognition in those dead eyes peering out of the car window?

Gathering himself, he moved forward, tried to ask, but other words came out of his mouth. "Boss, you go need foot soldiers for the elections, I'm your man oh!" Two-Scars smiled his best deferential smile.

A quick nod from the back window and the driver proffered a fifty-cedi note to him. Two-Scars hesitated before taking the money. But fifty cedis would buy a lot of forgetting. *Besides, who am I and what can I do?* he asked himself.

Nobody and nothing, nothing and nobody, came the sneering response.

Two-Scars leaned over the bridge and retched. He watched his spit mix with the filth of the Odaw River and flow toward the Gulf of Guinea.

East Legon, 6:15 p.m.

The constant hum of the cicadas has superseded birdsong as the sun casts its last light from below the horizon. Darkness begins to cover the scene. Just then the sound of a collective cheer rises up from the dwellings around the football pitch. Lights are back.

The men begin to leave the grave, silently, one after the other. Rashida is looking at the ground, which is covered now by leaves and twilight, as if nothing else was ever there. Her father watches her, putting his hand gently on her shoulder.

"You've seen a terrible thing today, Rashida." She bows her head and nods. "Don't be afraid, okay?" At this she looks up and gives her father a weak smile. "But you mustn't tell anyone, anyone at all." She nods slowly, hesitantly. "Rashida? Rashida! Do you hear me?"

"I won't, Dada" she says. "I promise."

"Best if you try to forget it ever happened," he says as he walks back to his herd.

Rashida hears a familiar whistle from the football grounds. She looks again at the place where the boy had lain, where she found him just a little while ago. There are too many feelings in her head. She's afraid and sad and guilty, but relieved too. In the end she decides to try to pretend it never happened, just like her father said she should.

The football park is free now, and for the last few minutes of daylight she and her friends will be able to play undisturbed and she can run and feel light again.

She is turning to go when a shiny object lying just beside a tree root catches her eye.

A silver bead.

Rashida bends down slowly, her hair falling forward, the baubles at the end of her braids clacking. She picks up the bead, rubs the dirt off, and puts it in her pocket.

INSTANT JUSTICE

BY ANNA BOSSMAN

High Street

"Hey, julɔ, julɔ!"

Hey, thief, thief!

Jane stared at Joe, lying there in the filth looking pitiful, his muddy shirt torn and soaked with blood and water, his face puffy and wet with snot and tears. He whimpered a little and twitched from time to time, but mostly he was still. The crowd had thinned, but there was still a small handful of stragglers, curious onlookers, pointing and staring at him.

A tall, thin woman with a bright-red satin scarf tied around her head spat at him. The spittle landed next to his head. Her companion, donning a similar scarf and holding tightly onto her cover cloth, shook her head, a look of disgust and pity creasing her face. She placed her hands on her hips and said—to Joe, to everyone standing there, to no one in particular—"Mɛni sane nɛ? Kwɛmɔ bɔ ni oka shi, mɛni kwraa otaoɔ?" *What is this? Look at you lying there. What is it that you wanted?* She curled her lips downward, shook her head again, tightened the cover cloth around her waist, then signaled to her friend that they should be on their way.

A woman walking by with a large wooden platter of smoked fish on her head stated, quite matter-of-factly, "Ebaagbo, mmm . . ." *He will die, mmm . . .* She then stopped and said, directly to Joe, "Mɛni ofee nɛɛ?" *What have you done?* After she had become a faint figure in the distance, three teenage porters, kayayei, holding large aluminum basins, scurried to and fro, chattering among themselves, looking at the man on the ground, and then at the people surrounding him who continued to stare and point. The kayayei's kohl-lined eyes easily identified them as being from the northern part of Ghana. They were on their way to one of the nearby markets, either Salaga or Makola, to look for shoppers who would hire them to carry their wares.

Jane stayed at the scene, waiting for the police to arrive. She knew that KB, Joe's friend, had called them because he'd mouthed this to her when they briefly made eye contact. She had been trying to catch his glance again, but he was busy pacing up and down, his eyes suspiciously darting from person to person and occasionally glancing behind and around him as though he were expecting to be ambushed or surprised in a similarly covert manner.

It was barely ten in the morning and already it was scorching hot, humid, unbearable. Earlier, Jane had asked the plantain sellers for water to pour on Joe; that accounted for his wet shirt. She thought it might soothe his pain. It was something, at least. She wished she could do more, but she wasn't sure what. The entire scene felt surreal. Working in downtown Accra, with all its hustle and bustle, market women and traders, hustlers and kayayei, she had witnessed this scene play out numerous times. A single angry voice would slice its way through the commotion, calling out, "Hey, julɔ, julɔ!" Everyone would stop what they'd been doing, as if called to attention, and soon enough a crowd of people would be running after the accused, their voices a rising chorus, shouting, "Hey, julɔ, julɔ!"

If the accused was caught, which was often the case, that

individual would be beaten to lifelessness, bathing in a small pool of their own blood and tears. It was an appropriate punishment for an appalling crime, so felt the ordinary workaday people of Ghana. These were people who toiled mercilessly to earn a pittance, and the only indignity worse than that was the knowledge that somebody would be vile enough to take from them what little they had. An eye for an eye; you take my livelihood and I catch you, I take your life. That was the unwritten law of these streets.

The irony of it all, which was never lost on Jane whenever she witnessed such scenes, was that they played out in the shadow of the Supreme Court and old Parliament buildings, which were only a stone's throw away. It only confirmed to Jane what she already suspected, that playing by the rules then waiting and praying for the best possible outcome was a process applicable only to a wealthy man's version of the game of life. The rest of humanity had to take what they could get, when they could get it.

Still, she'd never expected to see something like this happen to Joe. Not him of all people. And not today of all days, on this fine Saturday morning. She had gone to work early to set up her stall at the Arts Center for the young lady who would be working in her place that day. Jane had asked her boss for the day off, making up an excuse about needing to care for an aunt who had taken ill. The truth was that she knew Kwame would be coming today to collect his merchandise from the stall next to hers. She'd not seen him—though he'd been phoning her incessantly and she had rejected all of the calls since the night he made it clear that their relationship had no future.

Jane was eighteen when she first met Kwame. He'd returned to Accra to purchase land. After twenty-five years, he'd grown tired of America. He wanted to come back home, retire while he still had the ability to appreciate all the gifts Ghana offered. He'd gone to the Arts Center to buy gifts to take back to his friends and family in the US, and Jane had helped him navigate the maze of stalls. One of the wonderful things about the Arts Center is that the sellers work together, almost like a cooperative.

Kwame's attraction to Jane was obvious from the moment they said hello to each other. She enjoyed his attention, the way his eyes followed the movement of her curves, the way he twirled her braided extensions around his index finger or held his arm next to hers to see how much darker her skin was than his. "My black beauty," he would whisper. "My African princess." He made her feel like she was special, something to be cherished; in a city like Accra, where she so often felt dispensable, that alone was worth its weight in gold. It's true that she was young enough to be his daughter but, as he reminded her whenever they were together, she was not. She was a woman and he was a man, and years were only numbers. Every time Kwame came to Accra, which, after he started building his dream home, was fairly often, he and Jane resumed their relationship.

Five years passed quickly. Brick by brick, Kwame finished his home, started plotting his exit from America. His entire life had changed. Meanwhile, Jane's had stayed the same. Day after day, she got up from the same worn mattress, rode the same overcrowded trotro to work in the same stall at the Arts Center. The only time her life was different was when Kwame came back. He never expressly told her that he would take her to America, but he'd strategically dangle the possibility in front of her. "You would fit right in," he would assure her. "I can already see you managing your own shop on 125th

Street, or opening a small market in Clarkston or Decatur."

He often spoke of New York, where he'd first lived when he left Ghana. He'd worked as a taxi driver there and told the most fascinating stories of his passengers—millionaires who dressed like paupers and pretended to be streetwise and hardened; other Ghanaian immigrants who refused to reply in any of the native languages when he tried to bond with them. He also spoke, though not as much, of Atlanta and its surrounding suburbs, where he currently lived with his African American wife and their teenage children, a boy and two girls, not much younger than she was when they'd first met. Between his stories and the small research she'd done on the Internet, she felt as if she knew each place intimately.

Then, nearly a month ago, he'd shattered all her hopes of a future abroad when he told her that his family was arriving in a few days; Jane could no longer come to the house. His wife and children would be staying with him through the end of his four-week trip, as it was their Easter holiday, and then they would all return for good in a few months when the children's school closed for the summer. Kwame said he wanted to rent a small place where he and Jane could live together. He would come see her often, and once he and his family had settled into a rhythm in Accra, he would begin spending some nights and weekends with her.

It was then that she realized he had no intention of helping her make any significant changes to her life. His only intention was to take, take, and take from her, to use her as a toy, a thing to be played with, until he tired of her. She was crushed. She closed the door to any affection she'd ever had for him. If he was going to treat her like a prostitute then he should pay, as men did, for such services. That evening, she demanded that he give her all the cash that was in his wallet.

At first, he thought she was joking, but when he saw that she was serious, he complied.

"If you're in a difficult position or need help with something, just tell me. I will help you if I can," he said.

She smiled in his face but rolled her eyes when he looked away. While he was in the bathroom getting dressed to give her a ride home, she helped herself to everything in his bedroom that could fit in her handbag. Later, she'd hopped out of the car before he had a chance to kiss her good night—closed the door and walked away, without ever looking back or saying goodbye.

She never wanted to see Kwame again, which is why she'd asked to take leave from work that day.

She had finished setting up and was waiting for Hawa, her substitute, to arrive when KB came running into the stall. He quickly hid under the long wooden folding table they used as both a counter to display their wares and as a divider between workers and shoppers. The table was covered with a large piece of cloth that hung down and draped the front of it.

"KB, mɛni . . . ?" she started. *What . . . ?* Then she heard the mob's footsteps.

"Hey, julɔ, julɔ!" she heard. And suddenly she understood.

KB stayed under the table. He heard footsteps rushing by. It sounded like a stampede. He was about to come out when he heard someone walk into the stall. "Ona julɔ?" *Have you seen the thief?* He heard Jane say that she had only seen the others running past her, also in search of him. Then the man seemed to walk away. He heard Jane moving things around. She sat in the chair behind the table, reached down, and handed him a hat and some sunglasses, telling him to put them on.

He explained to her that the people who'd been chasing

him were only a small part of the mob. There were many others still in the car park. He began to explain what happened but all he could manage was his friend's name before he started crying. "Joe," he said. "They are killing him right now. We have to do something."

Jane instructed him to wait for a while before going outside. "Put on the hat and dark glasses. Wait for Hawa and tell her I had to leave. Call the police and tell them to come right away."

He agreed to follow her instructions, and then she left. He put on the hat, a touristy panama made of raffia, with a kente cloth bow. He slid the shades on and looked at himself in the handheld mirror that Jane kept inside a small box behind the table. If he were white, he could have easily passed for any one of the European tourists who'd be shopping in the Arts Center today. The black tourists usually tried to dress more like the locals, to fully embrace the African within them that the diaspora so often tried to force them to forget.

After putting on the disguise, he phoned the police and told them there were people in the car park beating a man they believed to be a thief. The voice on the other end said, with no discernible urgency, that they would come as soon as they were able. After KB, whose real name was Kofi Boakye, ended the call, he sat down and tried to figure out how everything had gone so wrong. When Joe showed up that morning in his small blue Peugeot to pick up him and Asante, it felt like every other morning. Yet here KB was, barely two hours later, trying to shield his identity to protect his life, calling the police to save one friend's life, and wondering if his other friend had managed to escape.

KB and Asante were business partners, at least that's what they called themselves. Some might describe them as "partners in crime." They moved merchandise from one place or person to another. It was illicit merchandise—drugs or black-market money or stolen goods—but their pickups and deliveries were all very straightforward and clean. They were not thugs. They didn't carry weapons, make threats, or engage in violence. They were never party to the transactions, merely the delivery people. But KB suddenly remembered, a little too late, that it was always the messengers who got killed.

One of their regular clients was the owner of the Forex Bureau inside the Arts Center. Whenever they went to see him, they stopped by the stall where Jane worked to say hello and, if she didn't have too many customers, sit and chat.

Joe was not in business with KB and Asante, though the three of them had known each other since they were in crèche. Though they all, in theory, came from middle-class families, from civil servants at that, KB and Asante were of a more modest background. Their families merely worked in regular government jobs with unimpressive titles. Joe's mother was a retired head teacher of a prominent school, and his father was a former high-court judge. They'd make it clear to Joe, and everyone else, that they felt KB and Asante were riffraff, and they didn't want their son hanging around them. That didn't stop Joe, especially after KB and Asante started paying him to drive them.

They never told Joe what they were doing, figuring the less he knew, the better. And Joe never asked, except on one occasion after they'd given him five hundred cedis for taking them around that day. He had jokingly asked them, while counting the crisp fifty-cedi notes, what the merchandise they dropped off was. KB smiled and told him that in time, he would know. But Joe already knew. He was also smart enough to know what not to know. So, if he was still curious about KB and Asante's odd jobs, he never let on.

That same afternoon that KB and Asante had shared part of their windfall with Joe, they stopped by the stall where Jane worked to say hello. Sometimes, if it was a slow day for Jane, and if the boys were done with all their errands, they would all pile into Joe's car and go to Asanka Local for a serious lunch of fufu and goat light soup or banku and grilled tilapia. The four of them had a very easy relationship. Jane had gone to the same high school as the three men, though her background was entirely different. Her parents lived in a village outside of Kumasi. They'd sent her to live with her aunt in Osu, a seamstress who fancied herself a designer, so that she could have a better education.

Jane's aunt was married to a midlevel bureaucrat, the sort who held little power at work but wanted others to see him as a big man. He had the requisite potbelly, wore gray and brown suits, was driven around town in a Mercedes that was neither new enough nor old enough to inspire envy. "Yessah, boss," his driver would say, after the big man had barked out a command, then the driver would salute him as though he were in the military.

The aunt had fulfilled her promise to her sister and made sure that Jane had received a decent high school education. But like her three friends, Jane had been unable to gain admission into any university. She'd started working in the stall at the Arts Center as a sales assistant. She contributed part of her salary to the household, but her aunt, suspecting that something was going on between Jane and her husband, had asked her to leave. Her aunt was only half-right; what was going on was that her husband was a lecherous man who was constantly making advances, but he was not a rapist and had always accepted Jane's refusal. Still, the woman wanted her to leave.

One evening, while her aunt was out delivering a dress to a client and then continuing on to her women's Bible-study group, the husband had approached Jane. He suggested that perhaps he could talk to her aunt, reason with her, make some assurances. Jane was thrilled; she thanked him profusely. "And how will you show me your gratitude?" he had asked, slowly taking her hand and pulling her toward him. She knew what he wanted, but she also knew what *she* wanted. Her aunt was the only family she had in Accra; this was not just a place to live, it was a home, and she didn't want to leave. She surrendered to his request, believing she would be rewarded with what she most wanted. The following day, her aunt's husband told her that he'd thought about the situation again and decided that maybe her living elsewhere would indeed be best for everyone. So Jane moved into a small apartment in Jamestown.

The last time the friends went to lunch together a few weeks back, two memorable things had happened. The first was a phone call that Joe received from his sister, Araba. She was hysterical, telling Joe that he had to go to Korle Bu Hospital, that he had to come right away. His mother had had a stroke. Joe, who was especially close to his mother, had not taken the news well. He'd started crying, asking what if she died. He somehow rationalized it in his mind that if he didn't go to the hospital, she wouldn't die. It took some doing, but the others eventually convinced Joe to get in his car and go. Thankfully, his mother survived and was expected, in time, to make a full recovery.

After Joe left, Jane had given KB and Asante a few items that she said she wanted sold. It was an unusual request from her, and for them. They didn't usually involve themselves in the selling of merchandise, but decided to make an exception for Jane. As a show of her gratitude, she gave a gold watch to KB and a gold money clip to Asante. She'd seen how the men had longingly eyed those objects when she'd placed them on the table with the rest of the loot.

Jane's next request was even stranger. She wanted to give them the location of a house where there was lots of brand-new merchandise. It belonged to a family that was returning to Ghana and had recently received a shipping container full of goods from America. She told KB and Asante who would be in the house, asked that they make sure the woman and her children were unharmed. "As for the man," she said, "I don't want him to need hospital but, abeg, tell them to make him suffer small." KB heard contempt in her voice, but her eyes were filled with pain and sadness.

"Did he hurt you?" KB asked. He silently vowed that if she answered yes, he would ignore Jane's directions and tell the ones doing the job to kill the man. But she said no, the man had not hurt her.

KB and Asante, enticed by the idea of an entire container of American merchandise at their disposal, decided to do the job themselves. They didn't tell anyone, other than the two criminals they'd enlisted to help them. They hadn't asked Joe to drive them because they didn't want to involve him in so risky a job. Besides, his mother's stroke had changed him. He was finally becoming the son she had always wanted. He had big plans to go to America and enroll in uni there. His older sister, who lived in Maryland and was married to a white American, was willing to sponsor him. He'd been spending most of his time getting his documents, and whatever else he needed to prove that he was worthy of a visa and an academic admission, written or organized and ready to be taken to the DHL.

The robbery was as effortless as Jane said it would be. The

family had complied with all their requests. The woman and children were visibly frightened. KB thought they might just melt into puddles of fear. The man, a Ghanaian, kept trying to make casual conversation with KB and the other armed robbers.

"Do you have families?" he asked them. "I'm sure you own things that have more sentimental value than cash value. Please leave us our passports and laptops."

KB and the others ignored him, but he kept talking.

"Shut up!" KB finally yelled, striking the man with a crowbar. "If you open your mouth again, I will beat you, saaaa." The man cowered, held his injured head in his hands, and began to whimper. KB hadn't hit him hard. If anything, his ego was more bruised than his head.

After they'd removed all the items they wanted, Asante and the other two men took the loot downstairs to be loaded into the van, leaving KB with his gun and crowbar to keep an eye on the family. All the necessary arrangements had been made with the staff. The house help had left suddenly for the village that morning. The night watchman, who'd opened the gate for them and was also helping them load items into the van, had been promised a small kickback. Before the men left, they would tie him to a chair and whip him just enough times to produce bruises, so he'd be seen as a victim rather than an accomplice.

Maybe, KB thought, he was being punished for taking part in that armed robbery. He and Asante hadn't stolen anything at all that morning. They'd come in and made a drop at the Forex Bureau, same as always. He'd given them their small percentage, and then they left the stall and entered the maze that was the Arts Center. Two men had rushed by and bumped into them, nearly knocking them over, then split off into different directions. KB figured they were pickpockets and told Asante to check his pockets. Asante pulled out the wad of cash that the al hajji at the Forex Bureau had just given him. KB did the same. It was right then, while KB and Asante were each holding a fistful of cedis, that a voice cried out, "Hey, julɔ, julɔ!" The two looked up and around to see this thief. When they realized it was them, they ran.

After Hawa came, KB rushed out of the stall, hat and sunglasses on. He wasn't paying attention to where he was going. He turned into the walkway and bumped into someone.

"Why don't you watch where you're going?" the man said in an accent that was not quite Ghanaian, but also not quite American. The voice sounded familiar. KB turned and looked at the man, fully intending to apologize, but when he saw the face, the still-raw scar on the side of his head, KB decided against it. *Oh God*, he thought. He quickly looked away, forced the image of the man and the thoughts that had followed out of his head, and allowed himself to focus only on getting to the car park and helping Joe.

Kwame was determined to see Jane one more time before he returned to Atlanta the following day. This was supposed to have been a happy, triumphant homecoming, but it had turned out to be the worst month of his life.

He didn't understand what had happened with her. He'd told her that he would rent a flat for the two of them to live in, effectively making her his second wife. She'd seemed unenthused by the idea and vanished like a ghost after that night. She wouldn't respond to his phone calls or texts. He'd even tried calling from an anonymous number. She'd answered the call but pretended she couldn't hear him talking. "Hello? Hello? Hello?" she'd kept saying. But he knew it was an act, because he'd called a few more times from various other anonymous numbers and she'd done the same thing.

After a few days, he became too distracted to worry about Jane. His wife, Mary, and their three children—Albert, Cristabel, and Annabel—had flown to Accra so that, together, they could christen their newly completed house. Mary and the kids had finally agreed to move to Ghana. Within days of their arrival, armed robbers had broken into their home, held them at gunpoint, and taken everything. It hadn't even been five days since Kwame had cleared their container of belongings from the port. They'd barely started unpacking the boxes they'd spent weeks packing and sealing and labeling back in Atlanta. And as if that wasn't enough, one of those hooligans had hit Kwame with a crowbar on the side of his face. He had a gash just above his ear, and his jaw was nearly broken. That incident was all it took for Mary and the kids to regret their decision to move. Within twenty-four hours, they were on a flight back to America. Kwame had stayed behind to sort out their affairs and, he hoped, find comfort in Jane's arms.

When Kwame first arrived, Jane had helped him custom order a set of Akuaba fertility dolls. He didn't want the mass-produced type that could be found on any street corner. He wanted a well-crafted work of art, made from the finest mahogany. The artisan had asked him to pick up the dolls that morning. Luckily, the people at the shop wrapped the carvings for him in padded brown paper. Though compact, the package was a little heavy, and he hoped he'd be allowed to carry it on the plane as hand luggage. After Kwame had paid for and taken possession of the carvings, he decided to pass by Jane's stall. Whatever he'd done or said to put her off, he was willing to apologize. As he was approaching the stall, some guy walked right into him, a typical tourist in his own world, completely oblivious to everything around him. Kwame entered the stall and saw that Jane wasn't there. Disappointed, he started walking toward the car park when he heard a lot of commotion, people chanting, "Hey, julɔ, julɔ!" He, along with several others, moved in the direction of the noise to find out what was going on.

It was just after nine a.m., still early, when Joe pulled into the car park at the Arts Center. Most markets in Accra, in the country, actually, came to life shortly after dawn; but the Accra Arts Center was mostly geared toward tourists, even though locals also patronized the place. It was an iconic place, right in the center of the city, on High Street, not far from the Kwame Nkrumah Mausoleum and a short drive, two minutes without traffic, to the old slave castle that had, until recently, been the official seat of government.

Whenever Joe drove KB and Asante down there to run their errands, which was more and more these days, he felt a sense of connectedness, a sense of purpose, both of which had been missing in his life. It reminded him that people had worked and sacrificed to build this country. He'd spent most of his youth aimlessly drifting through interests, experiences, and friendships. His sister Araba claimed it was because he was the last born and their mother babied him. She'd been actively campaigning their parents to cut him off financially.

"He's lazy and unmotivated, a useless sponger," Araba often said. Thankfully, his sister Lydia didn't share that view. She had offered to sponsor him for a visa. He would live with her and her family in Maryland while completing his studies. He'd initially scoffed at the idea because he liked his life in Accra. It was simple and carefree. But then his mother suffered a stroke. When he arrived at the hospital, there were already a dozen friends and family assembled in the waiting area. It was clear to him then, in a way it had never been before, that his mother had used all the time and resources given to her to build a life, to raise a family and create a career. She was part of a community. She was loved and respected. If, God forbid, she died, she would be sorely missed and well remembered.

He, on the other hand, had done nothing. He wanted people to one day speak of him in the same reverential way they spoke of his mother. And he wanted his mother, who, thank God, had lived, to be proud of him. He was ready to make something of himself, to do something with his life. He was saving the money KB and Asante paid him and trying to get a job so he could save even more money for when he was in America.

He'd promised his mother that he'd have her car back by midday, so he'd told KB and Asante that they had to be quick. "Make I no vex the old lady," he'd said.

While waiting for them, he watched the vendors at the front of the market getting their stalls ready. The Rasta boys were unpacking and hanging up their colorful T-shirts, baseball caps, and northern batakaris, exchanging jokes with one another. Joe was sitting in the car with the door open, one foot planted on the ground. He was fiddling with the heavy gold watch KB had recently started wearing. KB always took it off before his errands, though, because he didn't want the people who hired him to think he was becoming too big. The commotion began only seconds after Joe put the watch around his right wrist and closed the clasp

"Hey, julɔ, julɔ, eeiii!" he heard someone call out. He looked up and saw Asante and KB running toward the car and several people running behind them.

"Start the car, start the car!" Asante cried out. Thoroughly alarmed, Joe switched the engine on as he saw more people joining the chase. KB reached the car and tried to open the passenger-side door, but realized he wouldn't have enough time to make it inside the vehicle before being overpowered by those pursuing him. Asante didn't even attempt to stop. He ran right past the car and kept on going. With one foot still inside the vehicle, Joe stood up and looked in the direction his two friends were headed, so he didn't see the first blow coming. It landed on his head. He instinctively sat back down and tried to close the car door. A hand pushed through the window. Joe panicked and tried to roll it up, but now there were other hands reaching inside as well. There were too many people in front and around to drive away.

"Hey, julɔ, julɔ, eeiii!" came the individual voices, one right after the other. The car door jerked open and Joe was dragged out. Fear engulfed him as he scrambled to get off the ground. People started kicking him, spitting on him.

"I haven't done anything!" he screamed. "I beg you, I have done nothing wrong!" But they either couldn't hear him above the mob voices or they just didn't care. He curled his body into a ball in an effort to protect himself from the assault. He willed his mind to take him far, far away, and it did.

He saw himself at the airport, his family seeing him off. His father shook his hand with a firm grip, patted him on the back. *My son*, he said. His mother cried and congratulated him, even though he hadn't yet accomplished anything. *Ayekoo*, she said. Araba was so overcome with emotion she couldn't speak. She hugged him and cried into his shoulder, then she stood on her toes and kissed the center of his forehead.

Joe felt himself drifting off, falling deeper into what felt like a dream state. Then someone threw cold water on him and it startled him back to consciousness. He sensed the crowd moving away from him. He could even hear the footsteps, their sounds becoming softer, traveling to him from farther away. All except one set, which seemed to be thundering closer and closer.

"You fucking thief!" the voice boomed. And then something crashed down on his head. The pain was searing, causing him to see flashes of light, like bolts of white-hot electricity, behind his closed eyelids, before he was suddenly immersed in complete darkness.

Kwame approached the crowd and jostled his way to the front to see what it was they were gathered around. What he saw sickened him: people kicking and hitting and spitting on a young man curled up on the ground. He approached with the intention of protecting the man, of standing between him and the angry crowd, of making them stop. But when Kwame saw the watch, something shifted, unleashed a rage that had, unbeknownst to him, been building up inside his entire being. It was the gold watch his company had presented to him at his farewell party. Kwame knew it was his because the company's logo, the mythical phoenix, was emblazoned on its face. He had seen the robber wearing it the night they'd looted his house, and he'd wondered how the man could already be wearing it when they'd only just arrived.

Kwame insulted the man on the ground, the thief who'd stolen his entire life from him, made his family too scared to stay in the country. He began kicking him, each kick harder than the last, each kick a symbol of his frustration. Then he remembered the parcel he was holding, the wooden Akuaba dolls. He held the parcel high above his head and, with great force, brought it down on the man's skull. The crowd, as though they were one unified force, stepped away.

"Armed robbers," Kwame said by way of shorthand explanation while whacking the man, again, with the carvings. "My wife and children, gone!" Again. He could see blood flowing down the man's forehead. "You took everything!"

"Kwame, stop it, right now!" a woman's voice snapped. She stepped forward and grabbed his arm to prevent the next blow. "You are killing him. He didn't do anything. He is not a thief! KB, call the police now!"

Kwame looked at the woman. It was Jane. He recognized her, but her presence elicited no emotion. He was in a trance. He freed himself from her grip, pushed her so hard that she fell onto the ground right beside Joe. He raised the packaged carvings again. This time, several people from the crowd restrained him and led him away to a nearby communication center. "You have killed him," one of them said in a menacing tone. "We will hand you over to the police."

Kwame quickly realized that he was now the assailant and the fickle crowd could also turn on him. So he sat there quietly waiting for the police to arrive so he could tell his story.

The crowd had considerably thinned out, and he saw that Jane was still standing there looking at the lifeless figure on the ground. Kwame felt very ashamed that he had pushed her and wanted to tell her he was sorry. He saw a young man signal something to her, and just then three policemen arrived and moved toward the body on the ground. One of them prodded Joe with his foot before speaking to Jane.

Kwame felt cold as Jane looked on while the police approached him.

The events that followed were a blur. Kwame remembered the police telling him that he was under arrest. He remembered hearing arrangements being made to take Joe, the man he'd attacked, to the hospital in a taxi.

"I am not an ambulance," he remembered the taxi driver saying.

"We will pay," Jane had told the man. "We have the money. Asante, give the man money." A young man standing next to Jane reached into his pocket and produced a wad of bills secured with a gold money clip. It belonged to Kwame. He could tell because it wasn't an ordinary money clip, it was custom-made. The ends curled over like a pencil shaving, and Kwame's initials were engraved into the metal beneath the word *BOSS*. Kwame watched Asante remove a few bills from the clip and hand them to Jane, who handed them to the taxi driver. She then summoned another man wearing a hat and sunglasses, the same man who'd bumped into Kwame as he was on his way to her shop, to help Asante and the driver carry Joe into the taxi.

"Hey, julɔ, julɔ," Kwame said, pointing to the trio, but nobody minded him. "Julɔ!" he screamed, but everybody just went about their business as though they'd heard nothing at all.

Jane looked at Kwame as the police officers led him away from the scene. When their eyes met, she didn't turn away or flinch or even try to hide her contempt. She just kept staring. It occurred to him that he'd seen that expression before, on their last night together, when he'd dropped her off at her place. He'd been so lost in his own fantasies of the future that he hadn't been able to read that emotion in her eyes, on her face. But now it was so clear. Everything was crystal clear. The watch. The money clip. The man in the hat and sunglasses. The armed robbers. All the pieces, those tiny fragments of realization, were starting to come together.

Acknowledgments

I'm a huge fan of Akashic Books' Noir Series. It occurred to me one day that I'd never seen a collection of noir stories set in Accra. When I mentioned that to my friend Kenji Jasper, he wrote an e-mail introducing me to the publisher so that I could send him a proposal. Thank you, Kenji. Without you, this book might never have happened.

Accra, Ghana, is in the Greenwich Mean Time zone, but the joke there is that GMT really stands for Ghanaman Time. For one time-challenged editor and over a dozen time-challenged writers to actually make it through all the various deadlines and produce such a wonderful book is nothing short of a miracle. I have enjoyed every past-due minute of this experience.

Thank you to all the contributors for your creativity, perseverance, and, most of all, your love of Accra, with all its beauty, sass, and dysfunction.

It saddens me deeply that Kofi Blankson-Ocansey, who worked so hard on his story, passed away before it was published. Kofi's brilliance was impressive and his fascination with all things Ghanaian—especially the cultural history of neighborhoods like Jamestown, the one in which his story is set—was infectious. I am so proud to feature his work in this anthology. Kofi, you are sorely missed, my friend.

Thank you to my dear friend Greg Tate, and my daughter Korama Danquah, for offering their editorial skills when I wanted a second opinion or another set of eyes.

Ga, Twi, and Dagbani—the three indigenous languages that are used in some of these stories—are, quite sadly, spoken much more frequently than they are written. As a result, words, many of which have digraphs and diphthongs, are often (mis)spelled phonetically, or anglicized. Also, there are letters in our alphabet that do not exist in English or other Romance languages and cannot be found on most keyboards. In fact, African languages are often dismissively (and colonially) referred to as simple dialects. I would like to extend my gratitude to Mr. William Boateng and Mr. Lawrence Sandow with the Bureau of Ghana Languages, specialists in Twi and Dagbani, respectively; and Ms. Naomi Aryee, Ga teacher at Accra Girls' Senior High School, for their assistance with the spelling and grammar of words in our local languages. Meda mo ase papaapa.

This book could not have been completed without the support and friendship of my ride-or-die Accra girls: Ama Dadson, Christa Sanders, Aretha Amma Sarfo, Esta Twum, and Nana Oye Lithur. Thank you for all the banku and tilapia; for all the trips here, there, and everywhere around the city (and even to Koforidua) in search of beads and cloth, my two all-time weaknesses; for listening, laughing, and supporting me however I needed it.

Thanks also to Jeffery Renard Allen, my brother from another mother, for the daily chats and texts, the inspiration and wonderful advice with all things literary and life.

To Andrew Solomon: thank you for everything, the all of it, up and down, through and through. Love is this; friendship is this.

It has been a great privilege to work with Johnny Temple, publisher of Akashic Books. I so admire your vision for a reverse-gentrification publishing house and I am thrilled to be a part of what you have created. Thank you for offering me this wonderful opportunity to shine a spotlight on Accra.

A huge thank you to my cousin Kwasi Twum, for being such an amazing brother, friend, and human being; for always making me feel worthy; and for helping to heal so much of what was broken.

To everyone else who helped, in one way or another, to make this book come together, I would like to say thank you. I am very grateful.

—Nana-Ama Danquah

ABOUT THE CONTRIBUTORS

Ernest Kwame Nkrumah Addo

Ernest Kwame Nkrumah Addo graduated with a BA and MPhil from the University of Ghana, Legon. He has taught English at the University of Professional Studies, Accra, and has worked for the presidency as a speechwriter. Addo is currently pursuing a PhD in English at the University of South Africa.

Nii Armah

Gbontwi Anyetei spent his early years in Ghana, Nigeria, Zimbabwe, and Botswana before moving to Britain. A Pan-Africanist, he believes art can reframe our present and create a revolutionary future. His novel *Mensah* was short-listed at the 2017 Edinburgh International Book Festival, and his new novel, *For the Republic of Hackney*, is in progress. His essay "Writing for Africa from Britain" is featured in the 2019 anthology *Safe*. Anyetei relocated to Ghana in 2013.

Itunu Kuku

Ayesha Harruna Attah grew up in Accra and studied at Mount Holyoke College, Columbia University, and New York University. She is the author of the Commonwealth Writers' Prize–nominated *Harmattan Rain*, *Saturday's Shadows*, and *The Hundred Wells of Salaga*. Her writing has appeared in the *New York Times*, *Newsweek*, and *Asymptote*. Attah is an Instituto Sacatar fellow and won a 2016 Miles Morland Foundation Scholarship for nonfiction. She lives in Senegal.

Ameyaw, Multi Lens Prod.

Anna Bossman was born in Kumasi, Ghana. She obtained a degree in law and political science from the University of Ghana, Legon, and was admitted to the bar in 1980. She headed Ghana's Commission on Human Rights and Administrative Justice, and directed the Integrity and Anti-Corruption Department of the African Development Bank. Bossman has been writing short fiction since childhood and also writes poetry. Since 2017 she has been Ghana's ambassador to France.

Essie Brew-Hammond

Nana Ekua Brew-Hammond is the author of *Powder Necklace*, which *Publishers Weekly* called "a winning debut." Her work is featured in various anthologies, including *Africa39* and *Everyday People*. Forthcoming from Brew-Hammond are a children's picture book from Knopf and a novel. She was a 2019 Edward F. Albee Foundation fellow, a 2018 Aké Arts and Book Festival guest author, a 2017 Aspen Ideas Festival scholar, and a 2016 Hedgebrook writer in residence.

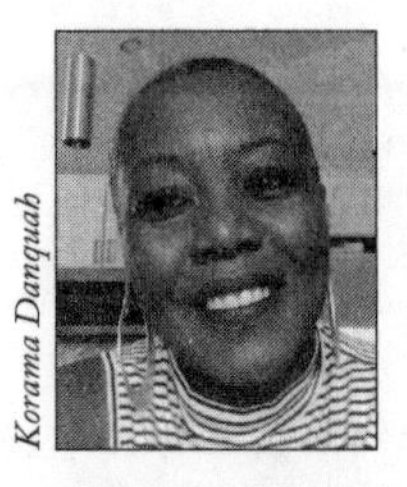
Korama Danquah

NANA-AMA DANQUAH was born in Accra and raised in the US. She is the author of *Willow Weep for Me* and editor of the anthologies *Becoming American*, *Shaking the Tree*, and *The Black Body*. Her work has been widely anthologized. Publications she has written for include *Essence*, the *Washington Post*, the *Village Voice*, and the *Los Angeles Times*. She has taught at Otis College of Arts and Design, Antioch College, and the University of Ghana.

Andre Lambertson

KWAME DAWES has published over thirty-five books, most recently the novel *Bivouac*. He was born in Ghana, grew up in Jamaica, and is considered one of the Caribbean's leading writers. Dawes is a chancellor of the Academy of American Poets, an honorary FRSL, and programming director of the Calabash International Literary Festival. At the University of Nebraska, he is the Glenna Luschei Editor of *Prairie Schooner*, Chancellor's Professor of English, and director of the African Poetry Book Fund.

Eric Gyamfi

BILLIE MCTERNAN is a writer and editor who experiments with literary and visual art forms and has an MFA from the Kwame Nkrumah School of Science and Technology in Kumasi. While living and working in Accra, she has published many articles and essays from her travels in West Africa. She is currently working on a piece that falls somewhere between a short story and a novel.

Eibhlín Ní Chléirigh

EIBHLÍN NÍ CHLÉIRIGH is a writer who left Dublin, Ireland, over thirty years ago; first to Malawi, then Zimbabwe, before settling in Ghana in 1994. Her background is design and communications, but she has always had a love of storytelling and the rich, vibrant oral traditions of both Ireland and Ghana. She has written a number of short stories and essays.

Dinesh Dhawan

KOFI BLANKSON OCANSEY graduated from Yale University and worked as a consultant and political speechwriter. He loved the Jamestown neighborhood in Accra because it is ground zero, rich with history and cultural syncretism. He lived in Accra with his son before passing away on December 6, 2019, at the age of fifty-nine.

A. Sackey

Anne Sackey lives in Accra. At the age of seven, quarantined with hepatitis C, she read many of the books in Kumasi's children's library to make the long days bearable. She escaped into the lives and worlds of the characters, and has been a voracious reader ever since. Sackey is the head of marketing at a pay-TV company, a job that allows her to satisfy her creative urges.

Jeune Afrique, Paris

Patrick Smith is a writer and journalist based in Paris, France. He contributes to *Africa Confidential*, *Jeune Afrique*, the BBC, and France 24. In the 1980s and 1990s, he lived and worked in Ghana and Nigeria, then investigated the links between the illegal exploitation of minerals and conflict in the Democratic Republic of the Congo for the United Nations. Smith is currently working on a book about the role of multinational corporations in Africa.

Oliver Doran, PhotoSolutions

Adjoa Twum was born and nurtured in Accra, as was her passion for vivid storytelling. After studying at Tufts University and Columbia University in the United States, she is back on African soil, managing public health programs in South Africa. Twum is currently working on a children's book series to promote Ghanaian culture and pride.